Good Girls Do

*Also by Cathie Linz
in Large Print:*

A Wife in Time
Continental Lover
Daddy in Dress Blues
A Handful of Trouble
One of a Kind Marriage
Private Account

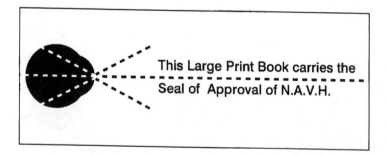

This Large Print Book carries the
Seal of Approval of N.A.V.H.

Good Girls Do

Cathie Linz

Thorndike Press • Waterville, Maine

LARGE TYPE
F
LINZ, C

Published in 2006 by arrangement with The Berkley Publishing Group, a division of Penguin Group (USA) Inc.

Thorndike Press® Large Print Basic.

The tree indicium is a trademark of Thorndike Press.

The text of this Large Print edition is unabridged.
Other aspects of the book may vary from the original edition.

Set in 16 pt. Plantin by Carleen Stearns.

Printed in the United States on permanent paper.

Library of Congress Cataloging-in-Publication Data

Linz, Cathie.
    Good girls do / by Cathie Linz.
      p. cm.
    "Thorndike Press large print basic" — T.p. verso.
    ISBN 0-7862-8515-X (lg. print : hc : alk. paper)
    1.Women librarians — Fiction.   2. Large type books.
  I. Title.
  PS3562.I558G66 2006
  813'.54—dc22
                           2006000138

For Jayne Krentz,
a wonderful writer
and the most amazing cheerleader
in the world!

As the Founder/CEO of NAVH, the only national health agency solely devoted to those who, although not totally blind, have an eye disease which could lead to serious visual impairment, I am pleased to recognize Thorndike Press★ as one of the leading publishers in the large print field.

Founded in 1954 in San Francisco to prepare large print textbooks for partially seeing children, NAVH became the pioneer and standard setting agency in the preparation of large type.

Today, those publishers who meet our standards carry the prestigious "Seal of Approval" indicating high quality large print. We are delighted that Thorndike Press is one of the publishers whose titles meet these standards. We are also pleased to recognize the significant contribution Thorndike Press is making in this important and growing field.

Lorraine H. Marchi, L.H.D.
Founder/CEO
NAVH

★ Thorndike Press encompasses the following imprints: Thorndike, Wheeler, Walker and Large Print Press.

Chapter One

Four years of college and two more of graduate school had gotten Julia Wright where she was today — wearing a too-tight Bo Peep costume and staring down the mayor's belligerent adolescent son.

"Unhand the goldfish, Billy, and no one gets hurt."

He stood at the edge of the artificially made pond and stared at her defiantly. "It's a koi, not a goldfish." His words bounced off the frantically wiggling fish poised right above his mouth.

Julia wanted to drop-kick him over the nearest rooftop. "Unhand the koi." Her voice was pure Cameron Diaz in kick-butt mode. "Put it back in the water. *Now!*"

Billy muttered something under his breath with the rampant disgust only a twelve-year-old boy could display. But he did toss the fish back into the pond that formed the centerpiece of the public library's grounds.

Halloween didn't always bring out the best in people, even in a small town like Serenity Falls, Pennsylvania.

Despite that, Julia adored this town. She had from the moment she'd first come here three years ago to interview for the reference librarian position. Then and now she admired the way the town appeared to be cradled by the surrounding hills, which retained some of their fall foliage. The landscape provided the perfect backdrop for the severely beautiful steeple of the All Saint Episcopal Church located right across the street from the library. She also welcomed the neatness of white picket fences enclosing manicured lawns and well-maintained homes along streets with names like Sleepy Hollow Lane or Sassafras Way.

Yes, Julia loved Serenity Falls.

As for her Bo Peep costume, complete with stupid bonnet and wayward hoop skirt covered by miles of ruffly white material bedecked with blue ribbons . . . well, she wasn't all that fond of it. She'd reluctantly agreed to wear it in the library's booth at the Fall Fun Festival being held in the town square tonight — the Saturday evening before Halloween.

The library couldn't expect more of her than that.

Plus, she'd just saved one of the library director's prized koi.

In her book, that all added up to going above and beyond the call of duty. Because wearing costumes and sounding like a Marine drill sergeant were not her normal modus operandi.

Julia led a very careful existence here. After experiencing a chaotic roller-coaster ride for most of her life, she was entitled to a little peace and quiet for a change.

And if there was one thing Serenity Falls excelled at, it was peace and quiet.

That peace and quiet was interrupted by the sound of a male voice drawling, "I thought Bo Peep's job was to watch the sheep, not the fish."

Julia didn't recognize the man or the big bad Harley parked nearby. The newcomer, dressed in black jeans and a T-shirt, was leaning against one of the oldest oak trees in Serenity Falls. She figured he must be passing through town, because he was much too dangerous-looking to be a native.

Not that she feared for her safety. The man didn't exude that kind of danger. No, this was something much more elemental, male to female.

She couldn't see much of his face in the shadows cast by the tree's massive trunk, but she could tell he was tall and well built. She squinted into the fast-approaching twilight, trying to get a better look at him. He had broad shoulders, a lean waist, and long legs.

Feeling guilty for staring, she looked away. Only then did she realize that while she'd been wool-gathering, Billy had taken off, which left her alone with the newcomer.

Julia shoved the stupid bonnet off her head. "The library is closed." She didn't know if he cared about the library. It was just something to say. Not that he looked like a regular patron to her.

"That what you do in this town to have fun? Dress up and eat live fish? You must be pretty hard up for entertainment around here."

She immediately defended her adopted hometown. "Serenity Falls has some wonderful entertainment venues."

"Venues, huh?" he drawled.

So, hottie biker-man was mocking her, was he? Probably thought she was easy game, given the fact that she was dressed like a demented Bo Peep.

Too bad she'd left her shepherdess's staff at home, or she could have yanked him right into the pond.

Okay, perhaps dunking him was a slightly intense reaction to his comment, but something about him got to her. Maybe it was the way he hadn't bothered to step out of the shadows, or the way he still leaned against the tree as if she wasn't worth straightening up for.

"This is a wonderful town." She said the words with the same emphasis she'd use to state her name.

"Right." He took a step closer.

Julia waved a cautionary hand. "You can't leave your bike there. It's a no parking zone."

"I'm not parking. Just stopping for a while."

"I doubt the police will see it that way."

"So you're trying to protect me from being abused by the local cops, huh?"

"Our police officers are all . . ."

"Wonderful," he interrupted her, his mocking smile flashing in the increasing darkness. "Just like the town and the fish and the library, too, I'll bet. All . . . *wonderful*."

Normally she'd introduce herself, but because he was annoying her, she didn't bother. "If you don't care for it here, you're welcome to keep on going. This road connects to the interstate in a few miles."

"Trying to run me out of town already?"

"No. It just appeared to me that you weren't very happy with your surroundings."

"Happy with my surroundings?" He was

doing it again, mocking her choice of words, although this time there was a touch of bitterness in his voice. "Yeah, you could say I'm not real happy with my surroundings at the moment."

"Are you lost?"

He laughed. It wasn't a happy sound. "Yeah, you could say that, too."

"Maybe I can help you."

"Why would you want to?"

Julia shrugged. "I'm a librarian. I help people find what they're looking for."

"That why you picked the Bo Peep costume? Because you're good at finding things that are lost?"

"I didn't pick it. This was the only one left that fit me."

The people of Serenity Falls took their Fall Fun Festival seriously. So seriously that they expected members of the business community to participate in the costume celebration. Granted, the library wasn't a business per se, but it was roped in on the event anyway.

"It fits you . . . well."

Something about the way he said that made her immediately look down to be sure that she hadn't had a "wardrobe malfunction." No, both breasts were still covered. Barely.

"Something wrong?" He had the kind of voice that would sound sexy even if he were reading the phone book.

"Wrong?" she repeated. "No. Not at all." Her voice was a bit squeaky, but then it was hard to sound totally professional when she looked like an escapee from a fractured fairy tale.

Note to self: No worries. I can handle this.

After all, Julia had plenty of experience at keeping her cool in the middle of a mess. Like the time her New Age mom had staged a sit-in at the San Bernardino Red Lobster, demanding it release its live lobsters.

She didn't know why that incident should suddenly pop in to her head. Maybe the image of Billy holding that flopping koi over his mouth had created the crustacean connection.

Julia quickly erased the image and instead focused on her watch. She was going to be late. "I've got to go."

"Want a lift?" He tilted his head toward his Harley.

The mental snapshot of her Bo Peep hoop skirt flying over her head had her quickly saying, "No, thank you."

"Hey, Julia, wait up!" The shout came from her left. She turned to find Pam

Greenley from Greenley's Garden Center waving at her from across the street. A quick glance back at the newcomer told her he'd turned and was headed back to his Harley.

Julia felt a touch of regret at his departure. She didn't even know the guy's name, but she couldn't look away. He had a way of moving — part sexy swagger, pure male — that was downright seductive. When was the last time she'd stared at a guy's buns?

Her younger sister Skye would have whistled. She'd always been the bad girl in the family.

Julia had tried to be the dependable one. It was a tough job, but somebody had to do it.

Reminding herself of that fact, Julia turned away from temptation and hurried over to the corner to meet Pam.

"Who were you talking to?"

"I don't know." Julia kept walking toward the town square, two blocks away. "He didn't tell me his name."

Pam, a runner, had no trouble keeping up even though she was wearing a Dorothy from *The Wizard of Oz* costume, complete with flashy red shoes that didn't look that comfortable. But then Pam was like that. Petite and perky. Cute and cheerful. She even had T-shirts printed with both descriptions and wore them often. The only time Pam got crabby was when someone called her elfish, although the truth was that with her short dark hair, high cheekbones, and pointed chin, she did look like she should be wearing green and helping Santa. "What did he want?"

"Directions."

"So did you tell him where to go?"

I wish. Now that he was gone, Julia's earlier aggravation with him returned, erasing her momentary lapse into sexual attraction.

"Well, did you?"

Julia nodded before changing the subject. "I'm beginning to think the selection process for choosing which library staff member has to attend this event in costume is flawed."

"You think?"

Julia stopped in her tracks. "Really? They set me up?"

"Come on, what are the odds of your name being pulled three years in a row?"

"Last year Maudeen Entmann was supposed to go," Julia reminded her.

"But she conveniently had to attend a wedding out of town so you took her place."

"Only because I'm a kind person beneath my tough exterior."

Pam laughed. "Tough?"

15

"Hey, I can be tough when I need to be. I'll have you know I just saved a koi from certain death at the jaws of the mayor's son."

"Yeah, that's you, defender of the underdog. Or underkoi."

"Too bad I left my superhero costume at home."

"The Bo Peep outfit is a nice cover. No one would guess that beneath all those ruffles lies the heart of a true superhero."

Julia nodded. "That was my intention."

Pam grinned. "It works for you."

"I thought so. Now I just hope I don't reveal anything tonight that I shouldn't." Julia tugged the material on the bodice.

"Just don't lean over at the Stump the Librarian booth, and you'll be fine."

In the town square, crowds of people were milling about, already collecting in groups in front of the booths that offered everything from hot cider to apple-bobbing.

Julia tried to remember her friend's advice during the next hour. Waiting at the library booth was a laptop computer provided by the library as well as a few reference books and a timer. She had ten minutes to get each answer. The questions came fast and furious.

"How many miles to the moon?"

"The moon is 238,851 miles from Earth."

"When is Britney Spears's birthday?"

"December 2."

"How many times have the Steelers won the Super Bowl?"

"Four."

"When did James Dean die?"

"September 30, 1955."

"Can the blue-footed boobie fly?"

This last question came from Mr. Soames, who had to be in his mid-eighties. He'd asked the same question of her for the past three years. And just about every time he came into the library as well. She suspected he merely liked saying *boobie*.

"Yes, it's a type of sea bird found in the Galapagos, and it can fly. The name actually originates from the Spaniards, who called the bird *bobo,* or Spanish for 'clown' because of its cross-eyed appearance." All of which she'd told him before.

Mr. Soames got this grin on his face. Julia knew what was coming, but short of duct-taping the old guy's mouth shut, she had no way of stopping it. "I bet it would fly better if it got some Viagra."

Which made the kid in line behind him ask Julia how to spell "erectile dysfunction" and snicker with his buddies.

Ah, the joys of being a librarian.

17

Finally, there was a momentary lull. Julia took a quick bite of the toffee apple Susan from the AAUW booth had brought her earlier. Yummy. She only now realized that she hadn't eaten anything since breakfast. *Mmmm.* The tart juice blended with the sweet caramel, thrilling her taste buds. She closed her eyes in ecstasy.

Julia opened them to find hottie bikerman standing in front of her booth. Blinking in surprise, she managed to quickly wipe the caramel from her chin with a paper napkin. If he mentioned Viagra, boobies, or erectile dysfunction, he was a dead man.

She could see him better in the well-lit area. He still looked tough and sexy in his white T-shirt, black jeans, and black leather jacket. But it was his face that held her attention now. There was a depth to his intensely blue eyes she hadn't expected.

"I'm surprised to see you here." The words were out before Julia could stop them. Damn. She thought she'd permanently cured herself of that trait. Since turning thirteen, she'd made a point of stopping to think before speaking, always making sure she said the right thing and avoided revealing anything too inflammatory or too intimate.

"I mean," she immediately corrected herself, "I thought you would have left town by now."

"So you've been thinking about me?"

He seemed entirely too pleased with the concept. Like she'd been sitting here mooning over him for hours. "Right. I've been waiting with baited breath." The mocking words just came tumbling out. The man clearly had a bad effect on her.

He smiled as if he knew it, too.

That stiffened her resolve. "How may I help you?" There, that sounded very professional. Very Marian the Librarian.

He glanced up at the sign, reading the ten-minute guarantee before asking his question. "So what do you do for fun around here?"

Julia relaxed. Okay, this was a question she could handle. "As I mentioned earlier, Serenity Falls offers a wide variety of things to do." She was about to list them when he interrupted her.

"Wrong answer. I asked what *you* do for fun."

"Me? Well, I read a book."

"Which wasn't the original answer you gave me. So what do I get for stumping the librarian?"

"Your choice of a mug or a keychain with the library logo." Julia refused to lose her cool and throw either one of them at him.

"The library has a logo?"

"Actually, it's the town logo."

"The town has a logo?"

"That's right." He made it sound like a criminal offense. "What's wrong with that?"

"If you don't know, I'm not going to tell you."

Jerk. She must have been an idiot to think he was attractive. Okay, so he was an attractive jerk. "Which would you like, the mug or the keychain?"

"You're not even offering a kiss for stumping the librarian?"

"Absolutely not."

"Too bad."

"You might want to take the keychain, because it's smaller and won't break when you pack it and leave." She dangled it in front of him.

He captured her hand with his. "What makes you think I'm leaving?"

"The fact that you don't seem to like it here." She didn't mention the fact that his touch was just as powerful as the rest of him.

"I like one or two things here just fine." His rough-and-tumble sexy voice turned dangerously inviting.

He leaned forward, slowly, inexorably.

Her right hand flew to her cleavage to prevent him from looking down her dress, before belatedly realizing that she was still holding the keychain . . . and that his hand was still clasped around hers. The backs of his fingers brushed against her chest, their heat blazing through the bare skin of her breasts.

And still he came closer. She tried to untangle her hand from his, her eyes from his, herself from him. But she couldn't.

Not because he held her by force. But because of the force zinging between them.

For one spotlight moment, his mouth hovered against hers, barely touching her lips in an almost kiss that was even more enticing than the real thing.

Oh yes, there was some incredibly powerful zinging going on now.

The only thing strong enough to tear them apart was the bellowing sound of the mayor's voice.

"Luke Maguire!" Walt Whitman — no relation to the poet — managed to instill those two words with an incredible amount of disapproval.

So hottie biker-man now had a name. And he had his hand back, because Julia yanked her fingers free.

Unfortunately, her hasty motion resulted

in the library keychain sliding down her bodice.

Too bad. She wasn't about to fish it out now.

"I'm surprised to see you here." Walt added the words as if they'd prod Luke into speaking. It worked.

"Oh?" Luke raised one dark eyebrow, which made him look even more bad-boy sardonic. "And why's that?"

"Well . . . I . . . That is . . ." The challenge caught the mayor off guard, which always made him sputter. "You didn't show up for your own father's funeral, so I didn't expect you'd ever return home."

"You better learn to expect the unexpected with me." Luke turned and walked away.

"Was he bothering you?" Walt was obviously concerned.

"Not really, no." Liar, liar. Luke had gotten to her, all right. Had he kissed her? Or seduced her? Her breast still zinged where he'd touched her. Unless that was the keychain she was feeling?

"He's a bad seed, that one."

Julia winced. She hated that phrase. And Walt certainly shouldn't be casting stones, not when his son had just tried to turn one of the library director's prized koi into sushi.

But she knew from past experience that Walt believed his model son could do no wrong.

"Luke Maguire was a real hell-raiser, pardon my language, as a teenager. I can't imagine what he's doing back here. Unless he's come to sell Maguire's Pub. Which would be a blessing. He's not the kind of business owner who would help us in our quest to get on the Top Ten Best Small Towns in America list. We really do have to focus our attention on our preparations, because we have some very stiff competition coming from other towns right here in Pennsylvania."

Julia nodded, although her mind was still on Luke . . . and kissing and zinging.

"This is an extremely important matter for our entire town."

She nodded again. "I'm not on the committee," she reminded the mayor. At least this was one job she hadn't gotten roped into. Instead, library director Frasier McGrady had that honor.

"You don't have to be on the committee to care about the outcome of this matter. It has the potential to affect us all in a positive way. Every resident of Serenity Falls. As I said, we have stiff competition from other towns in our state. Northumberland has the

Priestly House. He's the guy who discovered oxygen, as you no doubt already know." She did, but Walt loved proving how smart he was. "And Williamsport once had more millionaires than any other place at any other time. So they've got all those historic mansions on Millionaires' Row. And don't forget Mifflinburg. They've got their own buggy museum. All we've got is the Falls. And our town square, along with the downtown district." He waved his hand at their surroundings.

The gazebo did look particularly charming this evening, festively decked out with gold and purple mums. Rows of pumpkins were lined up like jury members at the feet of hay bales placed around the town square. All courtesy of Greenley's Garden Center.

"And I haven't even mentioned Lewisburg." Walt was clearly on a roll now. "They have woolly worms at their Fall Festival — worms that give a winter prognostication. We need a hook like that."

A hook like woolly worms? Only in Serenity Falls . . .

"See if you can't come up with something we could use to predict the future. Weatherwise, I mean. Look how well that Groundhog Day thing has gone for Punxsutawney — another Pennsylvania compet-

24

itor. So please do some research on the Internet and find something we can use here." Satisfied that he'd come up with a plan, Walt moved on to another booth.

Pam showed up as soon as he left and provided cover while Julia finally fished out the keychain. "I saw you with Luke Maguire earlier," Pam noted. "He was the guy back at the library, the one asking for directions, right?"

Julia nodded.

Pam sighed. "You two looked . . . close."

"I just met him tonight."

"Yeah, well, you've heard that saying, that there are two types of men? The good guys and the ones your mother warns you about."

The only type of men Julia's mother had warned her about were wealthy industrialists who polluted the environment and took advantage of third-world countries. And Republicans.

"Well, Luke definitely falls under the mother warning category," Pam continued. "When we were in high school, every mother in Serenity Falls was afraid of her daughter going out with him."

"Why?"

"Because he was a rebel, constantly getting into trouble. He was always so intense.

Skipping classes, drinking, smoking."

"Are you talking about Luke Maguire?" They were joined by Edith Peterson, who taught history at the high school and had since the Ice Age, according to her students. The reality was that she was in her early sixties and had no intention of retiring. "I just heard he's back in town. I had him in my class. He almost failed the course. Not because he was stupid, but because he didn't apply himself. He was a very disruptive presence in school. Was a great runner, though. He won several awards at state track meets. Then at graduation he refused to wear the cap and gown to the ceremony so he was barred from the event."

Pam nodded. "I'd almost forgotten about that."

"He drove his motorcycle right past the front door, into the high school hallway, clear to the principal's office to get his diploma and then he rode right out of town. No one has seen or heard from him since."

"His dad was the nicest guy. He ran Maguire's Pub," Pam added.

Julia had met Tommy Maguire a number of times. Serenity Falls was a small town, where everyone knew everyone else — and most of their business. Secrets were very hard to keep, but Julia had managed so far.

"Luke didn't even come back for his own father's funeral a month ago." Edith shook her head in sad disbelief. "His father's only child. To not pay your last respects . . . I just can't understand that way of thinking. How could anyone be that cruel?"

"What about his mom?" Julia asked.

"Oh, she passed away when he was eight or so. Very sad. She died of some sort of heart condition complicated by pneumonia. And so young. She was only in her late thirties. Apparently, she'd had the condition and never knew it until it was too late. Tommy was devastated. She was the love of his life, and he never remarried."

"What about Luke?" Julia asked.

"He was a handful even back then. I remember the time he knocked out the lights of the Hinkler Funeral Home sign so it read Fun Home. Shot them out with a BB gun."

"Why do you think he's come back?" This time the question was voiced by Pam.

Edith shrugged. "It must have something to do with Maguire's Pub, I should think. But enough about Luke. Let's talk about something happier. How has your evening been so far, Julia? Have lots of people stopped by the library booth?"

"A fair number, yes."

"I meant to tell you earlier that you look

so nice in your costume."

Rumors about Edith's vision not being very good must be true. "Thanks. Yours is lovely, too."

The teacher beamed and carefully rearranged the sleeve of her colonial period dress. "I made it myself, following a pattern that dates back to 1771."

"I saw lots of people at your Historical Society booth."

Edith nodded. "Because we were offering hot apple cider. That always draws people in."

"I volunteered to help out at the bake sale table, and they were almost sold out." Pam glanced at her watch. "Is that the time already? I'm supposed to be judging the pumpkin carving contest in three minutes."

"And I'd best get back to our booth as well," Edith said.

A moment later, Julia was alone with the vivid memory of the town's bad boy and the image of his lips touching hers, his warm fingers brushing against her breast. One thing was sure, Luke Maguire made a hell of a first impression.

Chapter Two

The devil must be mighty cold tonight, because Luke Maguire had always sworn that hell would freeze over before he'd ever step foot in Serenity Falls again. Yet here he was.

There were those in this uptight armpit of a town who'd likened him to a devil. He'd certainly done all he could as a rebellious teenager to earn his "bad boy" reputation. After a while, the stories got a life of their own, and got increasingly exaggerated with each telling.

Luke had never bothered denying any of them. What was the point? He didn't care what people in this town thought of him.

His dad was the one all wrapped up in that. The one who kept up appearances of being a caring father while behind closed doors he'd take off his belt and show Luke the real meaning of obedience.

When Luke had gotten big enough to best his old man in a fight, the beatings had stopped. He'd been maybe fourteen by then. After that, his father's anger and disapproval had merely taken another form.

Closed-fisted punches were replaced with verbal grenades launched to create the most damage.

And all the while, the customers at Maguire's Pub, his dad's pride and joy, had sympathized with Tommy Maguire for having to put up with such a hellion son.

So why had his old man left him the pub when he died? Why make him come back here by adding the stipulation that Luke had to run the pub for six months before selling?

Luke would have loved nothing more than to tell the crusty old attorney what he could do with the offer. But he couldn't afford to do that. Not now. He needed the money.

The reasons why didn't matter.

The bottom line was that he *did* need it. He wasn't proud of that fact. There were too damn many things in his life lately that he wasn't proud of.

He was far from perfect. Unlike Serenity Falls.

Luke's gaze wandered to the kids standing in a neat little line at the cotton candy machine. Even the rug rats had been trained to fall into place. Conforming was the rule around here, not rocking the boat.

If he was going to be stuck in this godforsaken place, the least he could do was have a little fun while he was here. Shake things up.

He was good at that.

Yeah, the narrow-minded residents of Serenity Falls were in for a few surprises.

One pleasant surprise since his arrival had been the sexy librarian. Not that he'd ever thought he'd link those two words together in this lifetime. Maybe he just had a thing for women in Bo Peep costumes.

She was kind of cute with her shoulder-length blond hair. Her eyes were green with a bit of hazel going on. Her name was Julia. He already knew she had great breasts.

But she'd aggravated him with her immediate defense of Serenity Falls. Just like the town, she had a controlled way about her that made him instantly want to shake her Bo Peep ruffles.

Maybe being stuck here wouldn't be as bad as he'd thought. Julia Bo Peep might just provide him with some much-needed distraction.

Not that he was looking for anything serious. Hell, no. He wasn't the settle-down type. Especially not in a place like this.

To Luke's jaded eyes, it appeared that nothing had changed. The sign over the Serenity Cafe still bragged they had the "Best Pies Around." The clock on the village hall tower was still five minutes fast, just as it had been ever since lightning hit it during a freak storm the day Pearl Harbor was attacked.

Time didn't stop here. Instead, it crawled by in agonizingly slow increments, like a form of water torture. Tick, tick, tick. Drip, drip, drip. A relentless monotony that could wear down the most solid of defenses.

"So the rumors are true. You are back in town."

Luke turned to find RJ Brandt III standing there, looking all self-righteous in his leather loafers and wool tweed sports jacket. Luke had disliked the guy in high school, and nothing about RJ's attitude now changed his opinion.

"You have a problem with that?" Luke countered.

"I had a problem with you not even bothering to show up at your own father's funeral."

"I'll bet you were there, right?"

RJ nodded. "Absolutely."

Right. No big surprise there. Luke's dad had always thought more of RJ than he had of Luke anyway. RJ, the high school class president and star football quarterback, was the kind of son Tommy wished he'd had.

"So why are you back now?" RJ demanded.

"To aggravate you."

RJ's expression reflected his disgust. "You never did take anything seriously."

Luke had worked real hard to make people think that. Apparently, he'd done a damn good job of it. Still was.

Fine by him. That was better than ever admitting what was really going on in his head.

Luke decided he'd had his fill of people. Needing some space, he headed for a relatively deserted corner of the square. Only when he got closer did he see the guy going through the garbage container placed there for this event.

Luke didn't recognize him. He had long, braided gray hair for one thing. That alone made him stand out in this podunk town.

"This location is mine," the guy said. "You have to find another one."

"Hey, it's all yours. Knock yourself out."

Luke watched the guy remove aluminum cans and drop them into a black plastic garbage bag he held in his other hand.

"So you're into recycling, huh?" Luke had no idea why he felt the urge to speak. He wasn't normally the kind to make small talk.

The guy just grunted in reply.

Luke recognized the sound. He'd made it plenty of times himself. It meant, *Go away, you're a pain in the butt.*

There was something about the guy Luke could relate to. A misfit. How rare to find one here. He doubted the guy's disheveled clothing of a flannel shirt and threadbare jeans were a Halloween costume.

"Come here often?" Luke asked.

Another grunt.

"Me, neither." Sighing, Luke turned away. He could use a drink. The Fun Fair didn't sell alcohol. But Maguire's Pub did.

So why didn't he just stroll on over there and meet up with good ol' Jack Daniel? What was stopping him? Fear?

No way. Luke had faced more than his share of life-and-death situations. No way he'd blink an eye at something as stupid as ghosts from his past.

He'd go later. When he was damn ready.

Coward!

The internal insult was actually delivered in his dad's voice. How crazy was that? And how like the old man to try to haunt him even after his death.

Luke's momentary insanity was interrupted by the strident sound of a kid's voice. "Yo, are you gonna tell my dad about the fish thing?"

Luke frowned before remembering this was the twerp Julia had caught red-handed by the library pond. "Who's your dad?"

"The mayor."

"Walt Whitman is your dad?"

"That's right. Whitmans have been in local politics for generations." The wanna-be juvenile delinquent suddenly sounded like he was forty.

Luke nodded. "I know. It sucks."

The kid, what had Julia called him? Billy? Yeah, that was it. Billy stared at him in surprise. But Luke saw the acknowledgment there. Following in a dad's too-large shoes wasn't a job for wimps.

"Most people don't think it sucks," Billy retorted.

Luke shrugged. "I'm not most people, kid."

"I heard you're a bad seed."

"I've been called worse."

"Maybe I'm a bad seed, too." Billy delivered the challenge with a swagger that Luke recognized all to well from his own childhood days so long ago.

"Maybe you are." If he were Dr. Phil, he'd ask how the kid felt about that. But he was no psychologist. And the kid's thoughts were none of his business.

That didn't stop Billy from continuing the conversation. "So what did you do that was so bad?"

"Too many things to list."

"You own that Harley by the library?"

Luke nodded.

"Sweet."

"Yeah, I think so."

"So what's it like to ride?"

"Sweet."

"Is it true you didn't go to your dad's funeral?"

"Yeah, it's true."

"How come?"

Luke shrugged. "It's complicated."

"Adults always say that when they don't want to tell the truth."

"Hey, watch who you're calling an adult."

"Well, aren't you one?"

"Not a responsible one."

"Why not?"

Luke shifted uncomfortably. "What are you, the Spanish Inquisition?"

"Whatever."

"Don't tell me you've never seen that comedy bit on *Monty Python*?" Luke had caught one of the episodes of the vintage British comedy on some cable station and had been hooked.

"Never heard of them."

"Your education is sadly lacking, kid. You got a video store around here?"

Billy pointed down the street with a negligent jab of his thumb.

"Wait here."

Of course the kid didn't do that. Instead, he nonchalantly followed Luke inside the store.

Luke could tell by the guilty way the two older women behind the counter moved apart that they had been talking about him. The tell-tale phrase "bad seed hell-raiser" was another giveaway.

He recognized the one on the right as Mabel Bamas because she had the same bubble-gum pink hair she'd had when she'd gossiped over the cash register at the 7-Eleven when he was a teenager.

"What are you doing with the mayor's son?" Mabel demanded as if he were a criminal or something.

"Helping him get abducted by aliens." Luke delivered the mocking comment with a straight face even as he strolled over to the comedy section and quickly grabbed what he wanted. "It'll be in the *National Enquirer* in a day or two. You could call the story in now if you want. Get a jump on the other papers."

Mabel looked at him in confusion. "The *Serenity News* office is closed now."

"Too bad." Luke put a *Monty Python* DVD on the counter.

"You want to rent that?"

"Affirmative."

"I'll need to see a credit card."

Luke fished one out of his wallet.

"This expired a month ago," Mabel seemed to take pleasure in informing him.

He took it back and handed over another one.

"Are you okay, Billy?" Mabel eyed the kid with concern. "Where's your dad?"

"At the festival."

"He know you're here with him?" Mabel asked.

"He's not really with me," Luke inserted.

"But you said —"

"That I was helping aliens abduct him. And you believed that?"

"No, of course not."

"Good. You have a nice night."

"You, too," she said automatically. "I mean . . ."

"I know what you mean," Luke said.

"Wow, they really *don't* like you here," Billy noted once they were outside.

"Affirmative."

The look Billy gave him indicated he was impressed but trying not to show it.

"Can I trust you to take that DVD back on time?" Luke asked Billy.

"Affirmative."

Hell, the kid was already sounding like a Mini-Me from one of those Austin Powers movies. Time to move on.

To Maguire's Pub? Why not?

"See you around, kid."

Billy nodded, apparently not at all upset at Luke's abrupt departure. Which was a good thing about guys, even rug rats like this one. They didn't get all huffy about stuff.

Not like females.

Thinking of females reminded him of Julia with the keychain down her breasts. Maybe he should go back and offer to retrieve it for her?

There had certainly been some major sexual chemistry going on there. She was a bodacious blonde in a Bo Peep costume. What more could a guy ask for?

Spending some time between the sheets with her.

Oh, yeah. That sounded good.

Too bad she wasn't the kind to fall right into bed with him. She was the kind who'd make him work for it. But it might be worth it.

Luke paused in front of Maguire's Pub. The building hadn't changed much. No surprise there. He entered, yanking open the door.

The air inside felt pre-breathed with all

the oxygen sucked out of it, a stark contrast to the fresh air outside. The smell of fried onions and beer overwhelmed him. Or was it the memories?

The past twelve years fell away, whipping him back in time.

You useless piece of shit. The world would be a better place if you'd never been born.

A second later, Luke found himself outside again, gulping in air even as he rammed into someone on the sidewalk.

It was the braid guy. Mr. Recycle Man.

"You got a name?" Luke demanded, itching for a fight.

"Tyler."

The anger seeped out of him. "Okay then."

"Glad you approve."

Hey, the guy had a sense of humor. Who knew?

"I hear you're the new owner of this place." Tyler jerked his head toward the pub.

"That's right."

"I do some handyman work if you're interested."

"You got a card?"

Tyler shook his head. "I'm not hard to find."

"The town fathers give you any trouble for picking cans out of the garbage?"

Tyler shrugged. "It's a free country."

"Parts of it may be. I'm not so sure about this place, though."

"I guess time will tell."

Luke nodded. That's what he was afraid of. No, not afraid. Never afraid. Never again.

"I'm telling you . . ." Edith leaned closer to Julia. "Mabel over at the video store called Stella, who called me and said Luke tried to kidnap Billy."

"I find that to be highly unlikely."

"I'm not so sure about that."

"Why on Earth would Luke want to do something like that?"

"Who knows why people do what they do?" Edith replied. "The world is filled with all kinds of twisted people."

"I agree," Luke said from behind Edith. "And plenty of them live right here in good ol' Serenity Falls."

Wanting to divert a confrontation, Julia quickly asked Luke, "Did you come back for your keychain?"

"That depends. Where is it?" His gaze lowered to her breasts.

"Not there!"

"Too bad. I was sort of looking forward to retrieving it."

"Sort of?" Damn. She'd done it again. Let her tongue get away from her.

His slow grin was her only reward. Or punishment.

"A man can only take so much anticipation," he said.

"I'll take your word for it." She handed him a keychain.

The zing was back. In his voice. In the way he looked at her from under those dark lashes of his. He had the kind of Black Irish looks she'd always been a sucker for. Dark hair and brows, intense blue eyes. Deep eyes. Not ocean kind of deep but brooding, I've-got-secrets deep. Dylan Thomas deep.

Edith cleared her throat. "I believe we're getting ready to close things down now."

Instead of staying and offering to help Julia, Luke just smiled and sauntered away.

Note to self: Hottie biker-men are not reliable helpers. Or reliable anything, for that matter. Nice eye candy. That's it.

"You seem disappointed that he's left," Edith noted.

"I was thinking about something else," Julia lied.

"Walt wanted me to ask you if you'd had time to check the Internet for that project he gave you." Edith was on the town council.

It took Julia a moment to recall what project that might be. Oh, right. The woolly worms/groundhog prognosticator. "No, I haven't had time yet."

"He seems very keen to get that done."

Walt was very keen about a number of things, most of them having to do with getting Serenity Falls on the Top Ten list of the country's Best Small Towns.

"I'll work on it the next chance I get," Julia promised.

"You do that." Edith patted Julia's hand. "And you work on staying away from Luke. He's nothing but trouble. Your mother isn't here to warn you, so I feel compelled to do so."

If they only knew. Julia's mother would never warn her away. Instead, she'd have hopped on the back of Luke's Harley in a heartbeat.

Luke couldn't believe how long it took for them to close down the so-called Fun Festival. Glaciers moved faster. Finally, his Bo Peep librarian was leaving the crowd, heading back down Main Street toward the library and the pond.

He'd left his Harley parked back there, so he might as well follow her. Even though it was dark, he could see the sway of her hips as she walked ahead of him. Or maybe that was just the ruffles on her dress. The thing seemed to have a life of its own, the skirt shifting back and forth like the hefty bell that tolled every Sunday morning over at the First Congregational Church.

He could have sworn he heard Julia swear softly as another gust of wind threatened to blow her off course.

A gentleman would take her by the arm and assist her. But he was no gentleman, and he doubted she'd welcome his assistance, despite her semi-flirtatious comments a short while ago.

So he just watched her, quietly following behind.

Luke had no idea why she headed for the pond instead of her home. Maybe she wanted to count the koi to be sure none had been eaten in her absence.

She did seem the ultra-responsible type.

Finally he spoke. "What are you doing?"

Julia wasn't expecting Luke. What was he doing, stalking her? She spun around at his question just as another even bigger gust of wind blew through. The billowing hoop skirt and her unsteady footing joined forces to make her fall backward . . . right into the water.

Julia had the presence of mind to grab the hoop skirt as she went down so it didn't fly over her head. But now it was soaking wet, preventing her from standing up.

"Here, let me give you a hand." Luke had his sexy voice on, the one hot enough to melt the polar ice caps.

It didn't work on her. "You're the reason I ended up in here!" She was tempted to yank him in right next to her.

The look in his eyes told her that Luke could read her thoughts. And he was practically daring her to act on them. But she refused to sink that low.

"Do you want my help or not?" Luke asked.

She tried to get out on her own but only ended up splashing them both and making herself even wetter.

An instant later, he'd grabbed both her hands and hauled her out. She stood before him a dripping mess.

The next thing Julia knew, he'd undone the ties holding up her skirt. It fell to her feet like an anchor sinking to the bottom of the sea.

"Oh, look, they're going skinny-dipping." Julia froze. Surely that wasn't her mom's voice? "I'm so proud of you, honey."

"Looks like we've walked in on an episode

of *Good Girls Gone Wild*," her sister Skye drawled from the darkness. "I can't wait to see what happens next."

Chapter Three

Julia yanked her skirt back up around her waist and slapped away Luke's hands.

"What are you doing here?" Julia demanded.

"Trying to help you." Luke reached for her again.

"Not you," she muttered, smacking his hands again. "Them." She pointed to her family, standing under the oldest tree in Serenity Falls. If she were the suspicious kind, she'd almost think the tree was conjuring up people to fluster her. First Luke, now her mother Angel and sister Skye. "What are you doing here?"

"What are you doing over there?" Skye countered. "All wet."

"I slipped and fell into the pond. I was *not* going skinny-dipping."

"That's a shame." Angel's curly brown hair glimmered in the moonlight, as did the amethyst crystal she wore around her neck. "It's so liberating to be free of these artificial restrictions that confine the natural beauty of the human body." She plucked at the floaty, tie-dyed Indian cotton dress she wore.

Julia was afraid Angel would start peeling off her clothing and step into the water. It wouldn't be the first time.

She had to get her mother out of here.

How fitting that her wacky family showed up out of the blue right before Halloween, the holiday that celebrated the weird and other-worldly. Both adjectives applied to her mother and sister.

She'd ask how they tracked her down to the municipal pond later. Her mother would probably tell her that she'd sensed Julia's vibes or something New Age-y like that.

Julia shivered. It had been unseasonably warm all day and evening, but now it was getting downright cold with the edgy wind. "I've got to get out of these wet clothes. Why don't you follow me home?"

"Works for me." Luke grinned.

"Not you. I meant them." She tilted her head toward her family.

"I'm Julia's mother." Angel moved closer, her clothing flowing around her like a cosmic cloud as she moved. "My chosen name is Angel."

"Nice to meet you, ma'am. I'm Luke."

Angel laughed. "You're very polite, Luke."

"You're the first one who's thought so."

Angel shrugged. "I often see what others don't. You should come over to the house, and I'll read the runes for you."

"Hello?" Skye waved both hands over her head, her multiple silver bangles jangling. Her neon red hair was short and spiky while her how-low-can-you-go jeans revealed the glint of a navel ring in the street light. "What am I, invisible here?"

Angel made the introductions. "This is my youngest daughter, Skye. And her daughter, Antonia."

"Also known as Toni the Biter," Skye added. "She just turned four, but she's got quite a grip with those baby teeth of hers."

"Be careful, honey." Julia watched nervously as Toni headed straight for the pond.

Skye wasn't the least bit concerned. "Don't worry. She can swim like a fish."

"Swimming isn't allowed in the municipal pond." Julia pointed to the sign.

"Still conforming to rules, huh, sis?"

"Still trying to break them?" Julia retorted, irritated as always by her sister's attitude.

"Oh, I don't merely *try*. When I put my mind to something, I get it done."

"Does that mean you've gotten yourself a job?"

"No way." Skye scoffed. "I'm not partici-pating in the corporate repression of the working classes."

"Capitalist pigs," Toni added. Her eyes widened as she caught sight of the koi gliding by. "Fishie!"

She made a beeline for the pond. Julia was too far away to stop her. But Luke wasn't.

"Luke, grab her!" Julia yelled.

"Me? Why me?" He looked panicked, like she'd just asked him to deactivate a bomb.

"Just grab her."

He did, holding her between his two hands as if she were some sort of alien life-form.

"Here," he hurriedly handed Toni over to the still water-logged Julia. But not before Toni tried to nip him. He moved fast enough to avoid her teeth. Just barely.

"Nice kid," he muttered.

"She's just expressing her frustration at not having the linguistic skills to voice her aggravation with the world situation," Skye said.

"She cannot go around biting people," Julia said. "No biting," she warned Toni with the same kick-butt voice she'd used on Billy earlier.

It had little effect.

" 'No' is a negative element we don't want

interfering with Toni's life energy force," Skye loftily stated.

Biting is a negative element I don't want in my life energy force Julia wanted to say but didn't. What was the point? Skye wasn't going to change. Neither was their mom.

"Here, I'll take her." Angel lifted Toni into her arms. "We really should be going."

"So you just stopped by to say hello?" Julia felt a huge sense of relief. This was the first time her family had come to Serenity Falls to see her. She deliberately hadn't told anyone much about her life before she came to town. She'd only been as truthful as she'd had to be — and as vague as possible.

"Stopped by to say hello?" Angel repeated. "No, we came to see you."

"And move in with you," Skye added.

Angel quickly patted Julia's damp arm. "I was going to break it to you a bit more gently."

Julia started shivering so hard her teeth were chattering. She was freezing, or it could be shock. Her family. Living with her? Stephen King couldn't have come up with a more horrifying scenario.

The next thing she knew Julia was encased in a warm leather jacket. "You're cold." Luke's voice rumbled near her ear. "How far away is your house?"

51

Julia pointed across the street. Or tried to. Her hands were shaking, making her think of the pointy-fingered stare of the haggard witch in one of those Disney movies. *Cinderella* was it? Or *Snow White*? Or *Sleeping Beauty*?

She hadn't seen any of them as a kid. Her mother hadn't approved of the fairy tales or the commercialization of them. She'd rented all three videos a few months ago.

"It's wonderful that you live so close by." Angel smiled. "Lucy and Ricky are tired after their trip."

Angel had brought more company with her? Skye and Toni the Biter weren't enough? "I only have one extra b-b-b-bedroom." Julia's teeth were chattering again.

"This is ridiculous," Luke growled.

Julia couldn't agree more and would have told him so had she been able to form words. Instead, she was concentrating on protecting her tongue from getting chewed by her chattering teeth.

Luke scooped her up, or tried to. The heavy, wet Bo Peep skirt didn't cooperate, the hoop smacking him in the face.

Rip.

The skirt fell to her ankles. He scooped her up again. His warm leather jacket barely covered her daisy-patterned panties. Why hadn't she worn those damn bloomers that had come with the stupid costume?

"Poomedoo."

Luke ignored her words, perhaps because he couldn't understand them. She'd been trying to say "Put me down," but it hadn't come out right. Her legs were shaking — all of her was. She felt like an ice cube.

"Which house is yours?" he demanded.

"The one with the g-g-g-green door."

"They all have green doors."

"F-f-fifth one from the corner."

The door was unlocked. He set her inside and reached for the lights. He was quickly followed by Julia's family.

Normally, Julia always felt welcomed by her home and the way she'd decorated it with items from places like Pottery Barn and Crate & Barrel. Dark woods. Cream walls and upholstery. And piles of books, neatly placed in stacks by subject or placed on Arts and Crafts–style bookcases that filled an entire wall.

Today was different. Today she felt like her quiet sanctuary was being invaded by a rowdy horde.

"You poor thing. I'll make some herbal tea to warm you right up," Angel said. "Skye, you'll have to take care of Lucy and Ricky on your own. Come along, honey."

Angel put her arm around Julia. "I'll run you a hot bath. Where's the bathroom? Upstairs?"

Julia nodded and mumbled, "Gilooja." She meant to say, *Give Luke his jacket.* But no one understood her. No surprise there. She'd always been the misfit in this circus.

Luke couldn't help noticing that the librarian had great legs. Supremo really. She looked incredibly sexy wearing his jacket, her creamy thighs a contrast against the black leather. She'd felt all curvy and feminine in his arms. Her breasts had rested against his white T-shirt, the leather slipping aside during one of her many shivers. And he'd been able to look right down the neckline of her Bo Peep top for an eyeful of cleavage. One lacy edge had barely covered the rosy tip of her nipple.

Oh, yeah, his body was on full alert, ready and reporting for action.

Apparently, he wasn't the only one to notice that. "So how long have you been having sex with my sister?" Skye demanded.

Julia heard voices. Which was strange because she lived alone. Had she left the television on last night? What day was it? A work day? No, Sunday. Today was Sunday.

Her brain hazily gathered the pieces of her

consciousness. She'd never been one to jump out of bed all bright-eyed and full of energy.

Then it hit her.

Last night. Luke carrying her home, half-naked. Her family. Here. In Serenity Falls. Disaster. Big time.

After her hot bath the night before, Julia had simply crawled into her bed and passed out from exhaustion. Or maybe sleeping had just been an avoidance technique for her. Or a coping mechanism.

It was barely seven in the morning, but she knew her mother loved greeting the sun every morning with a special chant she'd learned from an Indian shaman.

Julia didn't want to leave her bed. She sleepily gazed around the room, which was decorated exactly the way she wanted it in calming shades of soft blue. Antique David Roberts prints adorned the walls. Her floral sheets had a thread-count a queen would envy, pampering her every time she slid into bed. She loved her bedroom, which had taken her months to finally get just right from the crystal chandelier to the Victorian birdcage. Her surroundings soothed her . . . normally.

But today wasn't normal.

Reluctantly, she got up and peeked out

the window. The soft texture of the carpet was familiar beneath her bare feet. So was the view beyond the cream brocade drapes she cautiously moved aside. Daylight was just starting to break, the sun's rays creeping above Mrs. Selznick's roof behind her house.

There was no sign of her mother. Maybe Julia had dreamt last night? Maybe it had all been a nightmare caused by the corn dogs the Junior Women's League had been selling?

Then she caught sight of Angel, wearing a flowing purple skirt and a thick sweater along with her trademark hand-knit cap and scarf. This set was in shades of orange and fuzzy pink.

Julia needed caffeine. Badly. Yawning, she tugged on a microfleece baby blue robe and headed downstairs to her automatic coffee maker. Once in the kitchen, she could hear her mom talking outside the door.

"I hope you slept well last night, Ricky and Lucy. I know this isn't California, but I think you'll eventually settle in here if you leave yourself open to the experience."

Great. Her mom had people camping out in Julia's backyard last night.

Julia refused to feel guilty about that.

But she should offer them something for breakfast.

She opened the door and stepped outside. It was definitely nippy out. She could see her breath. "Mom, did you want to invite your friends inside . . . ?"

Angel turned. "Oh no, dear. The llamas aren't housebroken. Yet."

Julia blinked. "Llamas?"

Angel nodded. "Lucy and Ricky. Their previous owners named them. They were fans of *The Lucy Show.*"

"You put llamas in my backyard?"

"Of course. As I said, they're not housepets."

"What are they doing here?"

"Waiting for breakfast."

"What are you doing with llamas?"

"Feeding them."

"I mean, why do you have a pair of llamas?"

"Oh, didn't I tell you? I've started a new venture. Luna Llamas. I'm starting small, only two llamas. But I hope they'll breed and I'll have babies. Well, Lucy will. Ricky and I will be there for moral support."

Julia was speechless.

Her mother wasn't. "Llamas are excellent fiber producers. You shear them every other year usually. They have a dual fiber fleece. The fiber is hollow, which makes it excellent for creating warm clothing. And the fact

57

that it's oil free makes it a spinner's dream. We've got a spinning wheel out in the VW van. Aren't you proud of all the research I've done?"

Julia remained speechless.

Angel continued with her explanation. "We all just need a little time to gather ourselves, to regain our beginner's mind. You remember the Zen percept, right? Of bringing a clean slate and a pure mind to everything we do?"

Julia nodded. That's what she'd hoped to do in Serenity Falls. Start with a clean slate. Away from her wild family.

"I know what you're thinking," Angel continued. "But this time things are going to work out. Trust me."

If only Julia had a dollar for every time she'd heard her mother say those words. "What happened to your ice-cream store in Seattle?"

"Exotic Gellato was doing very well."

"Then why start raising llamas?" *And why say you're moving in with me? Please let that be a joke. Not that her mother had that kind of a sense of humor.*

Angel bit her bottom lip. "Well, I may have invested a little too heavily in the newest exotic flavor."

"Which was?"

"Garlic. Sales fell, and the next thing I knew, I had to close up."

Julia's stomach sank. Great. Her family was broke. That's why they were here. She was doomed. "Just like Friendly Franks. Remember that?"

"Of course." Angel tossed her scarf over her shoulder with a sense of flare. "The tofu hot dog stand did exceptionally well in California."

"But it was a bust in Fairbanks, Alaska."

"I still can't believe it didn't take off up there. There was such a crowd for the Ididerod. Other vendors have made enough in a few weeks to last them almost a year."

"Other vendors weren't selling tofu hot dogs."

"They eat moose and caribou burgers. How was I supposed to know they would turn up their noses at tofu? A much healthier and kinder alternative, I'd like to point out. You make it sound like I didn't have any successes. Being a New Age entrepreneur isn't easy these days, but I have made a go of several projects. I mean, Wicca Wiggs in Mendocino was a big hit."

"Because witches have to look good, too." Julia repeated her mother's pitch.

"They prefer to be called Wiccans. And

Friendly Franks was a hit in Mendocino after that."

"Until you moved us up to Alaska," Julia reminded her.

"All the signs, tarot cards, and runes said I'd excel at a new project."

What Julia's flighty mother really excelled at was moving on, from one wild endeavor to the next, one zany West Coast location to the next. She didn't have a practical bone in her body. Success was completely irrelevant to her. The "cosmic trip" was the important thing.

"Fall seven times, stand up eight." Angel recited one of her favorite Chinese proverbs.

Julia was tired of falling down. She'd come to Serenity Falls to get away from the world of chaos that surrounded her mother the way the scent of Chanel Number Five surrounded the mayor's wife. All she wanted now was peace and quiet. And a gallon or two of caffeine.

Luke sipped his coffee and reflected on his first night back in his hated hometown. Not that he was normally the reflective type. His philosophy was that too much thinking just made your head sore. Most things were better left alone. Forgotten. Erased.

"You want more coffee?" The question came from Adele Adamson, the cook at Maguire's Pub for as long as Luke could remember. Unlike the town, Adele had changed. She used to have long dark hair that she'd always worn in a braid down her back. Now her hair was cropped short. But she still had warm brown eyes and a crooked front tooth.

"Thanks for meeting with me this morning," Luke said.

"No problem. You sleep okay?"

Hell, no. He'd been awake most of the night.

From the moment he'd stepped foot into Maguire's Pub, he'd been hit with memories. The Marine Corps may have been maniacs about their rules and regulations, but they'd taught him one thing. Control.

So after that first episode when he'd exited the pub as fast as he'd entered it, Luke had zipped his emotions deep inside and focused on practical matters instead. But at night the memories had come out to taunt him.

Adele spoke into the silence. "You said you wanted to go over information about the pub."

"That's right."

"Look . . ." She twisted her fingers awkwardly. "I, uh, I know you and your dad never got along. And I feel badly for not saying anything about the situation when you were a kid. But I was raised not to stick my nose into other folks' business, you know? So I looked the other way when I saw the way your dad treated you those times he thought no one was around. Maybe I shouldn't have done that. I don't know. I've never said anything to another soul, and I never will. I just wanted you to know that . . . I guess just that I wish things had been different."

Her words had caught him totally by surprise. He didn't think anyone knew what had been going on. He wasn't sure that her knowing was a good thing. The bottom line was that it didn't change anything. "The past is gone. My only concern now is the present."

"So you've come back?"

Luke nodded. He would have loved to have added, *I've got to stay here for six months before I can sell this place.*

But the terms of his father's will were clear. He had to run Maguire's Pub for six months and not tell anyone that he wasn't back for keeps. If he did, he'd lose it all.

"I never thought I'd see this day," Adele noted.

"You and most of the folks in this town."

"Don't be angry with them. They had no idea how things really were. I'm sure even I only had a glimpse of how bad things got."

Luke hated this. Hated talking about this stuff. Hated remembering anything to do with this place.

But he'd lived through worse. He'd survive this, too. And then take the money and run.

"Here's a pile of mail I kept aside for you." Adele handed it to him. "I've been paying the bills out of the business account since your dad's death. I was actually doing most of that, the bill-paying, before he had his heart attack."

Luke looked over the account books Adele showed him, wishing he'd paid more attention to those damn math classes in school.

When she left him alone with the paperwork, his thoughts wandered. He'd called the meeting with Adele here, in the two-bedroom apartment above the pub where he'd grown up. There was nothing left from his old bedroom, which was now a home office with a table and a computer. And a depository for the beer can collection. His dad's pride and joy.

Luke had packed them all up last night.

No way was he looking at those. Or the talking mackerel hanging on the living room wall. They had to go.

He'd used a dozen boxes from the pub's storeroom, dropping stuff in as fast as he could. And he'd called a charity first thing this morning to come pick up most of the furniture.

It was bad enough stepping into his father's shoes at Maguire's. No way was he sleeping in his bed.

Luke had actually spent much of the night sitting out on the metal fire escape, like he had as a kid. He'd covered a lot of ground since leaving town. He'd joined the Marine Corps right after high school and had gone into the Special Forces as a Force Recon Marine.

After that, he'd eventually ended up as a Special Agent in the FBI, where he'd gone undercover so many times he'd lost himself. And maybe that was no great loss, but it left him with a raw emptiness inside that ate away at him.

Luke had been good at what he did. Too good. He'd started thinking like the people he was infiltrating. The lines between black and white, good and bad became blurred. To keep his cover, he'd had to do things that seared his soul until, burnt-out and broke, he'd had to leave.

Yeah, he was a real success story all right.

Enough wallowing in his past. Luke gathered up his empty coffee mug and headed downstairs to the kitchen, Adele's domain. While there, he sampled a piece of fresh bread still warm from the oven. "What do you know about a handyman named Tyler?" he mumbled with his mouth full.

"He does odd jobs around town, and he's a Rollerblading insomniac sometimes in the middle of the night, but he's not a bad guy."

"I never said he was." An insomniac Rollerblader? That must drive the mayor nuts. Luke's opinion of Tyler rose even higher. "Maybe he could help out here."

"The place could use a new coat of paint. I've been saying so for years. But we can't do anything to the exterior without the town council's permission."

"Since when?" Maguire's wasn't old enough to be designated a historic site.

"Since Walt has been trying to get us on the list of the Best Small Towns in America. He's really been clamping down on folks," Adele added.

"Let him clamp all he wants," Luke retorted. "No one is telling me what to do."

Angel watched the koi gliding around Serenity Falls municipal pond and wondered where she'd gone so wrong as a mother. What had driven Julia to come to a place so controlled and restrictive?

The signs were all over. No swimming. No fishing. No jaywalking. No standing. No trespassing.

Angel kicked off her hemp sandals and dug her toes in the grass. It was chilly, but she really felt the need to touch base with nature. So she sat down on the grass and studied her surroundings. The trees still had some of their brilliant leaves, but it appeared that someone had gathered all the ones that had already fallen. There were no piles of leaves to jump into. That was a shame.

This was her first trip this far east, and she'd been looking forward to a colorful fall display. She hadn't expected to see her daughter in a Bo Peep costume. That had cheered her up. The town hadn't.

Sure, it looked like something out of a Currier and Ives print, but Angel preferred Picasso herself. She'd never been one to color between the lines. Julia had.

Angel had not been surprised when Julia had become a librarian, because her first-born had always loved hanging out in libraries wherever they went. Angel had homeschooled both her girls for much of their school years. And she'd always thought she'd done a pretty good job of it, instilling in them the basic values of treating others with respect, honoring the environment, and exploring all the world's many possibilities.

So where had she gone wrong with Julia that she'd come to Anal City?

There wasn't a blade of grass out of place here. Not even a single autumnal leaf to crunch beneath her feet. The place was immaculate. It wasn't natural.

Angel didn't realize she'd actually spoken the words aloud until she got a response from someone standing behind her.

"It isn't natural," a male voice said. "It's a man-made pond."

She turned to look at him. Now this was someone Angel felt more comfortable with. His long gray hair was held back in a braid that went down his back past the collar of his flannel shirt. He looked to be around her age, in his late forties or early fifties. He had sad eyes. Brown but sorrowful.

"So the town is named for a man-made pond?"

The man shook his head. "Serenity Falls are natural. They're just south of town. The area is protected for now, but there's some talk of bottling the spring water and selling it."

"Big business trying to ruin yet another natural site." That issue was something Angel could sink her teeth into with all the force of her granddaughter Toni.

"You don't like the idea?"

"It's horrible!"

"You're not from around here."

"No. I just arrived in town last night. I'm Angel. Julia Wright is my daughter."

He just nodded as if he already knew that before suddenly turning around as if to walk away.

"Wait! You haven't told me your name. Who are you?"

"Nobody you need to know." And then he was gone.

"Julia, dear, I hate to bother you, but did you know that there are wild animals in your backyard?"

"They're not wild. They're llamas. And yes, Mrs. Selznick. I know they're there. But thanks for checking on me."

"I was going to call the police, but thought I should call you first."

"And I appreciate that."

"I'm not sure we're allowed to keep llamas in our backyards here in Serenity

Falls," Mrs. Selznick hesitantly pointed out.

"I'm looking into making alternative arrangements for them."

"Mr. Perkins runs a dairy farm outside of town. Maybe he could help you out. He's a second cousin of mine. Would you like me to give him a call?"

"Thank you. I'd appreciate it." She prayed that Mrs. Selznick hadn't seen Luke carrying her home last night, half-naked.

Ten minutes later, the mayor showed up on her doorstep. "I hear you've got llamas. Are you thinking of using them as prognosticators instead of a ground hog or woolly worms?"

"Possibly." Any excuse was welcome at this point.

Walt frowned. "They're not really indigenous to these parts."

"True."

"Well, keep me posted on the situation." Walt was studying the clipboard he often carried with him, his thoughts clearly already on the next item on his agenda.

"I'll do that," Julia promised.

"And find another home for them," he added. "I'm sure there's an ordinance against keeping livestock in a residential area."

"I'm working on it."

Luke was walking down Cherry Lane to Julia's house to retrieve his leather jacket and steal more kisses when he spotted Walt with a ruler in his hand. The middle-aged mayor had some kind of Mr. Rogers thing going on today, complete with baggy cardigan and khakis. He was even humming "Welcome to the Neighborhood" under his breath while he . . . it looked as if Walt was measuring the height of the grass in someone's front yard.

"Do you have a permit to carry that ruler?" Luke demanded in a mocking voice.

Walt frowned at him, clearly not appreciating his attempt at humor. "There is no regulation requiring me to have a permit."

"So what are you doing?"

"Official business."

"Since when does the mayor go around measuring peoples' lawns?"

"Since we passed an ordinance limiting the height of the grass."

"You're joking."

"I wouldn't joke about something this serious."

"Of course not. What about the number of leaves on the ground? Do you have an ordinance on that, too?"

"Not that lists specific numbers, no. I

tried to pass one, but the other members of the town council preferred more general language."

"Well, Walt, don't let me keep you from your official totalitarian duties."

Walt frowned at him. "Are you calling me a Communist?"

"No, I'm calling you an idiot."

As Luke walked away, he wondered how he was going to survive the next six months stuck here in this obsessive smallville. Then he got some news that made him smile. Julia Bo Peep was minding a flock of wildlife.

He found Julia in her backyard. "Your neighbor told me you were out here with your llamas."

"They're not *my* llamas."

"They're in your backyard."

"They belong to my mother. Meet Lucy and Ricky. Be careful. I read somewhere that llamas can spit if they get angry."

"Sounds like some of the customers at Maguire's."

"Really? I've never seen any spitting there. The place has been very tidy, and they have an excellent cheeseburger. The décor is a little dark, however. And the menu could use sprucing up."

"What? You want to turn the pub into one of those trendy tofu places?"

"Who said anything about tofu?"

"You keep llamas in your backyard. Don't tell me you're not some health-food addict."

She was actually addicted to Pop-Tarts and had a stash of them hidden in the cabinet above the stove, but she wasn't about to share that info with him. That reminded her that she needed to be sure her mother didn't find them. She'd throw them out for sure.

Note to self: Hide Pop-Tarts elsewhere.

"The fact that my mother has a pair of llamas does not indicate anything about me."

A lie, but he brought that out in her. The need to deviate from the truth. And the need to just stare at him. Luke looked even better in daylight than he had the night before. He was wearing black jeans and a T-shirt again.

"What about the fact that you like yellow daisies on your underwear?" Luke inquired with a wickedly slow smile. "Does that *indicate* anything about you?"

"No, but the fact that you brought it up indicates that you are deliberately trying to embarrass me," Julia retorted.

She met his stare head-on, refusing to look away from the blatant sexual heat he was aiming her way.

Note to self: You are immune.

Sure, there was something going on here,

but it took more than physical chemistry to impress her these days.

She narrowed her eyes in a female warning to back off.

Luke responded by slowly undressing her with his deep, Dylan Thomas eyes.

Their visual duel was interrupted by the sudden arrival of Toni, who proudly declared, "Girls have vaginas!"

And so it went . . . just another Sunday morning in Julia's now totally-out-of-whack world.

Chapter Four

Having completed her emphatic vagina monologue, Toni the Biter marched back inside, leaving Luke and Julia alone with the llamas.

Julia restrained from rolling her eyes, or tearing her hair out, or any of the many things she was tempted to do — including giving in to that hottie-biker-thing Luke had going on.

No, she maintained her decorum, her control, her cool.

She did allow herself one tiny sigh of relief that her niece was back inside, but that quickly evaporated when Luke said, "Your sister thinks we had sex."

Julia blinked. "You had sex with my sister?"

"No, she thinks *you* and *I* had sex."

Julia looked around, wanting to be sure they weren't overheard before replying. The llamas appeared to be eavesdropping, their ears inclined in her direction, but otherwise the coast seemed to be clear. She really didn't want any witnesses to a discussion about sex with Luke.

Julia kept her voice low and calm. "How do you know she thinks . . . that?"

"She told me so."

That sounded like something Skye would do. "What did you say?"

"Nothing."

"Nothing?" Her voice rose. "Why didn't you deny it?"

"I figured that was *your* job."

"You could have told her that we only met yesterday."

"That doesn't mean we couldn't have had sex."

"Yes, it does. I don't have sex with men I just met."

"So how long do you have to know them then? Two days? A week? A month?"

"I am not answering that question."

"Why not? Afraid the answer will ruin your reputation?"

"No." Julia was infinitely more afraid her family's wackiness would ruin her sterling reputation, one she'd worked so hard to create. "Look, I'm sorry my sister said anything to you. She won't be bothering you again."

"What about you?"

"What about me?"

"Will you be bothering me again?"

"I never bothered you in the first place. You're the one who approached me."

"I told you. I have a thing for women in Bo Peep costumes."

"I am no longer wearing that costume."

"Yeah, I noticed that." He'd been trained to notice a lot of things, like the tension on Julia's face at the mention of her sister. Definitely something going on there. Given his own family history, he could relate to having what the navel-gazers called "family issues." Not that he dwelled on stuff like that.

"Did you come here for a reason?" Julia asked.

"Absolutely."

"Care to tell me what that reason is?"

Instead of answering, he asked a question of his own. "How long have you lived here?"

"Three years," she automatically replied and then wanted to kick herself for responding to his bossy tone of voice.

"That explains it then."

"Explains what?"

"Why you still think this place is so great."

Julia looked up at the back of her house. "I realize it needs new gutters, but . . ."

"I wasn't talking about your house. I was talking about this town."

"If you dislike it so much, why are you here?"

"I was stuck between a rock and a hard place. This is the rock."

She didn't want to know where the hard place was. Her mental image was naughty enough. She had no idea if he meant to trigger such a response from her or if it was entirely her own fault. Either way, she felt herself getting all hot and bothered inside.

He'd had that effect on her from the first instant. Physical chemistry. Nothing more than that.

"Why are *you* here?" he asked.

"I live here."

"I mean this town. What made you come here?"

"A job at the library. I fell in love with Serenity Falls the first time I saw it when I came for my interview."

"So you're one of those."

"One of what?"

"The rose-colored-glasses crowd. The ones who always see the best in people, who always think the glass is half-full."

"And what are you?"

"A realist."

"Who always sees the glass half-empty?"

"Who knows there's nothing really in the glass."

"That's a pretty cynical way of looking at things."

"There's nothing cynical about the truth."

"There's a difference between your opinion and the truth."

"No, there's not. I see things as they are. You see them as you want them to be."

"And you learned all this about me after spending just a few minutes in my company. Amazing."

"So I've been told."

"Amazing and totally inaccurate. You're the one who has the distorted view of things."

"By *things* you mean this town?"

"You've been gone for what . . . ten years?"

"Twelve. I see the gossips have been busy at work filling you in."

"Someone mentioned who you were."

"And did they also tell you all about my evil-doings?"

"They may have related one or two high-lights."

"And probably warned you to stay away from me."

"It wasn't like that."

"Sure, it was." He shrugged, but there was something in his eyes, the flicker of a shadow that was there and gone. "Town bad boy. Trouble. Evil seed. I've heard it all before."

So had she, about her own family . . . but that was another matter and certainly not one she ever intended to share with him.

"So what are you going to do about it?" Luke demanded.

"About what?"

"About their warnings."

"I don't plan on doing anything. What about you? What do you plan on doing?"

"Raising some hell. Isn't that was hell-raisers do?" Luke considered hauling her in his arms and kissing her, but one of the llamas was eyeing him the way a con artist eyed an easy mark. Llamas spit, and the big brown one looked aggravated.

So did Julia.

"If you came into town to make trouble, that's your business," she said.

"Actually, my business is Maguire's Pub."

"Where you plan on raising hell?"

"Raising hell and the price of the burger on the menu. It's been the same for more than a decade."

"Sounds like an astute business decision."

"You say it as if you don't expect me to make many of those."

"No, I just meant that takes a lot of thought."

"What does? Raising prices?"

"Running a business."

"And you'd know this because . . . ?"

"My mother has run a number of businesses." Not that Angel put a lot of thought into her endeavors, instead relying on the runes, or fate, or karma, or a blind belief that everything would somehow work out.

"What kind of businesses?"

"The details aren't important. However, if you're interested in checking out some books on business administration, you can do so at the library."

Luke wanted to check her out, see if her lips were as smooth as they looked, her breasts as firm. He felt kind of weird having these thoughts about a librarian. Bookworms had never been his type before.

But there was always a first time for everything. And he was definitely looking forward to his first time with Julia.

"Are you crazy?" Julia confronted her sister in the kitchen a few minutes later. She'd somehow managed to evade Luke and send him on his way so she could come inside and set Skye straight.

"I can't believe you said something like that to him."

"And I can't believe you've got matching red towels in your downtairs bathroom." Skye frowned at her while dipping a tea bag into Julia's *Smart Chick* ceramic mug. "Don't you know that unbleached cotton is the most environmentally friendly?"

Julia waved her hands. "That has nothing to do with what we're talking about. Stop changing the subject, and answer my question."

"So you're saying that the welfare of the entire planet is of no interest to you?"

"I'm saying that I want to know why you said what you did to Luke."

Skye took her time wrapping the tea bag around a teaspoon before replying. "It's obvious."

"What is?"

"That you two are hot for each other."

Julia rolled her eyes. "Oh, please. I just met the man yesterday."

"So what? Time is irrelevant. I refuse to live in the world of time. It's too restrictive."

"Are you saying you'd have sex with someone you just met?"

"If I wanted to, yes."

"Well, I wouldn't."

"Wouldn't what? Want to?"

"Wouldn't do anything like that."

Skye shook her head, making her spiky hair stand even more on end. "You are such a prude. I can't believe we're sisters."

"Ditto."

"So how did you get this way?"

"What way?"

"All puritanical." Skye took a sip of her tea. "Is it from living here?"

"What are you talking about?"

"Has living in this town brainwashed you into believing their propaganda?"

"No one has brainwashed me. And there's nothing wrong with Serenity Falls."

"Not if you're into cloning. The houses all look the same."

"That's not true."

"They all have green doors."

"Walt thought it made them look more uniform, so it was part of a neighborhood improvement effort last year."

"You're living in a town that tells you what color to paint your doors. Come on. You don't think that's strange?"

"No, I don't. Having llamas in my back-yard is strange. Having a four-year-old tell me about her vagina is strange."

Skye grinned. "Toni is very proud of her female power."

"Good for her. But she doesn't have to go bragging about it in front of everyone."

"Define everyone."

"Luke."

"I'm sure he's heard the word *vagina* be-fore. And had intimate contact with a number of them, I'll bet."

Julia put her hands over her ears. "I am *so* not having this conversation with you."

Skye shrugged. "Hey, you're the one who started it."

Julia lowered her hands and gave her younger sister a firm look. "Just don't speak to anyone else about me."

"Why not?"

"Because I said so."

Skye just laughed.

"I mean it. Don't speak to anyone about me."

"Get over yourself." Skye took her mug and walked away.

"Wait a minute. Angel didn't say how long you planned on staying with me."

"Because we don't know. You know how Angel is."

"There's not enough grass in my backyard to feed llamas. Not to mention the fact that it's illegal to have them there."

"That doesn't surprise me. Everything in this town is illegal."

Too bad housing family from out of town wasn't illegal, Julia couldn't help thinking to herself. She did love her mother and sister. She just loved them more when they were on the opposite side of the country.

"Trust me, we wouldn't have come here if

there was any other option," Skye noted. "You were definitely our last choice."

Julia should have been pleased with this news, but somehow it ended up making her feel totally inadequate. But then Skye had been doing that since she was old enough to talk — making Julia feel incompetent. You'd think as an older sister, Julia would be the one who'd be more in control, more confident.

Au contraire.

Skye was always the one who marched right in and did whatever she wanted.

Julia was always the one who tried to clean up the mess afterward.

It stopped here.

Okay, maybe not right here right now at this very second, but in the extremely near future.

Julia would help out her family this one last time and then they'd have to take responsibility for themselves.

What a concept.

"I hear you were visiting the librarian with the llamas," Adele noted upon his return to Maguire's.

"The rumor mill at work again." Luke removed his leather jacket and tossed it onto a nearby chair. "Did you also hear we're raising the price of our burgers?"

"That her idea?"

"Who?"

"The librarian with the llamas."

"What makes you think it was her idea? You don't think I can come up with a business concept on my own?"

Adele shrugged. "I'm just saying that you go visit her and come back here announcing the price of the burgers is going up. Anything else you want to raise? Because if we're reprinting the menus, you might as well get it all done with at once."

"Who said anything about reprinting the menus?"

"How else were you planning on letting the customers know about the price change?"

"By writing it in."

Adele made a face. "That's tacky."

"So?"

"So my cooking deserves better than tacky menus."

"Printing new menus costs money."

"You have to spend money to make money."

"No, I don't."

"Yes, you do. It's a well-known fact."

"It's not known by me. We're writing on the menus. Get over it."

"You're just a regular bluebird of happiness today, aren't you?"

"I had a run-in with a sanctimonious idiot named Walt."

"And what did our illustrious mayor have to say?"

"The guy's a maggot."

"I believe he's a Republican."

"I thought they believed in government staying out of people's business."

"That's part of their national platform, I believe, yes."

"Then where does Walt get off telling people how high their grass can grow? He actually had a ruler in his hand."

"Well, they passed an ordinance, you know. To keep the town looking good."

"How did they get away with that?"

Adele shrugged. "It seemed like a good idea at the time."

"Lots of stupid things do. That's why you give them further thought."

"Hindsight is always twenty-twenty," she replied. "Listen, since you're redoing the menus, I think we should add sweet potato fries. They're always popular when I make them, but not everyone knows about them because they aren't listed anywhere."

Luke belatedly recalled Julia's comment about the menu needing some sprucing up.

"I'm not adding anything tofu," he warned Adele.

"Veggie burgers might be a good idea. I've got a file full of ideas." She hustled over to a small table in the corner of the kitchen. "Your dad refused to change anything."

Which made Luke want to turn everything upside down.

"I met the nicest man down by the library," Angel told Julia.

"What was his name?"

"He wouldn't tell me."

Don't let it be the library director, Julia prayed. "What did he look like? What did you say to him?"

"That big business was trying to ruin yet another scenic spot."

"What are you talking about?"

"Serenity Falls. The waterfalls."

"You went to see them?"

"No, but I was told they are beautiful. And that a big company wants to bottle the spring water and sell it."

"Those are only rumors at this point."

"That's always how these things start out. As rumors. Then, by the time you wake up and smell the coffee, it's a done deal."

"What did this guy look like?"

"He had the saddest eyes."

"That doesn't give me much to go on."

"He had long gray hair that was held back in a braid."

"That would be Tyler."

"Who is he?"

"He does odd jobs around town. No one really knows much about him."

"He seemed like someone I could really talk to. Aside from the fact that he also appeared to be a man of few words."

Julia could see how her mom could relate to Tyler.

"We should invite him over for dinner sometime soon," Angel said.

"I don't actually know him."

"Well, I do."

"You just met him today."

"Julia thinks you shouldn't have sex with a guy you just met today," Skye stated as she strolled into the kitchen and grabbed an apple. "Are these organically grown?"

"I don't think so," Julia replied.

"Where's the closest organic market?"

"I have no idea."

"Do you have any idea of what kind of pesticides are used on stuff like this?" Skye held up the apple as if it were radioactive and might start glowing any second.

"I'd have to get organic food before I could invite Tyler to dinner," Angel said. "I can check the Internet to find the closest organic market."

"Since when do you surf the Internet?" Julia demanded.

"Angel is a pro," Skye said. "That's how she got Ricky and Lucy. Via the Internet."

"You ordered them over the Internet?"

Angel nodded, looking quite pleased with herself. "More or less. I joined some listserves with other folks interested in llamas and got to know some people there. Those connections led me to Ricky and Lucy."

"They can't stay in my backyard."

"Of course not," Angel agreed. "That's only temporary."

That gave Julia hope. Her mother had been reasonable about the llamas. Maybe that meant she had a plan after all. One that didn't involve crashing at Julia's house.

But Julia couldn't rely on that. "My neighbor may have somewhere they can go. Her cousin owns a farm nearby." She paused as the phone rang. It was Mrs. Selznick.

"My cousin, the one who owns the dairy farm, is out of town at a funeral," Mrs. Selznick said. "I won't be able to reach him until the middle of the week. I could call him on his cell, but I didn't want to bother him at the moment."

"Of course not. I understand. We can wait a few days."

"What do llamas eat?"

"I'm not sure, but my mother knows. They're her llamas."

"They don't consume small house-pets, do they?"

"I'm sure they don't."

"Because I wouldn't want anything happening to my little Terminator. He's highly excitable, you know."

Mrs. Selznick's chihuahua got the shakes if anyone even glanced in his direction. "Yes, I know."

"And seeing another life form so large might be stressful for him."

"I understand."

"I got him from the lady who ran my Spanish class." Mrs. Selznick was addicted to taking classes. From Chinese cooking to tap dancing, you name it, she'd probably taken a class about it. "Her husband retired and was mean to the poor little guy. So naturally I had to take him and rescue him from such a bad situation."

"Un-huh." Julia's attention was wandering to where her mother and sister were huddled together — studying the contents of her fridge and shaking their heads. Not a good sign.

"I heard a rumor that you might be using the llamas as prognosticators. Does that mean that if there's a gas leak or something, that they'd die first and alert us? Like canaries in the coal mines?"

"No. The groundhog is a prognosticator, foretelling the future weather."

"And llamas can do that sort of thing, too? Tell us if we're going to have a longer winter?"

"That's a possibility I'm investigating."

"Well, that's exciting, dear. It may well be an advantage for us to have in our efforts regarding the Best Small Towns in America judges. I wonder if any other towns have llamas like that?"

"I'm going to have my mother research that on the Internet."

"I wanted to take a course about the Internet, but it was full by the time I registered."

"That's too bad." Julia waved her mother and sister away from her fridge, but they ignored her and opened a large garbage bag instead. "Listen, Mrs. Selznick, I've got to go now."

"Okay."

"Please let me know when you speak to your cousin and pass on my sympathies to him. Good-bye."

The instant she hung up the phone, Julia raced over to protect her food. "What are you doing?" She grabbed a container of Cool Whip from her mother's hands. "Put that back!"

"It's full of chemicals. And artificial sweeteners."

"I don't care."

"Well, I do." Angel yanked the container away from her and dropped it into the garbage bag that was already half-full. "Your body is a temple. You should honor it by only allowing pure foods to enter."

Julia stood spread-eagle in front of her open fridge, her hands gripping the edges.

"Step away from my refrigerator!" she ordered them both. Her kick-butt Carmen Diaz personality was back.

"Now, Julia, we're only doing this for your own good," Angel said in a soothing voice.

Skye was blunter. "The chemicals in all this processed food have clearly messed up your mind."

No, Skye and Angel were doing that. They were the ones messing up her mind.

"This is my house, and you've got no right to tell me what I can have in my own fridge." There, she'd made her stand. Drew her line in the sand. Made her feelings known.

Two seconds later, Toni walked up and bit

Julia right above her kneecap.

"Ow!" Julia had to hop away from the fridge over to a chair, where she sat and stared at the set of teethmarks on her skin.

Angel shook her head. "You see, even a small child realizes that this food is bad for you and should be removed."

Julia stared at her in disbelief. "She bit me!"

Angel shrugged. "Her way of communicating to you that you were behaving inappropriately."

"Me? She's the one doing damage. I told you, no biting." Julia fixed Toni with her best librarian stare.

Toni responded by sticking out her tongue at her. "I don't like you."

"I don't like you, either."

"That's not nice," Angel told Julia.

"She started it," Julia muttered.

How had she ended up like this, bitten and battered, so quickly? Her family hadn't even been in town for twenty-four hours, and already she'd been reduced to arguing with a child who could give that shark from *Jaws* a run for his money.

All in all, it was a sad state of affairs and one she resolved to get under control — right after she went to the store and got more Cool Whip. First things first.

"Are you Luke Maguire?" a nun asked him.

He eyed her suspiciously. He wouldn't put it past the loco mayor to have called in religious experts to perform an exorcism on him, so he wasn't really eager to identify himself without additional intel. "Who wants to know?"

"I do." She extended her hand and gave him an unexpectedly firm handshake. "I'm Sister Mary with the Sisters of the Poor Charities from over in Rock Creek."

"Oh, right." Luke remembered belatedly that he'd called them first thing this morning and been told everything would be picked up between four and five. "The stuff is all upstairs. I'll show you and then you can have the guys move it."

"There are no guys. There's just me and Sister Margaret." She tilted her head toward the beanpole tall nun beside her.

Neither woman was what you'd call athletic . . . or young.

"That won't work."

Sister Mary's eyes narrowed. "What do you mean?"

"I mean there's too much heavy furniture and other stuff for the two of you to carry it."

"I can assure you that Sister Margaret and I have hauled plenty of heavy items into the truck before."

Luke frowned at that news. He couldn't remember the last time he'd set foot in a church, but still . . . Nuns and little old ladies deserved certain courtesies. "It's not right."

"Well, perhaps not, but volunteers are hard to come by these days."

"You're telling me you can't round up a few guys to do the heavy lifting?"

"Are you telling me you're volunteering to assist us?"

Luke hesitated. The plan was for the charity to haul the stuff out without him having to deal with it or see it again.

"I didn't think so," the nun noted briskly. "Come along, Sister Margaret."

Luke put his hand out. "Hang on. For God's sake . . ."

She fixed him with a steely glare. "Do not take the Lord's name in vain, young man."

"Okay, fine. I'll go round up some guys. Give me a few minutes."

"You're welcome to try. Meanwhile, Sister Margaret and I will go on up and see what is involved."

"Don't lift anything heavy," Luke warned them.

It was Sunday. Who could he get?

He checked with Adele. She'd know what to do.

"Try Big Al a few doors down," she suggested. "He owns Cosmic Comics and should be closing up about now. I'll contact Tyler and see if he can come over."

The CLOSED sign hung on the door of Cosmic Comics, but the lights were still on so Luke banged on the door.

"Open up!" His years in the FBI guaranteed that the order was obeyed. But not happily.

"We're closed," a big black guy growled.

Luke actually had to look up to meet his eyes. The guy was a giant. He had to stand at least six-foot-five and weigh more than three hundred pounds. He had the build of someone who'd spent plenty of time doing physical labor, and he reminded Luke of that actor from *The Green Mile* — another bear of a man.

"You Big Al?"

"Who wants to know?" he repeated Luke's earlier words.

"Me and the Sisters of the Poor Charities."

"Look, I give to United Way once a year, and that's it." He went to close the door again, the overhead lights shining on his smoothly shaved bald head.

"No, wait." Luke shoved his foot in the doorway. "I need your help."

"And you are?"

"Luke Maguire."

"The new owner of Maguire's?"

"Yeah."

"So?"

"So I've got these two nuns at my place —"

"Whoa man, I'm not into those two nuns, a rabbi, and a priest walked into a bar jokes."

"I'm serious. I need help carrying some furniture out to their truck."

"Whose truck?"

"The nuns'."

"Since when do nuns drive a truck?" His look turned increasingly suspicious. "Is this some kind of Halloween scam?"

"No, look, I'm donating a bunch of furniture to this charity for the needy. Only they don't have anyone to carry it. I need another set of hands, Big Al."

"The name's Algee Washington," he said. "Only buddies are allowed to call me Big Al."

"Sorry. Adele sent me over."

"Well, hell, why didn't you say so in the first place? I'd do anything for her. Let me just grab my keys and set the alarm." A second later, he'd switched off the lights and joined Luke on the sidewalk. "Lead me to the nuns."

Of course the two sisters hadn't obeyed Luke's orders, and he and Algee walked into the upstairs apartment to find the nuns struggling at either end of a table. "Put that down," Luke ordered.

They obeyed. "I'm sorry. We thought all the furniture in this room was being donated."

"It is, but I told you two not to carry anything heavy."

"Which is why we didn't pick up the couch," Sister Mary retorted in exasperation.

"Allow me to assist you, sisters," Algee said with enough charm to stop an elephant in its tracks.

Sister Margaret giggled like a schoolgirl but Sister Mary kept her mind on business, directing them all with efficient orders.

Tyler showed up a few minutes later. Even with Algee and Tyler's help, it still took more than an hour to move all the stuff out.

"You sure you don't want this talking mackerel?" Algee asked.

Luke nodded. "Positive."

"And the beer collection? Seems the perfect thing for a tavern to have."

Luke shot him one of his don't-give-me-any-more-crap looks, one of several things he'd picked up in the Marine Corps. "The point is to get rid of this junk, not try in vain to talk me into keeping it."

"You could probably get good money for this beer can collection on eBay," Algee added.

"Hear that sisters?" Luke pointed to the three boxes. "You can get good money for the beer can collection on eBay. Go for it."

"Excellent idea," Sister Mary said before turning to Tyler. "We have warm meals at the shelter in Rock Springs if you need any assistance."

"He just looks homeless, but he's not," Algee said on Tyler's behalf.

"He's probably socking all his money into some investment portfolio on the stock market," Luke said.

"Is that true?" Obviously not one to be distracted from a possible noble cause, Sister Mary laid her hand on Tyler's arm, right above a tear in his flannel shirt.

"I'm not investing in the stock market." Tyler's voice sounded rusty. "Don't worry about me, sister. There are plenty of folks worse off than I am."

"If you ever want to talk . . ."

"I'm not one for much talking," Tyler said curtly.

Sister Mary nodded her understanding and removed her hand. "If you should change your mind, here's my card." She handed it to him. "The offer goes for you, too, Luke."

He frowned, not at all pleased to be lumped in the same category as Tyler.

But Luke still retained enough of a trace of manners not to reject the card the nun handed him. "I don't need any help," he said. "I just want to get rid of all this junk, that's all."

"Ridding yourself of the material goods doesn't mean you'll rid yourself of the memories," Sister Mary said.

The knowing look in her eyes remained with Luke long after she'd left, making him feel guilty for tossing the card she'd given him . . . but not preventing him from pitching it anyway.

Chapter Five

"Trick or treat!"

Angel smiled at the young girl standing on the doorstep. "And who are you supposed to be?"

"Cinderella."

"Really?" Angel bent down so she was eye-level with her. "Did you know that Cinderella actually went into the shoe business? She designed footwear that was environmentally friendly and didn't harm any animals. So obviously leather was out. Her business was so successful that she bailed out the king and queen, who'd driven the kingdom's economy into the ground with huge deficits caused by their excessive lifestyle. In return, Cinderella demanded free elections so every citizen could participate in the selection of their government. The Green Party won and opened the palace to everyone. And that's the way to get a happy ending." Angel paused to reach for a bowl.

The self-proclaimed Cinderella eyed it suspiciously. "What's that?"

"Organic apples."

"Yuck. Where's the candy?"

"Candy is poison."

The little girl's eyes widened. "Poison? You mean like what the witch gave Sleeping Beauty?"

"Of course not. And they prefer to be called Wiccans, not witches. Speaking of Sleeping Beauty, we've got a spinning wheel on display in the front yard. Did you see?"

"The witch had one of those."

"That was all a big mistake. Actually, she taught Sleeping Beauty how to spin the most beautiful things so she could be self-sufficient and not depend on some prince to support her or rescue her. Soon SB, as she was known in the business world, had an entire line of scarves and sweaters all woven out of the finest natural fibers. Hey, where are you going?"

"To find candy," the little girl stated in disgust.

Julia returned home from a long day at the library only to be almost mowed down by a mini-Cinderella tearing down the front sidewalk as if the hounds of hell were after her. She appeared more aggravated than frightened, however.

"What are you doing?" Julia asked Angel

the minute she reached the front door.

"Greeting the trick-or-treaters."

"Where's the candy I asked you to hand out?"

Angel shuddered. "I threw it away, of course."

"Then what are you giving the kids when they come to the door?"

"Knowledge and organic apples." She held out the bowl so Julia could check it out.

But Julia wasn't that interested in the fruit at the moment. "What kind of knowledge?"

"That witches aren't bad. And you'd be amazed how many children don't know the real story about Cinderella and Sleeping Beauty."

Julia sighed as she removed her coat and put it on one of the wooden pegs on the wall. "None of them know it, because you made it up."

"So did the male chauvinists who wrote the fairy tales in the first place." Angel planted her hands on her hips, which were covered by one of the filmy skirts she favored in colorful Indian cotton. "They made it up, so why can't I? Especially since I'm improving on the original story, which only perpetuates the myth of a woman's dependency on a man for happiness."

"The trick-or-treaters didn't come here for a lecture."

"I know." Angel beamed. "So it's a special treat for them to get one."

"Not really." Julia rubbed her forehead. She had a major headache drumming in her head. Halloween was always a wild day at the library, and today was no exception.

A glance in the mirror provided her with a revealing mental snapshot of herself standing there wearing a white blouse and brown pants and her mother who was wearing a colorful array of scarves wrapped around her upper body and a fluid skirt.

You couldn't find two more opposite females. Angel represented everything loose and flowing in the universe and Julia . . . well, she represented control and order.

Yet her mother looked happier than Julia did. What was with that?

Sure, Angel looked happier. She never worried about anything.

Wearing different clothing wouldn't change the way Julia felt inside. Would it?

Julia looked away, wondering if this new-found sense of dissatisfaction was a result of her mother's stay in her house.

The reality was that fashion choices were the least of her worries at the moment.

"Why is there a spinning wheel in the front yard?"

"Because your sister is demonstrating how it's used."

"And the fire pit next to her would be . . . ?"

"For light. It gets dark so early here. But getting back to the spinning wheel, it ties into the Sleeping Beauty story. You remember how she started weaving and developed SB Designs, right?"

"How could I forget?" Her mother had rewritten all the classics and made up a few of her own.

"What's Toni supposed to be?" Julia asked as her niece waddled by.

"An organic vegetable."

That explained the strange, bulbous look. "What is she, a rutabaga or something?"

"No, a yam. But the design didn't come out quite right. I was sewing it in a hurry because I couldn't decide whether to have her dress as a druid the way I am, or as a protestor from the sixties, or maybe as a tarot card. I was just bombarded with so many creative ideas that it was difficult deciding which one to choose."

Julia belatedly registered something she should have noticed first thing. "Why was there a sign on the front door about llamas spitting?"

"Well, I thought it might be nice for some of the older kids to see the llamas. After all, they probably haven't had the opportunity to see llamas close up before. But I didn't want you to get upset in case Ricky and Lucy spat at someone, so just as a precaution I put up that sign. Totally for your benefit."

"I'd have preferred that you leave the llamas out of the Halloween festivities entirely."

"Well, I didn't want them getting lonely."

Julia was almost afraid to ask. "Did they behave?"

"Admirably."

Julia sighed in relief.

"For the most part," Angel added.

"What's that mean?"

"Well, they didn't seem to care for one boy in particular. What was his name again . . . ?" Angel tugged on her right ear, something she always did when trying to retrieve a memory.

"It wasn't Billy, was it?"

"That's it. He was dressed as a football player, and that might have upset Ricky. He prefers soccer to football."

"Who does?"

"Ricky."

"He's a llama."

"Who likes soccer."

"What did he do to Billy?"

"Not much. Just set his boundaries."

"Billy is the mayor's son."

"So he told me."

"What exactly did he say?"

"I'd rather not repeat it. He was a bit upset at the time."

"Because Ricky set boundaries."

"And because of the wad of llama spittle on his chin."

"Ricky's chin?"

"No, Billy's."

Julia took a deep breath.

Note to self: Remain calm.

"When did all this happen?"

"About twenty minutes ago. But enough about me." Angel patted her arm. "How was your day at work?"

"Just peachy." The library director had brought her the news that Walt liked the idea of the llamas being Serenity Falls prognosticators and wanted research done on how that could be accomplished. Much of her day was spent on that, in between helping library patrons and working out glitches in the November staffing schedule for the reference desk.

Julia wondered if Walt would continue to be as keen on the llamas given what they'd done to his son.

She didn't have long to wonder, however, as Walt phoned her a few seconds later.

"I'm so sorry," Julia began, when Walt interrupted her.

"I should hope so. I would think your loyalties to Serenity Falls would take top priority in this situation."

Not knowing where he was going with this train of thought, she just paused and waited for him to say more.

"But now I hear that you're thinking of moving," Walt continued.

"Me?" Julia rubbed her forehead again and curled up on her favorite chair. She needed aspirin and Pop-Tarts. "I have no intention of moving."

"Not you, the llamas."

"You *told* me to move them."

"That was before I considered the idea of them being our prognosticators. The town council is going to have a special conference call about it later this week."

"But you said it's illegal to have llamas in my backyard."

"Yes, well, we can work around that, perhaps."

"Uh, Walt, have you spoken with your son recently?"

"What does that have to do with anything?"

"Well, he and one of the llamas had a slight misunderstanding."

"That wouldn't surprise me. He told me you shouted at him before the Fall Fun Festival the other day."

"Did he tell you why?"

"He may have. I wasn't paying that much attention."

Which could be one reason why Billy acted up so much — to get his father's attention.

"But getting back to the llamas," Walt said. "I thought we had an understanding."

"I'm sorry, but I'm still not following you."

"The word on the street is that your mother is going to move the llamas."

"Move them where?"

"To a farm."

"Right. My neighbor mentioned that her cousin, who's a dairy farmer, might have room on his property . . ."

"Oh no, we're not talking about him. I'm talking about one of the old-timers farms. The Amish. If she does that, we can't set up the publicity opportunities I had planned."

"She could always bring back the llamas for any special events . . ."

"But then they wouldn't be Serenity Falls llamas. They'd be *Amish* llamas."

"Are you afraid they're going to try to convert them or something?"

"I'm just saying that once they leave the confines of our lovely city, we lose control over them."

"Well, to be honest, given the fact that my mother owns them and she's not a resident of Serenity Falls, you've already lost control over them. Or rather, you never had control over them to begin with."

"But your mother seemed open to my ideas when I spoke with her earlier this afternoon."

"Did you ask her about the Amish farm then?"

"No, because I hadn't heard about it at that point. Hold on a moment, will you?" She heard the muffled sound caused by Walt putting one hand over the phone. "What are you boys doing out there?"

"Trick or treat!"

"Trick or treat in Serenity Falls ends at six p.m. and it's now four minutes past that time."

"*Awww,* come on . . ."

"Rules are meant to be followed. Now go home." More muffled sounds as Walt removed his hand. "I'm sorry about that. Now where were we? Oh yes. The llamas. What did you turn up in your research?"

"A lot about the care and history of llamas, which were first domesticated nearly six thousand years ago by the Quechua Indians. Did you know that they were first brought to this country by William Randolph Hearst in the 1920s for his personal zoo? They're good at guarding sheep and have a life expectancy of twenty to twenty-five years —"

Walt interrupted her. "Yes, but what about predicting the weather?"

"I haven't found anything on that yet."

"Well, keep looking. We need to have something special so we stand out. The competition is fierce, you know. Every town in the country wants to be the best. Except for Rock Creek, of course."

"Why are they different?"

Walt chuckled. "Come on, you know the answer to that. You just have to drive over there and take a look around. Half the commercial buildings in town are boarded up or for sale."

"I haven't actually visited Rock Creek yet."

"Smart of you. There's nothing to see over there. You do realize that the big game is coming up soon, right? Between our high school football team and theirs. I believe the library will be doing its part to show their support for our hometown boys. But getting back to the llamas, I want you to stay focused on this and stay away from Luke Maguire."

"What do you mean?"

"I heard that he was over at your place the other day. If he's bothering you, just dial 911 and have the sheriff deal with him."

"He's not bothering me." But Walt was beginning to, ordering her around.

"I'm just saying that there's no need for you to be afraid of him."

"I'm not."

"Good. Because he's been trouble since the day he was born. His departed father often said that, and it's true."

"That's a terrible thing to say about a child." Now Julia felt guilty for her fleeting similar thoughts about her own niece. She doubted the boyish Luke had bitten anyone by the age of four, however.

Walt shrugged. "Terrible but true. Listen, I've got to go. Remember what I said."

What she remembered was the shadowy look in Luke's eyes when he'd talked about the town warning her to stay away from him.

"What are your thoughts on Jell-O wrestling?" Luke asked Algee as the big guy took a seat at the bar.

Algee eyed him suspiciously. "Yo, I just want a Bud, man."

A minute later Luke set a beer in front of him. "Now back to Jell-O wrestling."

"I've got nothing against it. Why the question? You thinking of adding entertainment here at Maguire's?"

"I was kicking the idea around."

"You'd get kicked out of town if you tried that."

Luke just grinned.

Algee nodded. "Ah, I get it now. That's what you're after. Stirring things up. Well, I can relate. Don't think that a black man opening a comic book store in town didn't set off a few alarms."

"I'll bet."

Algee looked around. "You've got a nice crowd here, considering it's Halloween night."

"Yeah, well, offering a free beer if you come in wearing a costume helped, I'm sure."

"What are you supposed to be?" Algee pointed to Luke's black T-shirt and jeans.

"A bartender."

"Oh, yeah, wow. How could I miss that?"

"I was expecting you to come in as Superman or something."

Algee pointed to Superman's "S" logo

tattoo on his right bicep.

Luke shook his head. "Tattoos aren't considered costumes. That beer is not free."

"You owe me, man, for nearly breaking my back hauling out that furniture."

"I thought you were doing that for the nuns and because you and Adele are buddies."

Algee shrugged a pair of broad shoulders that would have done a defensive lineman proud. "Well, yeah, sure, that was one or two reasons."

"Where would I be if I gave out free beers to everyone who helps me out?"

"Two beers shorter than you were before? Unless Tyler doesn't drink beer? It's not like you've got folks lining up around the block waiting to help you out."

Luke was distracted from answering by the arrival of Julia's sister, Skye. She was wearing black biker boots and a strange-looking skirt over tight pants along with a tank top. She had a huge fuzzy sweater wrapped around her. He couldn't tell if what she was wearing was a costume or not.

She headed right for him. "My sister says I'm not supposed to talk to you. But I never do what she tells me."

Algee rolled his eyes and took off for safer ground with his beer in hand.

"Maybe you should listen to her in this case," Luke replied.

The multiple silver bangles on her wrist jangled as Skye hopped onto Algee's abandoned bar stool. "I think she likes you."

"I think you like making trouble."

"I've been told it's a natural talent of mine," she noted with cheerful pride.

"I've been told the same thing."

Skye nodded. "I know. I recognized that about you right away. Which is why I was so surprised that Julia is attracted to you."

"What makes you think she is?" Damn. Luke hadn't meant to show any interest. His lack of a good night's sleep since he'd landed back in this backwater 'burb must be catching up with him. Although he'd gotten rid of the contents in his father's apartment, the walls still talked.

Sleep deprivation, that was it. That was his problem.

"I just know." Skye gave him one of those looks women mastered when they thought they held the upper hand. "And I'm surprised because, frankly, I wouldn't have thought you and a belly-dancing librarian would have much in common."

"Julia belly dances?" The instant mental visual he got of that was enough to make him go hard in two seconds flat.

"Yes. And she's even better than I am, and I'm good enough to be giving lessons. Which is why I came in here."

"To belly dance?"

"No, to ask if it's okay to post a flyer about the classes we're offering."

"We?"

"Angel and me. She's teaching yoga, and I'm offering belly dancing."

"What's Julia offering?"

"To shoot us if we don't start bringing in some money. Not that those were her exact words. She's the polite one in the family. The responsible one. Which is yet another reason why her interest in you is so unusual."

Skye's comments were starting to aggravate him. "She told me you wouldn't bother me again."

"I never bothered you in the first place." Skye put her hand on his bare arm. "See? No chemistry."

She was completely right, but he didn't have to let her know that. Luke leaned closer . . . and that's when Julia walked in.

"Skye!" Her outraged voice clearly traveled to Luke's ears.

Skye just grinned and handed Luke the flyer before hopping off the bar stool and sashaying her way out the door. Luke expected Julia to follow her.

She didn't. Instead, she honed in on him with the accuracy of a scud missile. "What were you doing with my sister?"

He wiped an area of the bar he'd already cleaned twice. "What did it look like I was doing?"

"It looked like you were about to kiss her." Julia gave him two seconds to deny it before launching her attack. "Stay away from Skye."

"You like giving orders," Luke noted. "Must be a librarian thing."

"And you seem to like ignoring them. Must be a bad-boy biker thing," she immediately retorted.

"I'm not the only one who ignores your orders. Your own sister —"

She interrupted him. "I'll take care of my sister. You leave her alone."

"You know . . ." He leaned closer to prop his elbows on the bar. "If I didn't know better, I'd say you were jealous."

She raised her nose in the air as if avoiding a foul smell. "I'm not even going to dignify that with an answer."

He grinned. "Yeah, definitely jealous."

She lowered her head to glare at him. "Wrong."

"It's Halloween, you know. You really

should have worn your Bo Peep costume to-night." Leaning closer, he added, "Or you could have put on a belly-dancing costume."

Luke was close enough to see the expression in those hazel-with-a-bit-of-green-going-on eyes of hers go from disconcerted to embarrassed to resigned. "Skye told you, didn't she?"

"That you're an even better belly dancer than she is?" He grinned. "Yeah. She did."

"Well, keep it to yourself."

"Believe me, I will hold that image near and dear to my heart."

"I mean it."

"So do I," he solemnly assured her. "Scout's honor."

"You were a Boy Scout?" She sounded hopeful.

"Are you kidding?" he scoffed. "No way. Listen, how good are you at picking paint colors?"

The abrupt change of subject clearly threw her for a second. "Paint colors?"

"Adele thinks the place could use some sprucing up." Luke glanced at the dingy walls and the display of mounted plastic fish and had to agree that the décor could use some updating. The equipment behind the bar and in the kitchen had been modernized, but nothing else had been.

"Then you should be asking Adele about paint colors."

"She's color-blind."

"Oh."

"I don't want anything weird or pastel."

"You could go with a warm neutral color. Or a nice hunter green like this." She pointed to one of the colors on the paint chart he'd pulled out from beneath the bar before scooting onto a bar stool to get a better look.

A customer required Luke's attention, but when he returned to Julia a few minutes later, he found she'd already filled two paper napkins with notes and was still busily writing away.

Standing there, he noticed the way her blond hair curved against her cheek. She had most of it tucked behind one ear but one bit had come loose, and that made him want to reach out and see if the strands were as silky as they looked.

She was such a golden girl sitting there, all proper and responsible as she studied little squares of paint color with weird names like Canyonlands and Divine and Penny. He couldn't blame his desire on the Bo Peep costume this time. She was wearing regular clothes tonight — jeans, T-shirt, fleece pullover. You couldn't get more L.L.Bean than that.

Yet he still wanted to peel that T-shirt off her shoulders and find out what color her bra was and how it looked against her creamy skin.

She merely had to exist, and she got to him. "So what brought you out on Halloween night?"

"My mother told me Skye was coming to see you."

"Did she tell you why?"

"I didn't stick around long enough to hear that part," Julia admitted.

"Too bad."

"I promised you Skye wouldn't bother you anymore."

"So you came charging in here to protect me from your sister?" he drawled. "How . . . *sweet* of you."

"I did not come charging in here. You make me sound like a rhino or something."

"No, the rhino is the guy in the corner over there, the one sitting with the giraffe."

"Why are all these people in costumes?"

"Hello . . ." He gently tapped her temple. "It's Halloween."

"I know that."

"I'm offering a free beer if you come in wearing a costume."

"Oh."

"Oh. That's it? No comments? No insults?"

"When have I insulted you?"

"Too many times to count."

"Oh, please. That is *so* not true."

He raised an eyebrow. "Really?"

"Yes, really. I've been exceptionally nice to you, especially considering how rude you've been to me."

"Me. Rude to you?"

"Absolutely."

"Yet you're still protecting me from your sister."

"More like I'm protecting *her* from *you*."

"Because you want me for yourself."

"Right," she mocked him. "I don't know how I manage to keep my hands off you."

"It's difficult for you, I'm sure," he noted with pseudo-modesty.

"But I manage."

"Yeah, I noticed that about you. That . . . and your mouth."

"What about my mouth?" She lifted her hand to be sure there weren't any Pop-Tart crumbs stuck to it.

"I like your mouth. I want to kiss it." He reached out and brushed his thumb across her bottom lip. "Slowly. Over and over again."

The costumed crowd faded into the background as Julia was bombarded with a tidal wave of desire. A simple touch, yet her reaction was totally intense.

Her parted lips positively hummed with excitement while shivers of irrational pleasure danced down her spine.

And those eyes of his. They did things to her. Looked at her with such brooding eloquence. Sent her visual messages that bypassed mere words and went directly to visceral passion.

I want you. Naked. Here. Now.

Not that he was stripping her with his gaze or anything tacky like that. This was totally magnetic, like a force field locking on her and *only* her . . . pulling her in.

Julia had abandoned the prim white blouse in exchange for a light blue velvet trimmed V-neck T-shirt she'd owned for ages. The brown pants had been replaced with a comfy pair of jeans. Clothes for relaxing at home in, not for inspiring a guy like Luke to seduce her. So what was going on here?

She'd noticed Skye's absence when Toni had refused to go to bed by eight, which seemed more than a reasonable bedtime for a four-year-old in Julia's opinion and that of the various experts who posted such things on parenting sites on the Internet that Julia had checked out.

When she'd asked her mother where Skye was, she'd heard the alarming news that her sister had headed off to speak to Luke.

Julia hadn't waited to hear more. She'd grabbed a fleece pullover from a peg by the door and headed straight here.

Only to find Luke leaning toward her sister as if he were about to kiss her.

The memory made her jerk back from his tempting touch. "Oh, no, you don't." Her words were meant as much for herself as for him. "What were you talking to my sister about?"

"You."

She wasn't really sure she wanted to know more than that. But she had to ask anyway. "What did she say?"

"That you're attracted to me."

"And you believed her?"

"I believe what I see when I look in your eyes."

Aggravating as he might be, Luke did have a way with words when he wanted to. And then he had those deep Dylan Thomas, I've-got-secrets blue eyes. He only had to look at her to make her want him.

"Don't." Her voice was unsteady.

"Don't what?" He gently traced the line of her jaw with his index finger. "Don't notice your mouth? Don't believe what I see in your eyes? Don't long to kiss you every time I see you?"

"All of the above," she croaked.

He just smiled and shook his head before cupping her cheek in the palm of his big hand. "Sorry, but I don't do well following orders. One of the reasons I didn't re-enlist in the Marine Corps when my time was up."

"I didn't know you were a Marine."

He shrugged and let his hand slip away, looking as if he regretted letting that bit of information slip. "There's a lot about me you don't know."

"I'd like to change that sometime." The words were out before she could stop them.

"You might be able to kiss a few more secrets out of me. It's worth a try. Care to give it your best shot?"

"Here?" She looked around. "In the middle of Maguire's?"

"Wherever, whenever."

His gaze captured hers, and she had a hard time breaking that visual bond. Knowing when it was time to retreat, she slid off the bar stool. "I'll think about it."

"You do that." He sounded ultimately

confident that she'd come around to his way of thinking.

As she walked out of Maguire's, Julia reminded herself that it was Halloween night, a time of madness. That was the reason for her momentary foolishness in flirting with Luke.

Tomorrow things would calm down, and everything would return to normal. That's what she wanted. Not Luke.

Chapter Six

Julia had just finished going through the three most recent issues of *Publishers Weekly* for selection purposes when she happened to look out the library window, the one located beside the reference desk.

Blinking, she removed her reading glasses and scooted her rolling chair around the deep bookshelves that created a half-wall behind the desk. She needed to get closer to the window . . .

What Julia saw made her want to turn and run in the other direction. Or hide in the rarely used anthropology section back in the 572 area of the stacks.

But that would be irresponsible of her.

Her house was located right across the street. The sun was shining down on it . . . and on the mob gathered on the sidewalk in front.

The rolling chair zoomed across the floor as she leapt out of it. On her way out the library's front door, Julia told the part-time assistant at the circulation desk, "I'm taking my lunch now."

Without even bothering to grab her coat, Julia raced home to find out what was going on. People blocked her way. "Excuse me . . ." she said.

"Hey, no cutting! The line starts back there . . . Oh sorry, Julia. I didn't realize it was you," Mabel from the video store said. She had a bright red-and-black tartan cap jauntily perched atop her pink hair.

"What's going on?"

"Sue Ellen says she saw the image of Jesus in the fur of one of the llamas."

This might sound more impressive to Julia had she not known that Sue Ellen Riley was several pancakes short of a stack. She was also someone who loved the limelight. "Where is she?"

"Up there." Mabel pointed toward the head of the line.

"Well, Sue Ellen is mistaken. These are just two llamas named Ricky and Lucy."

"Do they have a manger? Maybe we should use them in the Christmas pageant at St. Mary's?"

"The pageant at our church is better and bigger," someone else stated. "The llamas should be at First Baptist."

"Everyone is welcome at the Unitarian Church," another person piped up.

"Listen, everybody," Julia said, "this is all

just a big misunderstanding."

Mabel's expression turned rebellious. "Are you charging money to see the llamas? Is that it?"

"No, of course not. At least I don't think so . . ." With her family, anything was possible. "Let me go sort this out."

"You do that. And see if you can't get this line to move a little faster," Mabel told her. "I've been standing here longer than I do at Wal-Mart on a crowded Saturday afternoon."

Julia had no trouble spotting Sue Ellen, who still sported the big hair look so popular in the '80s when she was a cheerleader. The sunshine glowed off her golden hair like a huge halo.

No wait, she *was* wearing a halo.

"Sue Ellen, this is getting out of hand."

"Not my doing. A greater force is at work here."

"I don't see it," Dora Abernathy from down the street was saying, squinting through her bifocals at Lucy. The female llama stood primly by the fence, looking perplexed by all the attention. "All I see is a bunch of fur."

"Because that's all there is to see," Julia said in exasperation. "Remember that incident with the Rueben sandwich?"

Sue Ellen's expression turned defensive. "That image was easy to see."

"Because you rigged it that way to increase sales at your brother-in-law's diner," Julia retorted.

"Those were all false accusations. And I certainly didn't rig this. Why would I?"

"How should I know?"

"I'm telling you, I still don't see it!" Dora's voice turned querulous.

"Oh, for heaven's sake, it's right there." Sue Ellen pointed, the glitter stars on her lilac acrylic nails reflecting the sunlight. "Here, on the right side."

"Whose right?" Dora demanded. "The llama's or mine?"

"The llama's."

"When she's facing me?" Dora continued her questions.

"Yes." Sue Ellen paused a beat before adding the kicker. "Maybe only *true believers* are able to see it."

"Well, now that I know where to look, it does resemble a face . . ."

"Enough already!" Julia had had it. "Sue Ellen, I want you to tell all these people that you made a mistake and they should go home."

"Why would I want to do that?"

"Because you're all trespassing on private

property. Why isn't my mother out here? Where is she?"

Sue Ellen shrugged. "She said she was going inside to meditate."

"Maybe you should sic Toni the Biter on them." The suggestion came from Luke, who appeared out of the blue at Julia's side.

"What are you doing here?"

He gave her that slow grin of his. "Enjoying the circus."

"Who's Toni the Biter?" Dora demanded. "Some mob enforcer?"

"She's my four-year-old niece," Julia replied.

Dora frowned. "Your niece is named after a mob enforcer?"

Julia gritted her teeth. "There is no mob enforcer."

"But Luke just said —"

"Listen, everyone . . ." Julia waved her hands in the air to get the crowd's attention. "Just go on home. There's nothing to look at here."

"I wouldn't say that," Luke countered.

"So you see the image, too?" Sue Ellen said.

"I see a pile of crap," he said bluntly.

"That's not possible," Angel said as she emerged from the house. "Llamas are excellent digesters. They leave pellets, not piles.

Or so it said on the Internet."

"Either way, there's nothing pretty about llama shit," Skye stated as she joined them. "Trust me, I know. I've had to clean it up more than my fair share."

"It can be used to fertilize the garden," Angel said.

"Not my garden," Julia said, already noticing the odiferous cloud arising from her backyard.

"What are you doing here?" Angel asked Julia. "I thought you had to work today."

"I did. I looked out the library window and saw that a crowd was amassing around my house so I came home for my lunch hour."

"Is the sheriff standing by to call for reinforcements and crowd control?" Luke asked.

"Of course not." Julia gave him a warning glare. "And don't you say anything to make things worse."

Not the least bit intimidated, Luke had the gall to actually grin. "How can they get worse?"

"Ten dollars to see the image of Jesus today," Skye suddenly called out to the crowd. "Last chance to behold this miracle!"

"Stop that!" Julia hissed, grabbing her sister's arm. "What are you doing?"

"Trying to make some easy money. You said you wanted us to contribute to the household income."

"By legitimate means."

"Well, my belly-dancing class doesn't start until next week, so I won't get any money from my students until then."

"I never said you should promote this kind of thing," Julia protested.

"That call for dollars thinned out the crowd some," Luke noted.

Skye nodded. "Of course it did."

"You should try charging twenty tomorrow," Luke suggested. "Makes it seem like a more valuable experience."

"Stop that." Julia was so aggravated she smacked Luke's leather-clad arm. She didn't care if he was a hottie biker-man, he was aggravating her beyond belief. "Do not encourage them. They're perfectly capable of starting a riot all on their own."

"I told you, that incident in Orange County wasn't entirely my fault," Angel said. "I didn't realize things would get out of hand that quickly."

"I don't want to talk about that," Julia said, instead focusing her attention on Luke. "You." She jabbed her finger at him. "Inside."

"I just love it when you speak librarian to me," he drawled.

Once they were alone in her kitchen, she barely took time to notice how incongruous Luke looked — tough and sexy in her warm and cozy kitchen with the heart-stamped canisters that had been a gift from the town welcome wagon — before asking him, "What are you really doing here?"

"You ordered me inside."

"You know what I mean."

"I heard about the riot and had to come check it out."

"Oh, please." She rolled her eyes. "Like you care what goes on in this town."

"When it involves you, I do."

"Why? So you can have a good laugh at my expense?"

"Well, that's part of it, sure."

"I'd prefer if you just left me alone." It was all she could do not to grimace at how prissy and Marian the Librarian she sounded. She needed a Pop-Tart. Pronto.

She still had a hidden stash that her health-maniac mother and sister hadn't found.

But no way she was stuffing her face in front of Luke.

"And I'd prefer not to leave you alone," Luke replied, reaching to slip a loose strand of her hair behind her ear.

Help. She was coming completely undone here.

And okay, so it wasn't entirely Luke's fault. Her family was playing a huge factor in her unravelling. But Luke wasn't helping matters any by tempting her to do something she'd regret.

She could still feel the warmth of his thumb brushing her lower lip from the night before. Feel his fingertips grazing her jaw. Both were minor incidents that didn't merit the attention she'd given them.

He didn't seem the least bit affected by her presence. Not that her outfit — khaki pants and navy polo shirt — would impress anyone. But he appeared to get a kick out of pushing her buttons, out of making fun of her. Was she just some big joke to him? Was that it?

"I don't care what you prefer," she said, belatedly getting back to his previous comment.

He raised one eyebrow. "No?"

"No. I'm tired of being pushed around in my own house, in my own backyard. If I say I don't want something, then that's what I mean. And if I say I like Cool Whip, then that's also what I mean."

"I like Cool Whip, too." His voice turned

rough-and-tumble sexy. "Spread all over you, it would be especially sweet."

She had no comeback for that comment.

Which was the only reason it was quiet when her sister popped her head in the back door and said, "I hate to interrupt you two, but the media has arrived."

Julia blinked. "What media?"

Skye shrugged. "Looked like the local CBS affiliate, but I didn't pay that much attention to what was written on the side of the TV van. The reporter is a Diane Sawyer wannabe right down to the haircut and black turtleneck. She's chatting with Sue Ellen now. She's already spoken with Angel."

"No!" Julia raced outside.

The glare of the spotlight pinpointed the reporter's location immediately. She was speaking into the microphone. "The holidays are fast approaching. And here in Serenity Falls, a miracle may be unfolding."

"This is my daughter Julia," Angel told the reporter. "She's a librarian."

"Really? In that case, how would you *classify* today's events?"

"As fiction."

"You aren't a believer, then?" the reporter asked.

"I *believe* this is all a big mistake."

"There you have it." The reporter returned the mike to her perfectly lip-lined mouth. "Two sides of this llama legend. A miracle? Or a mistake? This is Sondra Delaine, reporting from the small town of Serenity Falls. Back to you in the studio."

"How did you get out here so fast?" Julia demanded.

"I faxed them a press release this morning." Sue Ellen proudly buffed her acrylic nails against her hot pink angora sweater.

Julia gave the Diane Sawyer wannabe an accusatory look.

The reporter just shrugged. "What can I say? It was a slow news day."

Julia didn't have to wait long for the reaction to the segment on the noon news to set in. The first call came within minutes from Fred, a reporter with the *Serenity News*, wanting an exclusive interview . . . with the llamas if possible.

The next call came from Walt, and he quickly made his opinion known. "Did you see that segment on the noon news?"

"No."

"Well, I did. The story depicted us as wacky. The station called me, asking if I knew that Sue Ellen was referred to as 'Our Lady of the Outlandish' in town. I'm telling you Julia, we do not want the description

136

outlandish attached in any way, shape, or form to Serenity Falls. The Best Small Towns in America judging committee isn't looking for wacky or outlandish. There's no place for that on their form. No place at all."

Walt only paused long enough to draw in a breath before barreling on. "To have the llamas as possible prognosticators is one thing. I mean we already have the precedent of the groundhog over in Punxsutawney and even the woolly worms in Lewisburg. But to bring Jesus into this . . ." Walt almost wheezed in the middle of his hissy fit. His voice lowered to a semi-whisper. "People take religion very seriously. I know I do, and I certainly don't want anyone thinking we're committing blasphemy or anything like that. People are very touchy about these things."

Julia sighed. "I realize that."

"Then how could you allow this to get so out of hand?" His voice was booming once again.

"Me? I had no idea Sue Ellen was faxing out press releases to the media this morning. In fact, I didn't even realize until this morning that she knew I had llamas in my backyard."

"Oh, please. Everyone in town knows you have the llamas. They have to go."

"I agree. Everyone in town needs to go home."

"Not the townspeople. The llamas. They have to go."

"Again I agree. There isn't enough room in the backyard. My mother plans to move them within the next day or two." Angel didn't exactly work on a time schedule.

"No, I mean they have to go *now*. Before midnight. Before more media shows up."

From where she was standing in the hallway, Julia could see out the front picture window that two television vans had just pulled up. "It may be too late for that."

"I don't want to hear that."

"I'm not real thrilled with the news, either."

"The news? More television crews? Oh, no. Hold on. I've got another call."

Julia walked into the kitchen with the cordless phone and stood on her tiptoes. Pop-Tarts. She *had* to have Pop-Tarts. *Now*. She didn't care who saw her scarfing them down at this point.

"Here." Luke placed a balancing hand on the curve of her hip, his thumb brushing her bare skin at her waist where her polo shirt separated from her khaki pants. "Let me help. What do you need?"

What did she need? Him. Touching her. Skin to skin. Mouth to mouth. Tongue to tongue. Tongue to skin. Mouth to skin.

The possible erotic combos made her go all warm and squishy inside. She suddenly yearned for the pleasure Luke promised her with every teasing touch and seriously hot look. She wanted him to tumble her to the kitchen floor — or better yet lift her to the kitchen counter — and have his wicked way with her. Maybe then this powerful need would stop burning deep within her.

She glanced over her shoulder, fearful that she might be conveying her thoughts to him like some kind of blinking neon sign glowing on her forehead.

Uptight librarian wants you. Take me now.

Almost afraid of what she would see in those eyes of his, Julia was surprised to find a similar passion there and a matching confusion.

What did *he* have to be confused about? The fact that she wanted him? Or that he wanted her?

And he did want her. He let her see that, but he kept so many other things secret in his increasingly complicated gaze.

Julia stared at him, at his mouth, at the tiny scar along his jaw, at his mouth again.

His fingers branded her bare skin with their warmth as he moved her closer to him. Was he going to kiss her? Have his wicked way with her?

The moment was shattered by Walt's bellow over the phone she'd forgotten she still had pressed to her ear. "Disaster! Julia, are you there?"

"Yes." Her voice was unsteady. So were her knees. But she managed to grab the foil packet of Pop-Tarts anyway and rip it open.

"That was the *National Enquirer.* They want an exclusive."

"Too late. I already gave an exclusive to Fred."

"Fred?"

"Over at the *Serenity News.*"

"You don't understand. The *National Enquirer* is calling me. This is totally unacceptable! Do something!"

"Like what? What am I supposed to do?"

"You could always send Luke streaking across the front lawn." Skye joined them with Toni in tow. Her suggestion was accompanied by a wide grin in his direction. "That might provide an interesting distraction."

"Is Luke there?" Walt demanded. "I should have known he'd have a hand in this."

"He didn't have anything to do with it," Julia stated.

"I wouldn't put it past him to put this entire idea into Sue Ellen's head."

"She was called Our Lady of the Outlandish long before Luke returned to town," Julia pointed out.

Walt ignored her. "The important thing now is to do some spin control."

"Fine. You send the Serenity Falls spin doctors right over."

"As mayor, I'm also head of the publicity committee."

"Then it looks like controlling the media is your job, not mine."

"You're on-site, so you'll have to do it. It would take me too long to get over there. They're your llamas. You deal with it."

"There not my llamas." But Walt had already hung up. Julia's aggravation was building, had been building since the moment she'd looked up from "New Releases" in *Publishers Weekly* and looked out the library window. "Okay, fine. Everyone out of my way!"

"Uh-oh. She's got that look in her eye. Better watch out," Skye warned Luke. "She's really pissed now."

"Do not use language like that in front of your daughter," Julia instantly reprimanded her.

"It's just a word. I have no trouble with

my daughter using whatever words she wants to express herself."

"Well, I do, so stuff it."

"My big sister has such a dirty mouth." Skye ducked as a Pop-Tart sailed through the air at her. "And she throws like a girl."

"First a riot out front and now a cat fight." Luke rubbed his hands with anticipation. "Is this a great day or what?"

"Where's the cat?" Toni demanded.

The little girl's question returned some semblance of sanity to Julia. The red mist was lifting from her vision. No way she was wasting another Pop-Tart on her sister.

She was a librarian. An information professional. She could leap tall mountains of data in a single bound and answer reference questions on everything from algebra to zoology.

The bottom line was that she could kick butt as well as the next bibliophile. Probably even better.

Too bad she wasn't wearing those Librarians Have Tighter Buns briefs Pam had given her last Christmas.

It didn't matter. She'd go out there and set these idiots straight.

She just had to think of something brilliant to say.

Something both charming and decisive,

powerful and persuasive.

Piece of cake.

Note to self: You rock!

Second note to self: Restock Pop-Tarts ASAP.

Taking the doorknob firmly in her hand, she pulled the back door open and stepped outside.

Several hours later, Julia was in the mini-mart, frantically filling her shopping basket with boxes of Frosted Brown Sugar Cinnamon Pop-Tarts.

Her intervention with the media had *not* gone well. Not at all.

Just thinking about it made her toss in a box of chocolate donuts and a package of Oreos.

Instead of calming the crowd down, she'd seemed to just get them riled up even more. Not that she could really get them or the reporters to listen to her in the first place. Her sound bites were "too boring" one had proclaimed before ordering, "Go back to the babe with the big hair."

Okay, so maybe citing llama statistics and history hadn't been the right tactic to use. No one seemed to care about the connection between William Randolph Hearst and llamas. They were completely indifferent to the fact that the animals were originally domesticated more than six thousand years ago.

Julia had returned to work for the remainder of the afternoon, hiding out in the stacks doing weeding, removing books from the collection that weren't being circulated. She hated doing that. But she hated dealing with her own failure to handle the llama issue even more. Then she'd come here for food. Comfort food.

Julia paused in front of a display of Hostess Twinkies. How much was too much? Should she . . . ?

You bet.

Into the basket went three Twinkie packages.

"Julia, I'm so glad I found you." Pam waved at her from the healthful section of the store, where the fresh vegetable and fruit items were stacked. "I just saw you on TV."

"I don't want to talk about it. I just want to binge eat and pig out." Unfortunately, it appeared that the only place she could do that was in her car.

How had her life ended up here? With her in the mini-mart, hoarding junk food, and forced to retreat to her white Honda Accord for a little peace and quiet?

That's why she'd come to Serenity Falls. For the peace and quiet.

Where had it gone? It seemed to have evaporated the moment her family arrived in town. Nothing had been the same since then.

Or maybe it had started even earlier, when Luke had rolled up on his Harley and eyed her the way a football fan would eye a big screen TV before Super Bowl Sunday. With lust in his heart.

Julia had to regain control somehow. And soon. Hopefully the sugar binge would help her cope and come up with a plan. She always felt better when she had a plan.

Two hours and half a dozen Pop-Tarts later, she was still struggling to work out a coherent course of action as she sat cross-legged on Pam's comfy couch. No wacky relatives here at her friend's house. Instead, there were cheerful floral slipcovers and warm oak antiques, lending the place its English cottage style and charm.

She and Pam had finished off a good portion of an excellent Pinot Noir over a heated discussion of the flaws of the male population and whether or not the plumber or the gardener was the hotter guy on *Desperate Housewives*. All very important issues.

"Okay, how about this one," Pam said. "The future of the world depends on you having sex with the last man on Earth —

Tommy Lee or Ozzy Osbourne?"

Julia frowned. "Where do you come up with these questions?"

Pam wagged a finger at her. "You're avoiding the topic."

"The world can blow up for all I care. No way I'm getting down and dirty with either one of those two."

"I'm talking worse-case scenario."

"No kidding." Julia waved half a Twinkie at her. "And no thanks, I've already got a worse-case scenario on my hands. I mean, where did Sue Ellen come up with this idea about the llamas?"

Pam took a sip of wine. "Who knows where she comes up with anything or why she does the things she does? She grew up in Rock Creek."

"So?"

Pam shrugged. "So I'm just saying . . ."

"What is it about Rock Creek and Serenity Falls?"

"You've lived here several years. You know how things are. The two towns are very competitive and not at all alike."

"What's so bad about Rock Creek?"

"It's just not Serenity Falls. But getting back to Sue Ellen, she's someone who craves attention, and this has certainly given it to her."

"Why couldn't she have picked someone else's animals to have a vision about?"

"I recently heard about a farmer who had pig with the number of his favorite NASCAR driver on it. He was just born that way. The pig, not the farmer."

"Or how about Mrs. Selznick's dog Terminator? Why not pick the Terminator? Why me?"

Pam grinned. "Just lucky I guess."

Julia sipped her wine. "Did I tell you that I threw a Pop-Tart at my sister?"

"You did mention it, yes."

"That's not like me."

"I know," Pam noted solemnly. "You value your Pop-Tarts."

"And my self-control."

"I hear you." Pam gave her a reassuring hug. "Tomorrow will be a better day, you'll see."

What Julia saw the next morning was a *Good Morning America* truck outside.

Could things get any worse?

Apparently they could, because she found a nun outside her back door. A nun with an attitude. And a microphone in front of her.

What now? Had she been called in to bless the llamas? To condemn them all as blasphemers? What?

"It's a shame that people with nothing

better to do make up this kind of story," the nun was saying. "Especially at this time of year."

"You don't think it's a miracle then, Sister Mary?" the reporter asked.

The nun shook her head. "A miracle is a single mom who works two jobs to care for her kids and still help them with their homework at night. A miracle is a child donating all the money in their piggy bank to help victims of Hurricane Katrina. That's where you'll find the hand and the face of God. Not on the side of a llama."

The gathered crowd broke out into spontaneous applause, with one or two wiping tears from their eyes. Or maybe it was the bitter cold getting to them.

"There you have it." The reporter smiled into the camera. "Is that the final word from here in Serenity Falls? Only time will tell. This is Leslie Burbank reporting."

Five minutes later a beaming Walt approached her. "Isn't this great? Our town featured on *Good Morning America*."

Julia frowned at him. "Last night you were appalled by all this attention."

"That was before the *Late Show With David Letterman* called me. Can you believe it? David Letterman! I've been a fan for years. He wants the llamas."

"Too bad," Angel wrapped one of her scarves around her neck with agitated emphasis. "He can't have them."

"But this is a great chance . . ." Walt sputtered.

Angel stood her ground. "Forget about it."

"Whose idea was it to call in Sister Mary?" Julia asked. "That was brilliant."

"I'm glad you think so." Walt preened. "She stopped things from getting too out of hand. As I said yesterday, we certainly don't want to be known as outlandish. But standing out from the crowd, putting our name on the map, appearing on the *Late Show* — that's not a bad thing."

"Walt had nothing to do with me being here," Sister Mary said as she joined them. "Luke was the one who called me."

"Luke?" Julia couldn't hide her surprise.

"That's right."

Walt frowned. "Since when have you and Luke been so close?"

"Oh get over yourself, Walter," Sister Mary was clearly aggravated with him.

He looked affronted. "All I did was ask a simple question."

"With a lot of innuendo behind it. Don't you have something better to do than stand around taking credit for things you didn't do?"

"No." Walt's face turned red as he belatedly realized what he'd just said. "I mean, of course I do. And I'm going to go do them right now."

"Smart move," Sister Mary said. "I've got to be moving along as well."

"I'm going to go help Sister Mary serve meals to the needy in Rock Creek," Angel told Julia.

"I have to work today," Julia said apologetically.

"I understand." Sister Mary patted her hand. "I believe there's someone right here in Serenity Falls who needs you more than he lets on."

Julia still had an hour before she had to be at the library so she had time to swing by Maguire's to see Luke. She had so many questions. What had Sister Mary meant? Why had Luke called her in?

Maguire's appeared to be closed, which she should have realized because they were only open for lunch and dinner. A sign by the door listed their hours as noon to eleven p.m., but she saw someone moving around inside.

She tested the door. It was open.

"Hello?" she called out.

"What do you want?" The irritated question came from Tyler, who was opening a can of paint.

"I was looking for Luke."

"He's upstairs." Tyler jerked a thumb toward a doorway at the back of the bar.

Julia walked through the open door and up the flight of scuffed wooden steps. The door at the top was slightly ajar.

She knocked, which pushed the door wide open, revealing Luke working out in gym shorts and no shirt in front of a punching bag.

She just stood there, frozen, fiercely reminding herself that drooling over a guy was so tacky. But she was only human, and he was pure muscle packed into a powerful package — the hardened ridges of his chest and six-pack abs. The sheer physical impact of him was enough to take her breath away.

As if sensing her presence, he suddenly swiveled to face her — a man ready to confront danger. Was that from his days as a Marine? Or was there another reason for his response?

"Sorry." She laughed nervously. "I didn't mean to interrupt you. Tyler told me you were up here and . . ." She had to stop to draw in air. "Uh, I can come back later."

"I wouldn't think a woman who throws Pop-Tarts at her sister would be afraid of a guy and his punching bag."

"I'm not afraid. And don't leave out facing the maddening hordes of the press."

"Right."

"Which is what I wanted to talk to you about."

"Are you gonna get riled up?"

"What?"

"Because if you're gonna get riled up, you might as well put one of these on." He unlaced a boxing glove. "Here, give me your hand. These will probably be way too big on you, but it'll give you the idea . . ." He bent his head to fasten the glove on her hand. As he did so, she noticed the way his dark hair covered his nape. She also noticed he was tanned all over. Then he strolled back to the punching bag and braced it against his hip and shoulder. "Okay, come on, take a swing or two."

"No, I . . ."

"Pretend the bag is one of those reporters. Or Sue Ellen . . . Whoa . . ." He took a step back at the unexpected force of her punch. "Hold on there, tiger. Keep your wrists straight." He gave her a few more tips ending with, "Aim *through* the bag, not at it."

"That sounds like Zen boxing." She took his suggestions, however. They worked.

"I gotta tell you," Luke admitted with a wicked grin, "there's something about a librarian and a punching bag that makes me hot."

"You were hot when I got here." *Right. Why not just tell him you want to have sex with him?* "I mean you were working up a sweat . . . Yes, well, uh, I really must be going now."

"Wait a second. You never told me why you came here in the first place."

"Oh. I wanted to thank you for sending Sister Mary over to handle the situation at my house. The one with the llamas, I mean."

"What makes you think I did that?"

"She said you called her."

"God save me from chatty nuns," Luke muttered.

"Well, *you* saved me. That was nice of you. Why did you do it?"

"Simple. Because I want to have sex with you."

Chapter Seven

Julia blinked at him. "Yes, well . . ." *Brilliant. That was a brilliant, totally bumbling response.*

"Yes, you want to have sex with me, too? Great. Let's get started."

She put her hand out, forgetting for a moment that she still had the boxing glove on it. Which meant it accidentally rammed into Luke's stomach.

The air left his body with a rush. Damn. Sucker-punched by a librarian. It was humiliating.

"I'm so sorry." She yanked off the glove and dropped it to the floor. "I didn't mean to hit you like that. Are you okay? Did I hurt you?"

"Town bad boy KO'd by local librarian," Algee noted from the doorway behind them. "News at eleven."

Bracing his hands on his knees, Luke lifted his head and glared at the big guy. "Very funny."

"Help him," she appealed to Algee. "He's hurt."

"I doubt that," Algee said. "Embarrassed, yeah. You sucker-punched the guy."

"That's not what happened," Julia denied.

"No?"

"No." She shook her head. "The boxing glove on my hand accidentally collided with his stomach."

Algee grinned. "Not a move Rocky Balboa would approve of."

Julia couldn't help smiling back. "I don't think Sylvester Stallone has anything to fear from me."

"Not sure the same thing is true for Luke here though." Algee jerked a thumb in his direction.

"He doesn't have anything to fear from me, either," Julia maintained.

"Hey, people, I'm standing right here," Luke reminded them, his aggravation obvious.

"Bent over," Algee added with a grin.

Luke immediately straightened, his posture military upright. His glare was equally pure Marine with a bit of FBI mixed in.

"I've got to go, or I'll be late for work," Julia hurriedly said.

"You go ahead," Algee said. "My store doesn't open for another hour yet. I'll stay here and look after Luke."

Algee waited until she'd left before turning to Luke. "Looks like she's your kryptonite."

Luke frowned and wiped his face on the towel he'd grabbed from a nearby chair. "What are you talking about?"

"You know. Superman and kryptonite. It's his one weakness. Every superhero has one, you know. A weakness of some kind."

"Trust me, I'm no superhero. Far from it."

Algee ignored his caustic comment. "Sometimes their weakness is their own mortality. Under the costume, Batman is only human. Ditto for Spiderman. Both have to protect their secret identities at all cost."

Luke knew all about protecting secrets. He'd had to do plenty of that in the course of his undercover work. Had to do it growing up, as well. *Protect* might be the wrong word to use in that case, though. It was more like being forced to keep secrets because no one would believe the truth, so what was the point in revealing it?

Even now he was still tied up by secrets, and once again they involved his dad. To get his inheritance, he had to stay silent about the terms of the will and the fact that he had to remain here for six months.

Stuck. Incarcerated. A prison term. But one made more interesting by the belly-dancing librarian with a mean right hook.

She'd caught him unprepared today. It wouldn't happen again. No way was she his kryptonite, his one weakness. Not in this lifetime.

Angel walked into Maguire's and paused to blink at the darkness in comparison to the bright November sunshine outside.

"What is it with people today? The place isn't open yet," an extremely irritated male voice growled. "Not for another ten minutes."

Angel smiled and studied Tyler for a moment. Normally she wouldn't try to read his aura without permission, feeling she didn't have the right to tune in to other people's energies without their permission. But there was something so compelling about this man, something that spoke to her soul.

There was a deeper shade of blue in his aura that indicated loneliness, and also black, which seemed to act as a shield of protection from outside energies. A man who had secrets.

She'd seen a similar aura around Luke.

But she wasn't here to interpret their energy fields. She was here for a much more pragmatic reason.

"I hear that you're an excellent handyman."

Tyler shrugged and kept painting the trim.

"I was wondering if you could help me with a project. The thing is, I can't pay you. Not with money that is. But I could barter with you."

"Barter?"

Angel nodded, aware of the door opening behind her but not paying much attention to the newcomer. "You know, perform a service for you."

"What kind of service?"

"Whatever you'd like. Aura reading? Tarot card reading? Or massage maybe? I'll bet it's been a long time since you've had a good massage, right? I don't consider it bragging to say that I can make you feel like a new man." She wiggled her fingers. "It's all in the hands, you know. And having the touch. I can give you *such* pleasure . . ."

Angel paused at the sound of a thump behind her. She turned to find a stunned postal worker standing there, a pile of mail dumped on the wooden bar.

"Are you okay?" Angel asked in concern. "Did you drop the mail? I'll bet your back is aching because of that huge bag you're carrying. I can help . . ."

The woman shook her head and backed away from Angel as if she were warding off the devil.

"Well, if you change your mind, let me know . . ." Angel cheerfully waved at her before returning her attention to Tyler. "Now, where were we?" She tapped a fingernail on her bottom lip. It felt slightly chapped — her lips, not her fingernail. Which reminded her that she needed to get more of her favorite all-natural lip balm.

"You were offering to make a new man of me," Tyler prompted.

"Not that there's anything wrong with the present one," she hurriedly assured him. "I wouldn't want you to think I was passing judgment on you or anything."

Tyler shrugged. "You wouldn't be the first."

"No, really. I'm very much against that sort of thing."

"What sort of thing?"

"Being judgmental. Some people might think it unusual that you Rollerblade in the middle of the night, but I don't. Really I don't."

"I Rollerblade when I can't sleep."

"I have some excellent homeopathic remedies for insomnia you might want to try."

"Rollerblading works for me."

"And that's fine, too. After all, the middle of the night is an excellent time for reflection and meditation. It's so nice and peaceful. On a clear night like last night, you can see the stars."

"I don't look up much."

"Why not?"

"Don't see the point."

"So you like to keep your focus on terra firma. You must be a Capricorn. I'm an Aquarius myself."

"I thought asking someone's sign went out as a pick-up line a decade or two ago."

"Just because we're in a pub doesn't mean I was trying to pick you up. Not today, anyway. Who knows what the future might hold? At the moment I'm just trying to help my daughter."

"By picking me up?"

"No, by trying to exchange your skills for those I have. I am hopeless with home repairs. Not that I haven't tried, because I believe you should be open to new experiences. I've even read some of those Time-Life books, you know the ones with all the diagrams and pictures and direct titles like *Electricity* or *Plumbing*. But things didn't work out. One time I actually flooded the entire kitchen because I did something wrong with the shut-off valve."

"Sounds like you forgot to turn it off."

"That may have been it. Anyway, are you interested?"

"In?"

"In fixing Julia's leaky bathtub faucet. As I said in the beginning, I can't pay you in a monetary fashion, but . . ."

Tyler held up his hand to stop her explanation. "I'll stop by when I can."

"That would be wonderful. Thank you so much. If you let me know ahead of time, I'll make some granola bars for you."

"You don't have to feed me."

"So you'd prefer the massage then?"

"We'll wait and see how things go."

"An excellent plan. Thank you, Tyler. It's been nice chatting with you. I really feel like we've made a connection."

"I don't do connections."

The sadness in his aura made her heart ache, but she didn't say anything. Sometimes there was no way of making something right. She knew that all too well.

Luke saw Sheriff Norton walk in to Maguire's but didn't take much note beyond that until the town's lawman said, "You know that soliciting is not allowed here in Serenity Falls, right?"

"Someone handing out flyers advertising free video rentals or something?"

"By soliciting, I was referring to the world's oldest profession, as in prostitution. We don't allow that sort of thing here."

Luke raised an eyebrow. "And you're telling me this because?"

"Because someone overheard a woman soliciting one of your patrons earlier today."

"What patron?"

"Tyler."

"He's not a patron. He's doing some work for me."

"Either way, soliciting isn't allowed."

"So I can kick those Girl Scouts out if they come around selling cookies?"

Sheriff Norton fixed him with a stare.

"Who was the woman?" Luke demanded.

"The llama lady."

"Julia's mother?"

The sheriff nodded.

"That's almost the stupidest thing I've ever heard. Comes in second to Walt wanting to measure the height of a guy's grass."

"Now there's no need to take that tone of voice with me, son."

"Bud, you're only ten years older than I am, so don't go trying to get all paternal on me."

Adele interrupted them, bursting out of the kitchen. "Here, Bud, try the sweet potato fries. I used something new on them."

Bud removed his hat and his face turned all red. "It's, uh, real good to see you, Adele."

"You, too, Bud. Here, have a fry."

She held it to his lips.

Luke observed all this with a frown. Was he hallucinating, or was Adele actually flirting with the sheriff?

Fine by him, if it distracted the lawman from continuing this ridiculous line of questioning.

What was it about small-town law enforcement that made them so territorial and insular? He'd run into the problem before during his time with the agency. Some local badges had bristled at having the Feds show up. Others had worked well with him.

He couldn't see Norton working well with him, but he'd seen worse. None that had warned him about prostitution, however.

"Remember what I said," Sheriff Norton told Luke when he left half an hour later, having eaten a meal specially prepared for him by Adele.

Luke confronted her as soon as he left, following her into the kitchen. "What's with you and the flatfoot?"

Adele sighed. "I've been trying to get that man to notice me for two years now, ever

since his wife up and left him for an aluminum siding salesman."

"I'd say he noticed you."

Adele perked up. "You think so?"

Luke regretted having said anything. No
way he wanted to get into any kind of discussion about personal relationships with
Adele, or anyone else for that matter.

So he just shrugged, snagged a handful of
fries, and headed back to the bar. At least
there, most folks stayed out of his face.

But when Julia showed up a few hours
later, he decided that having her in his face
might not be such a bad thing. She had a fire
in those eyes of hers. She still looked like an
ad for L.L.Bean with her tidy wool sweater
and jeans, but the expression on her face
was ballistic.

She placed both hands palm down on the
bar as if slapping down a challenge. "Someone is spreading rumors about my mother."

"So I've heard." He set down the glass
he'd been wiping.

"Who is it?"

"Like I pay attention to that kind of thing?
Although I have to say that having the
sheriff pay me a little call about it was unexpected."

Julia frowned. "I don't understand."

"He wanted to let me know that prostitution and soliciting are frowned upon in these parts."

Julia marched clear around the corner of the bar and right behind it to stand before him, a spitfire. "No one accuses my mother of something like that," she growled.

Luke never knew that a growling librarian could turn him on so fast. There were so many unexpected angles to her — like that belly-dancing thing.

"Nothing happened." Tyler said as he joined them. "Just a misunderstanding."

"Yeah, this town excels at those," Luke noted.

"Your mom said she needed me to help her with a project," Tyler explained to Julia. "But she couldn't pay me with cash and offered her services instead. Like massage. In a barter situation."

Julia knew her mother liked the bartering concept and often used it with her New Age friends. However, the idea didn't go over nearly as well with the practical capitalists who populated most of the country.

Not that Tyler appeared to fall under the practical capitalist category.

As for Luke, she wasn't sure how to categorize him. Bad boy, yes, certainly. Troublemaker, absolutely. Incredible kisser?

Note to self: Irrelevant.

She looked away from his mouth as if just staring at it might be enough to make her do something she'd regret.

"Thank you, Tyler, for clearing that up for me."

"I'm just sorry her interaction with me caused trouble."

"You didn't cause any trouble. This town did that," Luke growled.

"Did you tell the sheriff about the misunderstanding?" Julia asked Luke.

"Do I look like I'm on a confiding-buddy basis with lawmen?"

He looked dangerous and sexy. "Never mind. I'll go talk to him myself."

"You do that."

As she turned and walked away, Luke couldn't help admiring the way the denim cupped her butt.

"Busy day," Tyler noted dryly.

"Yeah, it's not often I get a visit from a tight-assed sheriff and an angry librarian in the same day."

"Lucky you."

"Yeah." Luke grinned. "Lucky me."

"How could you do that?" Julia faced her mom, who was calmly brewing herself a cup of her special blend herbal tea in Julia's kitchen.

"How could I do what?"

"Talk to Tyler that way."

"What way is that? I have no idea what you're so upset about, but it isn't good for your auric field to express such anxiety."

Julia had plenty to be anxious about. First, she'd had to stash her junk food in a locked armoire in her bedroom. She'd also put her breakables there, away from little Toni's inquisitive hands. She'd even installed child-proof latches onto the kitchen cabinets and drawers. Did anyone else think of that? No. Of course not. Apparently she was the only one with nightmares of Toni downing a bottle of Drano or yanking a knife out of the drawer.

"Here, try a celery root cookie. I baked them this afternoon."

"No, thanks. Look, Angel, just don't go offering any other men a massage."

"Why not? I've got the touch."

"I know you do. But stick to yoga lessons, okay?"

Angel frowned. "You really think Tyler would be interested in taking yoga lessons?"

Julia ignored the question. "He said you asked him to do some kind of project. What project?"

"I wanted it to be a surprise."

"I hate surprises."

"You didn't always."

Julia sighed. "Yes, I pretty much always did."

"Really? I never noticed that."

"I know. Now about that project . . ."

"I wanted Tyler to fix your leaky bathtub faucet."

"Oh." Now Julia felt guilty for giving Angel a hard time.

"I wanted to do something to help you, and I know that drip drip drip noise bothers you, so I thought I'd do something to remedy the situation. Not that I'd attempt such a thing on my own, not after the last incident."

"Which one? The one where you nearly set the rental house on fire when you tried to restart the pilot light on the old stove?"

"No, the one where I flooded the kitchen that time. Where were we when that happened? Was it Washington state or Oregon?"

Before Julia could answer, there was a knock on the back door. It was Tyler. "This a good time?"

"Any time is a good time if you make it so," Angel answered. "Come on in. Can I offer you some tea?"

Tyler shook his head. "Just show me the leaky faucet."

"It's right this way."

Noting the way her mother's face lit up when she saw Tyler, Julia's heart sank. She'd seen that look many, many, many times before. Each time her mom took some social misfit under her wing and into her heart. Most recently it had been Aiden, the poet who wanted to write Celtic rap.

He'd mooched off Angel for six months before taking off. That's what they all did in the end. Take off.

Julia had no reason to believe Tyler wouldn't do the same thing. She wanted to warn her mother, but knew there was no point. Angel never listened to her advice anyway.

"As most of you know, this Friday is the big game between Rock Creek and Serenity Falls High." Library director Frasier McGrady paused to study the staff members in the meeting room with him. "The rivalry between the two towns makes the Capulet and Montague feud seem like a petty upset. Of course, our library is far better in every possible way than Rock Creek's. So is our football team. Which is why I want all the staff members to wear their GO TIGERS buttons this week. Any questions? Comments?"

Alice raised her hand. "No one has mentioned the issue of one of our staff members appearing on the local news in a sensationalized story about the animals in her backyard."

Frasier nodded as he closed the folder he'd been consulting for their meeting. "That's correct."

Alice sniffed her disapproval. "Well, I think it reflects badly on all of us when one of us behaves in such an unprofessional way. It's bound to have offended a number of our patrons as well."

Frasier frowned. "Has anyone said anything to you?"

"They don't have to. I can tell by the way they're looking that they're uncomfortable."

Julia wished she had a Pop-Tart handy to toss at her. The reason patrons were uncomfortable was because Alice was such a pain in the butt.

Ever the peacemaker, Frasier said, "Yes, well I'm sure that now that things have settled down, we won't have to worry about a repeat performance. Right, Julia?"

"Right."

Long note to self: Why did you let her talk about you that way? Why didn't you defend yourself? Why didn't you cut her off at the knees and take her down like a defensive lineman from the Serenity Falls Tigers? Why did you just sit there and take it?

Where was her backbone? Her Carmen Diaz kick-butt persona? The one that had put Billy in his place when he'd tried to swallow the library director's koi? Where had Alice been then, huh? Not out there on the front lines, that's for sure.

Julia spent the rest of the morning as disgusted with her own lack of spunk as with Alice's cheap shots.

At lunch in the staff room, Julia discussed the incident with Patty Miller, head of circulation, and Laurie Wachowski, the part-time children's librarian. Patty was in her forties and had super-short red hair and an outgoing personality. Laurie was in her mid-thirties and wore her long brown hair loose around her shoulders almost as a shield to protect her from the world. But she was fantastic with kids. The three of them sat around a square table squeezed in between the sink, the fridge, and the side counter housing an old coffee maker and microwave.

"Alice seems to be going out of her way to make your life difficult," Patty noted in between bites of salad.

"That's my family's job," Julia said.

Patty shook her head. "I can't believe the

way she picked on you like that."

Julia still couldn't believe she hadn't defended herself. This after having had boxing lessons from a hottie like Luke.

"The town council desperately wants Serenity Falls to be chosen as one of America's Best Small Towns," Patty continued. "I think Alice is feeling the pressure, because Frasier made her liaison on that project. That's why we have to wear these buttons. Because she heard that the judging committee has ten points on which they select their top towns. One of them is the high school test, because they consider it to be the heart and soul of a small town."

"I would have thought Edith would have the high school situation totally under control," Julia noted. "I mean she's taught there since the dawn of time, and she's on the town council."

"You know how Alice is."

"Anal."

Patty nodded. "Enough said."

"I thought the library was the heart and soul of a town."

"Not the week of the Serenity Falls/Rock Creek game," Laurie said.

"Not any time during football season, actually," Patty added.

"So does the judging committee look at

the library at all?" Julia asked.

Patty nodded. "Of course, it does."

"So high school and library. What are the other eight points?" Laurie wondered.

"No one knows for sure," Patty admitted. "I think the downtown area is something else that's judged."

"I heard a rumor that there was even a local restaurant test," Laurie added.

"In which case Maguire's would win, hands down. Have you tasted Adele's sweet potato fries?" Patty made a dreamy face, one she usually reserved for chocolate. "They're to die for. And have you heard that they're on the new menu permanently now? Before she only had them occasionally."

"I heard that was Luke's doing," Laurie said. "His dad would never approve of changing the menu one iota. But Luke liked the change."

Julia made no comment, keeping her attention on her carton of cherry yogurt. Hey, she could eat healthy when she wanted to.

"I hear he's hired Tyler to do some kind of painting work for him," Laurie added.

"The members of the town council aren't happy that he didn't tell them what color he plans on using," Patty stated. "You know how they are about that kind of thing."

Julia nodded, but her attention was actually focused on how incredibly good Luke had looked in front of that punching bag, muscles glistening with sweat. No, *glistening* sounded too girly somehow. He'd been the picture of male power.

So why didn't she have female power? Why had she wimped out with Alice?

"I hear Walt described it as bordello red," Laurie said.

"It certainly is a bright color," Patty agreed. "What do you think, Julia?"

"That I was a failure at defending myself earlier. It's not as if I wanted those llamas in my backyard to begin with. And it's not like I'm the one who called in the media. Sue Ellen did that. I should have said as much to Alice. Put her in her place."

"She's Walt's sister-in-law," Patty reminded her. "I don't think there's anything you could have said that would really make an impression. She knows that with her family connections there's no way she'd ever lose her job here."

"There's one bad apple in every batch," Laurie said.

"On a happier note, the new Jayne Ann Krentz hardcover is in now." Patty adored romance fiction and was an expert at steering patrons to the best authors and books.

"I know. I read it already," Julia said with a grin as she licked the last bit of yogurt from her plastic spoon.

"How did you manage that?" Patty demanded.

"I have connections in tech services." Andrea the cataloger had let her have the book overnight the other day. "I also bribed her with chocolate."

"No fair!" Patty lobbed a crumpled paper napkin at her.

At which point Alice walked in. "Food fights are not allowed in the staff room," she stated with disapproval.

Julia barely managed to keep a straight face at the Alice impersonation that Laurie was doing behind the open door to the fridge as she replaced the jug of lemonade she'd brought with her from home. Laurie was big on citrus.

"Whew, that was close," Patty noted as Alice departed as quickly as she'd arrived.

Laurie had the final word. "Let's just hope that Serenity Falls wins this football game on Friday, or everyone will be in as bad a mood as Alice."

Serenity Falls did win the game against Rock Creek Friday night, which had to go into overtime. But Julia was more interested in the Wiener Dog Races the next day, the first Saturday in November.

Once again the town square was decorated, this time with banners of dachshunds hanging from the iron lamp posts. The race route was a straight line from the front steps of the gazebo to the park bench at the north edge of the park. Well-wishers lined the short route, waving handmade signs proclaiming "Our Frank Is a Wiener!" or "Go Oscar, Be a Winning Wiener" or "Our Wiener Is a Hot Dog!"

The smell of steaming hot dogs and grilled bratwurst filled the air. Bavarian-style pretzels dotted with salt were also available. That's what Julia was here for. The food. Not the canines, despite the fact that her friend Pam had her puppy Rosebud entered in the Little Smokies category for dogs under a year old.

The emcee of the event was Walt's youngest brother, Phil the dentist. Julia had only recently noticed that most people in town were known by their first name and profession. Walt the mayor. Ethel the teacher. Pam the flower girl, even though she was nearing thirty and was no longer a girl. But the fact that she'd opened a flower shop within the nursery made her Pam the flower girl. She'd gained a reputation for her gorgeous floral wedding displays.

Always a flower girl, never a bride, Pam liked to say.

"Is this thing on?" Phil tapped the microphone before beginning. "Welcome everyone to the tenth annual Wiener Run. We've got to be *frank* with you, we've got an exciting series of races lined up today! We'll kick off with the Senior Sausages event. You might think these dogs would be waddling like the wind, but they really know how to pour on the mustard." Phil was one of those guys who liked cracking himself up. "Our judges this year are the town council members. The rules are the same as always. First dog that *dashes* across the finish line wins."

"Everything in this town is the same as always. Or it was until I met you and your family," Luke noted as he joined her.

When Julia made no comment, he said, "Aren't you going to ask me what I'm doing here?"

She shook her head. "I saw the booth selling Adele's sweet potato fries."

"Her idea," he said.

"You should give her a raise."

He was wearing jeans, a denim shirt, and his perennial leather jacket — and he looked too good to be real.

The last time she'd seen him, she'd been protecting her mother's reputation. Or trying to.

She'd gone right behind the bar and confronted him. Been so close she could see his dark eyelashes. She stole a quick sideways look. That Black Irish thing he had going on was still a weakness of hers.

Brooding, complicated, secretive. None of these were good adjectives to apply to a guy who turned your knees to mush.

Julia made a serious effort to ignore him and to concentrate on the event.

The first race went well, with Mabel's dog Tubbie taking the honors.

"These dogs are on a roll today!" Phil cheerfully proclaimed from the podium. "Let's give them a round of applause as they step into the wiener's . . . I mean the *winner's* circle."

"That Phil, he's just a laugh a minute," Luke mocked.

"He's having fun."

"Look at the buns on that dog," Phil said with a belly laugh.

Mabel was not amused at the insult to her beloved Tubbie.

The look on her face had Phil hurriedly backing away. "Let's move on to the next event. The Little Smokies."

"Go Rosebud!" Julia shouted with a wave at Pam. Even if she did come for the food, she should still show support for her friend and her puppy.

The younger dogs didn't have a clue as to what was going on. Some of them were even running backward as their owners tried to coax them to get moving; others just pranced around in circles.

Rosebud came in third. Not bad for her first appearance.

"Now on to the main event." Phil's voice boomed over the rickety sound system. "I know the winner will *relish* a wiener victory here. Just a reminder that any dog who veers from the course will be disqualified."

Scanning the crowd, Julia was surprised to see her sister Skye on the other side of the race route. Toni was next to her, but not for long.

No sooner had Phil proclaimed the race begun than Julia's four-year-old wild child niece ran into the track, distracting the dogs who scattered to the winds.

For the first time in Wiener Race history, not one dog crossed the finish line.

Only Toni the Biter did.

Luke cracked up. "You're right. This town is marginally more interesting than it used to be," he noted with a grin at the chaos surrounding them. "Let's give them all something else to talk about, shall we?" Taking her in his arms, Luke kissed her.

Chapter Eight

Luke was kissing her. On the mouth. His tongue parting her lips and tangling with hers. Right there in the middle of the town square.

Julia should have been upset. Outraged. Not delighted. Or exhilarated.

Maybe she was demented, but she was savoring every delicious moment.

Luke tasted like spicy mustard and forbidden temptation. He caught her bottom lip between his teeth and drew it into his mouth to suck and nibble. Rough yet gentle, he took his time. The kiss was full of surprises, like the dart of his tongue in a feathery caress across the roof of her mouth. Shockingly seductive.

Tilting his head in the opposite direction, he targeted her mouth again in a continuation of his kiss that made her toes tingle and curl. It blossomed into an erotic exchange between his skillful tongue and hers, eager to catch up and learn more.

Her hands were on his shoulders, his on her waist. She vaguely recognized those facts, but her main focus remained on his mouth covering hers.

This was everything she'd anticipated and so much more. First kisses weren't supposed to be like this. They were supposed to be sweet, or gently exploring, or tentative. Awkward, even.

But she and Luke and been building to this moment for weeks. Ever since that first day when he'd shown up in town on the back of his big, bad Harley, looking so male-to-female dangerous.

The sultry taste and touch of him instantly went to her head, making her dizzy with desire.

Julia had never really understood the appeal of French kissing before because she'd never been handled by a master in the fine art. As Luke leisurely unleashed his tongue in a moist probing of every curve and corner of her mouth, she truly became a convert. He convinced her that there was incredible gratification to be found in this oral thrust and parry.

Awesome, awesome. The words echoed in her head like a mantra.

Now he was adding slow reverent strokes to his repetoire. Julia would have moaned in pleasure, but that would have meant breaking off the contact, and she couldn't face that.

A wild ecstatic surge of sexual energy consumed her entire body. He nudged his knee between her legs, and she lifted her knee to enable him to come closer.

"Stop that!" The order came over the loud speaker system and eventually worked its way into Julia's consciousness. "Stop that right now!"

The real reason she stepped away from Luke was because she needed some oxygen or she'd pass out.

"Humans are not allowed in the dog race," Phil barked into the microphone.

Slowly Julia became aware of her surroundings once again. Like one of those stop-action scenes in the movies, where everything else faded, telescoping in and out of reality.

A second ago her reality had been focused on Luke's mouth on hers, his tongue dancing across the roof of her mouth.

"You're breaking the rules," Phil continued as the crowd scattered in disarray.

Julia slowly nodded. That kiss had definitely broken all the rules she'd set up for herself here in Serenity Falls.

She looked at Luke. He looked at her. And smiled. She knew what his smile tasted like now. And that changed everything.

For her.

But was it the same for him?

"Why did you do that?" Her lips felt swollen from his touch.

"Because I wanted to. You wanted it, too."

Yes, she had.

But did she want Luke's kisses enough to risk everything else she'd worked so hard to obtain here in this quiet town? That was the million-dollar question and one she had no immediate answer to.

"We've been shopping all morning," Pam declared, "and you have yet to mention the kiss that shook the world."

Once a month Julia and Pam went antiquing, hitting their favorite spots within a hundred-mile radius before stopping for lunch at a little French bistro they loved. The quaint dining room with its lace curtains and warm colors created a warm and cozy environment that was perfect for "girls who lunch."

Julia had to admit that it felt good to get out of Dodge — or Serenity Falls — for a little while. Away from her zany family, away from the memory of Luke kissing her yesterday afternoon.

"It's not right. It's very wrong," Pam vehemently stated.

Julia realized that she shouldn't have allowed Luke to kiss her, but even so, she was surprised by her friend's intense reaction.

"It's wrong for you not to talk to me about it," Pam clarified. "I'm your friend."

"I already know you don't approve of Luke."

"That was before I knew that Sister Mary liked him."

"Ah, the nun with the attitude. She's from Rock Creek," Julia reminded her, recalling Pam's comments from the last time they'd gotten together.

Pam grinned. "I know, but I don't hold that against her."

Julia made no comment, instead focusing her attention on the excellent lobster bisque soup in front of her.

But Pam was not easily dissuaded. "All kinds of things have been happening this past week. Sue Ellen sees mystical faces in your llamas and is busted by Sister Mary. Toni disrupts the wiener races. And Luke disrupts the entire town by kissing you."

"They're not my llamas."

"You know what I meant."

"Now you know why I never talked about my family."

"They do seem a little . . ."

"Wacky?"

"That wasn't exactly the way I was going

to put it, but if you say so I'll go along with *wacky*. After all, you know them better than I do."

"Yes, I do. And I had no idea they were coming."

"Would it have made things easier if you had known?"

"It would have given me a chance to prepare. Although there's really no way to entirely prepare for them, because I never know what they're going to be into or what they're up to." Julia shook her head. "You couldn't possibly understand."

"Why is that?"

"Because you come from the perfect All-American family. Totally normal."

"Every family has their issues to deal with. Even mine."

"Has your mom ever been arrested for starting a riot?" Julia demanded.

Pam sat back in surprise. "Well, no."

"Mine has. Not that I even call her mom. She prefers that I call her Angel."

"Okay, so she's a little unusual."

"More than a little. She has llamas in my backyard."

"They seem kind of cute."

"You want them in *your* backyard?"

"Not really."

"I rest my case. I've really tried to make a

new life for myself here."

"And you have."

"Until I disrupted the races yesterday."

"Well, actually your niece did the disrupting. You just did the kissing."

"I didn't start that. Luke did." Julia groaned. "Listen to me. I sound like a five-year-old."

"Are you falling for Luke?"

"Do I look that stupid?"

"Hey, I was just asking."

"If I'm stupid?"

"No, if you're falling for Luke."

"Well, I'm not. Despite the fact that he's an awesome kisser."

"He is, huh?"

"That's hardly a surprise. He's had tons of experience."

"Mmmm."

"What's that supposed to mean?"

"Nothing. I was just agreeing with you."

"I suppose everyone is still gossiping about it."

Pam nodded. "That and the lack of a winner at the wiener races. Your niece was the only one who actually crossed the finish line, but humans aren't allowed in the race."

"And now we know why."

Pam nodded.

Julia groaned. "I can't believe my sister

just let Toni loose like that. She has no idea of discipline."

"Who doesn't? Your sister or Toni?"

"Either one of them. Skye believes that saying 'no' introduces negative energy into Toni's world."

"So she never says 'no'?"

"Not unless Skye is talking to me. Then she has no problem saying 'no.' We don't always get along very well. Maybe because we're so different."

"How so?"

"She's always been the wild one. I've always been the one to pick up the pieces."

"That's got to be tiring."

"Tell me about it."

"Let's get back to Luke . . ."

"I already told you I'm not falling for him."

"Just kissing him for fun?"

"You think he was kissing me in front of half the town to make a fool of me, is that it?"

"Is that what you think?"

"No." Julia didn't want to have those thoughts. But that didn't stop them from creeping into her mind like a dark sludge.

Wishing didn't make it so, despite her mother's New Age philosophy to the contrary. Wishing that Luke wasn't trying to make a fool of her didn't mean it wasn't true.

Okay, now her thought process was getting muddled, and Julia hated that, almost as much as she hated the doubts nibbling away at her insides. She knew Luke liked making waves, shaking things up. He'd told her so himself plenty of times. And she'd heard it from others as well.

"What do you think?" Julia asked Pam.

"I don't know. When it comes to Luke I thought I had him figured out. Maybe there is more there than meets the eye. Not that what meets the eye isn't mighty fine."

"He's not that easy to figure out," Julia said. "Believe me, I've tried."

"Sister Mary isn't easily conned. If she thinks Luke is worthwhile, then she must see something there."

"You could try not to sound quite so doubtful."

Pam shrugged. "I just don't want to see you get hurt because of him."

"That's not something I want either."

"What about his kiss? Was that something you wanted? It sure looked like it."

"He caught me by surprise."

"And . . . ?"

"And he's an awesome kisser, like I said. I forgot where I was for a minute or two."

"Four."

Julia blinked. "What?"

"Mabel timed it. The kiss lasted four minutes, twenty-three seconds."

Julia felt her face heating up. Putting her hands to her cheeks, she could feel the warmth there. "I don't believe this."

"Mabel had her stop watch out, so I think her time-keeping is pretty accurate."

"I mean I don't believe they were timing my kiss!"

"I believe only Mabel was."

"Then they might as well all have, because she'll tell everyone in town anyway."

"At least Luke erased the digital picture that Billy took of you two and wanted to post on the Internet."

"Where did you hear that?"

"From Mabel, so again, it must be true."

"If Luke wanted to humiliate me, then he wouldn't have gone out of his way to delete that picture."

"That's one way of looking at it. But in my book, he shouldn't have kissed you that way in front of everyone to begin with if he didn't want people gossiping about you. He may be used to the gossip, but you're not."

Actually, Julia *was* used to it, just not here in Serenity Falls. But all through her childhood and teenage years, there had been plenty of gossip about her family and their unconventional ways.

One of her most painful memories was being in school, kindergarten maybe or first grade, and being given a workbook her first day there. The other kids had already been together for months, but Angel had just moved into that area of Washington state, so Julia was the new kid in class. The teacher had told Julia to circle the things that were different from the others.

One of the other kids had laughed and pointed at Julia, with her tye-dyed skirt and too-big Mother Earth T-shirt, loudly declaring that she was the one different from all the rest.

That feeling of being the odd one had stuck with her, even though Angel had chosen after that to homeschool Julia and Skye until their teenage years.

Julia wasn't just the odd one as far as the rest of society was concerned; she was the odd one within her own odd family. She never felt like she fit in.

Her mother and sister had no problem living in what they always called the "eternal present moment."

Julia worried where they were going to get food the next day or pay the rent the next month.

Somehow Angel usually came through,

but there was never any security in knowing that everything would be all right. Somehow Julia lacked those genes that assured the other two women in her family that there was never anything to worry about.

Or maybe they didn't worry because that was Julia's job. She'd never asked them. Maybe she should.

Julia's thoughts were interrupted by the arrival of their waiter asking them if they wanted dessert.

"Of course. I'll have the chocolate mousse," Julia said.

"And I'll have the crème brûlée."

"We are *sooo* predictable," Julia noted with a grin. "Every time we come here we order lobster bisque, the chicken dijon crepes, and our desserts."

"We just have good taste," Pam stated.

"You have outstanding taste. That's why your floral wedding design business is such a hit at the nursery."

"My parents weren't convinced it was going to work out, but it has."

"So things are going well?"

Pam nodded. "You'd be surprised how many people are planning a December wedding. Maybe they want the tax deduction for the year."

"You're such a romantic."

"Not me. I like having my feet on the ground."

"Me, too." Seeing Pam's look, she added, "Okay, okay, for one moment —"

"For four minutes, twenty-three seconds," Pam inserted.

"— I let Luke sweep me off my feet."

"You actually lifted your right foot clear off the ground and were up on your tiptoes with the other foot . . ."

"I don't need to hear the play-by-play, thank you very much."

"I'm just saying that it looks like Luke is already halfway to sweeping you off your feet."

"Halfway doesn't count," Julia firmly stated.

"Stop looking at me like that," Angel said. "I'm not abandoning you. Really I'm not."

The llamas blinked their long lashes at her.

"I explained it all before. Remember, Lucy? Ricky? You're going to love it here. Look how much room there is for you to wander around and explore in this pasture. You two have it all to yourselves. And your own stalls in the barn. The Millers are very nice people. You're going to have a great time here."

She paused to pat Ricky's neck reassuringly.

"And I told them how much you like bananas and cookies, Lucy." The llama's long hair draped over her spectacular dark eyes and eyelashes. Her fluffy pure white wool was clean now, but that might not last long with the threat of rain in the grumbling gray skies.

"I'll come visit you as much as I can. At least a couple times a week."

Lucy moved closer to "snuff" her face with her black nose. Angel bit back a sob as she buried her face in the soft fur she dampened with her tears.

She wasn't just being emotional with llama separation anxiety. Her issues with Julia were always there at the back of Angel's mind. And now they were bubbling up as she hugged her llamas.

"It's just temporary." She reassured them and herself. "We're going to have our own place soon, and everything will work out for the best. I can feel it. I just need to trust my inner guide."

Angel took a healing deep breath. When she got in her vintage VW van, she had to take time to do a whole body chakra meditation. She worked hard to focus her power of attention directly toward her entire energy system, but the fear and anxiety were hard to remove.

And so it was that later that night, she found herself unable to sleep. Getting up from the futon mattress she'd placed on the floor of the den, she recalled how dismayed Julia had been when she'd seen her there. Julia had been looking dismayed a lot lately.

Angel had reminded Julia that she liked sleeping on the floor, like they did in Japan.

Julia hadn't been reassured.

Angel pulled on wool leggings and tugged on a coat. She added her favorite fuzzy knit cap and scarf in hot pink and navy blue before heading for the door.

The skies were clear as she quietly let herself out of Julia's house and walked down the deserted street. Midnight and not a soul around. The place was quiet as a tomb. All the houses were dark, no lights shining in any windows.

Yes, some people had their porch lights on. But it seemed they did so more with the desire to keep strangers away than to welcome anyone.

Angel kept walking, trying to escape her thoughts.

She heard him before she saw him. Tyler. Rollerblading.

Angel hadn't spoken to him since he'd come to Julia's house and fixed her bathtub faucet. Julia had gotten so upset about her offering Tyler a massage that Angel had felt reluctant to make any waves.

But that didn't mean she was going to welch on their agreement. She still owed Tyler.

"Nice night, huh?" she said.

She'd startled him; she could tell by the way his body stiffened. Wanting . . . no, *needing* to keep him nearby, she said, "I couldn't sleep. I moved the llamas from my daughter's backyard tonight. That was hard. Not that moving them was hard. They went into the trailer without any trouble at all. But it was hard for me to leave them at the farm I'd chosen for them. Not because I don't think they'll be well cared for. But it seemed like I was abandoning them." She shivered. "I told them I wasn't, but I'm not sure how much llamas understand. Well, I know they understand a lot, but I'm not sure if I was communicating effectively with them. Maybe I should have said something else. Maybe there's a Peruvian phrase that would have reassured them."

"Sounds more like you're the one needing reassurance."

She was surprised by his insight.

196

"Have you ever had a secret so big you didn't know how to fix it?" The words tumbled from her lips.

There was a long pause before Tyler spoke. "Yeah." His voice was gruff.

"Really? What did you do about it?"

"Nothing."

"That's what I've been doing for the past . . . well, thirty years now. Nothing. But that's not working for me anymore. I have to do something to make it right."

"Thirty years is a long time."

"I know."

"Goes by fast," Tyler said.

"Yeah, it does. Scary, huh?"

"I would have thought a New Age woman like you would have a positive perspective on the subject of time."

"I do most of the time. There's that word again. *Time.* A strange concept, isn't it? It's just one way of marking our shared planetary presence here on Earth."

Tyler made no comment.

"Anyway, I haven't forgotten that I still owe you a massage. Unless there's something else I can do for you? Some way I could help you the way you helped me?"

"I'm beyond help."

His words wounded her heart. "Don't say that. No one is beyond help."

197

"Now you sound like Sister Mary."

"Do you know her?"

"Our paths crossed."

"I helped her at the food pantry over in Rock Creek. I liked her."

Angel liked Tyler, too, but for once she was cautious in telling him so.

"Dog races." Angel shuddered as she spoke to Julia after work the next day. "Seems barbaric to me."

"This from a woman who was keeping two llamas in my backyard."

"I wasn't whipping them in a race."

"Trust me, no one was whipping any of the dogs. They were all pampered pooches. But Toni totally messed things up."

"She was just playing."

"In the middle of the race. Disrupting it completely."

"I heard that you kissing Luke did that as well. Disrupted things," Angel said. "That made me proud."

Julia was clearly at a loss for words, so Angel changed the subject. "I found the perfect place for Lucy and Ricky and moved them yesterday to an Amish farm less than an hour's drive from here. In case you were wondering why the llamas weren't here any longer."

"What was wrong with the dairy farmer's place?"

Angel shuddered. "He uses chemicals and growth hormones."

"Well, he wouldn't use them on the llamas."

"Ricky and Lucy wouldn't flourish there. What have you got against the Amish farmers? You've never even met them."

"I don't have anything against them."

"Some people do, you know. Because they're Amish."

"Well, I'm not some people."

"I'm glad to hear that. I didn't raise you to be *some people.* I raised you to be open to all the possibilities in the world. To realize that the unknown is just another term for creation."

Great. Her mother was quoting Deepak Chopra to her. Well, that might be his view of things, but in Julia's book, *unknown* simply meant "chaos."

And she'd had enough of that to last her a lifetime.

Or several reincarnated lifetimes.

"By the way, did I tell you that your neighbor signed up for my yoga class today?" Angel asked.

"Mrs. Selznick likes taking classes. She's taken everything from Spanish to tap dancing to introduction to opera everywhere from the park district to the library. If there's a class offered, she takes it."

"What's wrong with that?"

"Nothing if you're not the owner of the Candlewick Store. Mrs. S almost burned the place down when she took a candle-making class there."

"She probably lacked a good teacher, that's all."

"And an asbestos vest."

"Asbestos is poisonous."

"But inflammable. Don't light any candles around her, that's all I'm saying."

"But you know I like to use aromatherapy in conjunction with my yoga . . ."

Julia shook her head. "No open flames."

"But I could use those tiny hurricane lamp things . . . And I may have to smudge to rid the space of any negative energy."

"You've already done that once and set off all my smoke detectors."

"Yes, well, there seems to be a lot of negative energy around, so it needs another smudging." Angel paused to study her a moment. "You look tired. Have you been using that herbal remedy I gave you?"

"No."

"How about the sea kelp?"

"No."

Angel sighed. "You always were a stubborn one."

Julia was thirty, had a mortgage, and contributed to a 401(k) plan. She shouldn't have to hide her Pop-Tarts in her own house.

If she were really stubborn she'd make a stand, lay down the law.

Problem was, it wouldn't make any difference. Her mother would just continue doing what she wanted.

There was no changing her.

Angel stared at her daughter and wished she could read her mind. Julia had never been an easy one to decipher. Angel could read other people's auras, the energy emanations of the physical body, but not her oldest child's. Knowingly or not, Julia blocked her out.

Angel tried not to be hurt by the barricades, reminding herself that Julia had always maintained a stiff-upper-lip approach to life. Even as a toddler, she wouldn't cry when she fell down, but would instead set her jaw with determination and simply get up again.

Angel, who freely admitted to being sensitive and not at all stoic, knew her oldest child hadn't inherited that toughness trait from her. When a bird hit the window of their apartment last spring, Angel had cried for an entire afternoon. She hated seeing others in pain or upheaval.

Not that Julia was indifferent to other's suffering. Not at all. But when Angel "felt your pain," she showed it. Julia hid it.

Julia hid a lot of emotions.

Even so, Angel was fully cognizant of the fact that her daughter was going through a period of upheaval right now. And that Angel was partly to blame. True, Julia tended to take things too seriously while accusing Angel of taking them too lightly.

And although it was true that Angel was low on monetary funds at the moment, she had come to see Julia for another reason. The guilt of not being completely honest with her oldest daughter was starting to eat Angel up inside.

Normally, Angel led a very truthful life. That was a cornerstone in her belief system. Except in this case.

Angel desperately wanted to do the right thing. She just had to figure out what that was.

The tarot cards and runes were clear about one thing. Angel needed to reconnect with Julia on an emotional level before she could reveal her darkest secret.

What happened beyond that was anyone's guess.

★ ★ ★

"If you'd rather not talk about it, we won't," Patty told Julia in the library staff room.

Julia looked up from the *Library Journal* article she was trying to read during her lunch break. "Talk about what?"

"The Wiener Races."

"And the kiss," Laurie added.

"I'd rather not talk about it." Julia took a bite of her salad. She'd decided she was becoming entirely too dependent on junk food as a crutch in dealing with her family . . . or her attraction to Luke. At this rate, she'd soon have health issues to go along with all her other issues.

Not that she was about to trade in her Pop-Tarts for tofu or soy milk. Not going to happen.

But she was a believer in the Socrates school of thought regarding moderation in all things. Even Pop-Tarts.

"It's a good thing that Alice is on vacation with her family at Disney World," Patty noted.

"They were driving down and stopping in Washington, D.C., so Alice could speak to our representative there. She wants to tell her what she's doing wrong," Laurie said.

"That certainly is one of Alice's specialties," Julia conceded.

"It's sort of sad that she doesn't get pleasure out of anything aside from being critical."

"I'll tell you what's sad," Patty said. "That a library board member wanted to know why we're carrying 'those trashy romances' in our library."

"How many of their bones did you break?" Laurie asked.

Patty scowled. "Believe me, I was tempted. Instead, I gave her my biggest smile." She paused to demonstrate. "And asked politely if she was referring to the most popular fiction on the planet. I added that those unfamiliar with the genre had a lot of misconceptions about it. Then I handed her a copy of the article in last year's January/ February issue of *Public Libraries* on the romance novels' appeal and suggested she read it."

"Did she?" Julia asked.

"Surprisingly, yes. She came back to me this morning and thanked me for—"

"Not killing her?" Laurie inserted with a grin.

"For the information."

"That was generous of her." Laurie took a bite out of the peanut butter cookies Patty had brought for them.

"She just couldn't resist your awesome

powers of persuasion," Julia noted.

Patty grinned and preened at the compliment. "Ain't that the truth."

Julia spent the rest of the afternoon at the reference desk. She liked helping people find what they were looking for, and she liked the fact that a library was designed to make finding information easier. No putting a purple book on the shelf by the window just because it looked pretty there. No sticking another tome on the bottom because it had bad energy.

No, in a library, there was a logical plan. Call her weird, but Julia loved the Dewey Decimal System. At one time she'd considered becoming a cataloger before deciding she preferred working with the public.

Because the Serenity Falls Public Library wasn't large enough to have a separate readers' advisory librarian to deal with fiction requests, Julia handled those as well. Which is how she came to be speaking to Mabel about a mystery she was looking for, one she'd seen in a book display the library had a few weeks ago.

"It has a red cover." Mabel fingered her pink curls as if doing so might prompt her memory. "I do remember that much. And the title had something to do with a place."

Julia was able to track it down eventually, thanks to a list of book titles she put on the weekly bookcart display for the past six months. She was in charge of both the fiction and nonfiction new books displays, as well as those spotlight displays she did on topics ranging from animal care to Hollywood bios to natural disasters to scrapbooking.

Book list handouts were also her responsibility, and she had a dozen of them currently on display. After helping Mabel, she refilled the flyers for an upcoming library program — "Origami with Joy" — and added more "True Stories of Survival" handouts.

During a brief mid-afternoon lull, Frasier stopped by for a chat. "Walt informs me that the folks who decide this best small town matter look at the local library as part of the package. And they look pretty closely, including investigating how many books we order each year. I'd like to see you up the orders this month to help those figures out some. I'm not suggesting we go over our budget, just that we order now instead of waiting."

Julia nodded her understanding.

Frasier started to walk away but then turned back to her. "By the way, interesting race the other day. Glad to see you did your bit to make the day memorable." He flashed her a surprising smile, which left her wondering if he'd been mocking her or not.

And that got Julia thinking about Luke again. She'd been doing so well, too, ever since she'd come up with the idea of punishing herself every time he came to mind — one carrot stick for every "Luke thought." So far this afternoon the score was Luke and the carrot sticks two, Julia zip.

She could do better . . . and she would. Or she'd add brussels sprouts to the mix.

Wait, she was one of the few people on the planet who actually *liked* brussels sprouts. So she'd have to come up with something else.

What vegetable did she really dislike? The only one she could think of was bok choy. She wrinkled her nose. Yes, that should do it. Thoughts of Luke were bound to disappear now thanks to that adjustment.

Maybe all it took were a few adjustments, and Julia would get the rest of her life back to normal.

The pessimist in her thought that would be about as likely as the Village Hall Tower clock being accurate again for the first time in sixty years.

Just think bok choy, she reminded herself. Bok choy. Not bad boy. Simple.

★ ★ ★

"So you're kissing librarians now." Algee issued the statement and then took a huge bite of the famous Maguire's burger.

"Only one," Luke drawled. "I hear the others are married. I don't have many rules, but I don't poach on other men's property."

"You do know that she was seeing the banker before he got his trophy wife."

"Who was?"

"The librarian you kissed. She and RJ were an" — Algee paused to do hand quotes — "item." He reached for a few sweet potato fries and then looked up. "Hey, speak of the devil. There he is now."

Luke's eyes narrowed as he watched RJ approach.

"I need to speak to you, Maguire."

"Go ahead, Brandt." He could use surnames as well as the next guy.

"In private."

"Algee is a bud. You can talk in front of him."

Algee scooted his chair closer so he could drape one of his huge arms across Luke's shoulders. "Call me Big Al. We're buds," he told RJ.

"Fine. I'll be blunt then. Stay away from Julia."

"Ah. I heard the two of you used to be an"

— Luke paused to use the same hand quotes Algee had — "item."

"Is that why you were trying to humiliate her in front of the entire town?"

"PDAs are frowned upon around here," Algee told Luke.

"PDAs?"

"Public displays of affection."

"There was nothing affectionate about what he did," RJ said.

"True," Luke agreed. "Nothing luke-warm like affection. Listen, Brandt, does your wife know you're in here, warning me off your old girlfriend?"

There was a pause, long enough to make the warning hairs on the back of Luke's neck stand up, but it was too late.

"I am *not* old, and I was *never* his girl-friend," Julia said in an icy voice from behind him.

Chapter Nine

Damn. This was why Luke usually sat at a table in a corner, so no one could sneak up on him.

But he'd forgotten that when he'd joined Algee at his table.

Big mistake.

Julia had a way of sneaking up on him when he least expected it. Like when he was in bed at night, unable to sleep. She'd come to him then, a man's X-rated fantasy woman. But she'd also come to him when he was going through the piles of paperwork required to keep a place like Maguire's going. He'd remember her smile, or the sound of her laughter. And he wasn't happy about that. It smacked of being sappy.

"RJ and I went out on a few dates," Julia was saying, "but that's it. Not that it's any of your business."

Damn, he got hot and hard when she put on that Miss Prim persona. He wondered if she was wearing her daisy underwear today under those nifty jeans. She really did have great legs. Long and curvy. Just the way he liked his women and their legs.

"I do not appreciate being the topic of conversation over a few brewskis," Julia added.

"Brewskis?" Luke repeated.

She waved her hand at the beers on the table. "Alcoholic beverages."

Luke couldn't resist teasing her as he stood to face her. "So it's okay if you're the topic of conversation, as long as we don't drink when we talk about you?"

She narrowed her eyes at him in a gesture intended to warn him off. It had the opposite effect on him, however.

"You know what I mean." Her voice was as sharp as a barbed wire fence intended to keep out intruders.

But Luke was an expert at getting past outer defenses. "I know exactly what you mean." He leaned a little closer with every word he spoke, until his lips hovered just above hers.

He kept his gaze focused on her eyes, even though he was tempted by her mouth. He wanted to see the attraction she felt for him. He wanted to know he wasn't the only one in this mess.

She allowed him just a brief glimpse before shoving him back into his chair. The only reason Luke let her get away with it was because he liked the feel of her hands on his body and because she then turned her ire to RJ.

"I expected better of you, RJ."

"I was trying to protect you from this scumbag." RJ jerked a thumb in Luke's direction.

"I can protect myself," Julia said.

"I can attest to that," Algee added. "She has a mean sucker-punch."

Luke shot him a dirty look.

Undeterred, Algee added, "So you don't have to worry about the librarian."

"I do have a name, and it's not 'librarian,' " Julia stated. "How would you like it if I called you the Comic Book Guy?"

Algee shrugged. "Doesn't bother me a bit. I've been called much worse."

"We're straying from the subject here," RJ said. "Julia, I need to speak to you privately."

"How do you think your wife is going to like that?" Luke said.

The banker ignored his question and instead cupped Julia's elbow with his hand. "Come along. Let's get out of here."

"Want me to punch him for you?" Luke asked hopefully.

Julia glared at him. "Don't you dare."

"A little advice — you might not want to

dare a guy like Luke," Algee said. "Just trying to be helpful here."

"You." She pointed to Luke. "Stay here. I'll speak with you later." She turned and left with RJ.

"Doncha just love bossy women?" Algee noted before munching on a crisp dill pickle.

Love? That four-letter word was definitely *not* in Luke's vocabulary.

"Let's go over to the Serenity Cafe and talk over a cup of coffee." RJ voiced it as an order, not a suggestion. A polite order.

"I'm paying for my own coffee," Julia stated. Actually, she could really use a slice of pie about now. Her mother had made her try one of the pumpkin-applesauce-bran muffins she'd baked this morning, and her stomach was still in cement shock.

Julia noticed the curious looks she was getting from the other customers as well as the waitress, who was Alice's squeaky-clean eighteen-year-old niece.

After ordering a slice of today's special, strawberry-rhubarb pie, and coffee, Julia made sure that no part of her body came in contact with any part of RJ's. A little tough to do given the tight space under the booths here at the cafe, but Julia worked hard and was successful.

She wasn't avoiding the contact because of any lingering feelings she had for RJ but because she didn't want to "set tongues wagging," as Edith would put it.

Of course, if gossip was a real concern to Julia, she should never have returned Luke's kiss at the Wiener Races the other day.

He'd taken her by surprise, that was her excuse. A feeble one, granted.

If RJ had tried to kiss her, even if he had taken her by surprise, she would have pushed him away, no problem.

Everything about Luke was a problem.

"Just tell me one thing," RJ said. "Why did you let Luke kiss you in front of the entire town?"

"You mean it's okay if he kisses me in private?"

He gave her a reprimanding look. "You know what I mean."

It did not escape her notice that he'd used the same words she'd used with Luke a few moments ago. "I really don't think this is an appropriate topic of conversation between the two of us."

"Why not?"

"Because you're married now, and who I kiss is none of your business."

"He's bad news. I realize you're new in town —"

"I've lived here more than three years now," she interrupted him to point out.

He waved her words away. "Still new in town. So you might not realize what kind of trouble he is."

"I've heard the gossip going around."

"But you don't believe it?"

She shrugged.

"You should." His expression was stern.

"What does everyone have against Luke? I mean, he's been gone for a long time."

"Stole his diploma and left."

"He was just a kid then."

"He was never just a kid. He was always trouble. In school and out. Picked up for various acts of vandalism."

"Charged with them or just picked up?"

"Does that really matter?"

"Was he the only wild teenager in town?"

"Pretty much, yeah."

"So he was different." She knew only too well that meant you stood out like a sore thumb.

Julia stood out — in a different way than the rest of her family.

They studied Zen koans; she studied math. They explored auras and chakras; she explored the local library of whatever town they were living in at the time.

Her mother and sister explored and experimented their way through life with no thought whatsoever to the consequences of their actions. They accused her of being rational and hard-headed, as if these were the deadliest of sins, while warning her about being too judgmental of others.

It wasn't as they said . . . that she belittled their beliefs. She'd been raised with certain truths — and they were good truths to have. Be kind to others; be good to animals and the earth; do no harm.

But she was also a firm believer in common sense — a trait that was definitely lacking elsewhere in her family tree.

She'd been so involved in her own thoughts that she'd lost track of what RJ was saying. "No one has any idea what Luke has been doing for the past twelve years. There are rumors that he was in the state penitentiary, so I had the sheriff check and he couldn't confirm that."

"You had the sheriff digging into Luke's past? That's a huge invasion of privacy."

"He refused to do much, but regardless, security is more important than privacy."

"Easy to say when it's not your privacy that's being messed with," Julia said. "And I fail to see how Luke could be a security risk of any kind."

"Has he checked out any suspicious material from the library?"

"Do you have a warrant?" she shot back.

RJ blinked at her. "Of course not."

"Then drop this."

"I just asked you a simple question."

"No, you were snooping around, looking for trouble where none exists."

"I was not snooping around. You make it sound as if I were pawing through the loser's garbage or something. And those rumors about Mabel doing that behind Maguire's have nothing to do with me."

"You're setting up a situation like the Salem witch hunts, making people suspicious and playing on their worst fears. That always brings out the worst in human beings, not the best."

"Are you actually defending the guy?"

"I'm defending his right to peaceably live here, the same as any other citizen."

"But he's not the same as any other citizen."

"He doesn't have to be to have the *same rights*. That's what our country is all about!"

"Walt doesn't think so. He's on my side about this."

"There shouldn't be sides. That just causes more divisions between people instead of bringing them together."

"So you think Luke is the underdog and

your job is to be his champion, is that it? Is that why you kissed him?"

She refused to answer.

RJ shook his head. "You're too naive for your own good. Fine, be that way — but don't say I didn't warn you." He tossed a few dollars onto the table and walked out.

Julia exited the cafe to find Luke waiting for her outside. He was leaning against the brick wall, one knee bent, wearing his customary black jeans, T-shirt, and leather jacket — and looking every bit the bad boy his reputation generated.

Well, no, not a *boy*. Definitely a man. But not a bad man. Just one with wickedly tempting intentions. Or so she suspected. "What are you doing here?"

"You ask me that a lot, have you noticed?"

She didn't know how to answer that so she stayed silent.

"What, no fast response?" He raised a dark eyebrow. "I'm shocked."

Ignoring him, she turned and headed south toward home. When she'd first bought her house, she'd loved the fact that she merely had to cross the street to get to work and that she could walk the few blocks to the downtown area to shop without having to use her car.

Her mother had raised her to be enough of a conservationist that Julia paid attention to things like miles per gallon and saving gasoline by walking.

"Still have nothing to say?" Luke joined her. "No problem. I'm not a fan of gabby women anyway."

"Gabby women?" she repeated in disbelief.

"You have a problem with that?"

"Lots of problems." She'd lecture him about being a chauvinist but doubted he'd change, so she needled him in a more subtle way. "The least of which is that it doesn't seem like the kind of word you'd use."

"What's wrong with *gabby?*" He sounded defensive.

"Nothing. It's just well . . . more of a feminine adjective."

"And I used it about females." He stopped in his tracks. "Wait a second. Are you accusing me of using *girly* words?"

His outraged expression cracked her up.

"It's not funny. Lucky for you, I might forgive you."

"Why's that?"

"Same reason I gave you before. Because I want to have sex with you."

"*Shhh.*" She put her fingers to his mouth and frantically looked around. Luckily, they were now past the downtown area and on a quiet residential street.

"Mmmm." Luke nibbled on her fingers and then dabbed at them with the tip of his tongue. "You can *shhh* me anytime."

She narrowed her eyes. "Don't even start with the librarian jokes."

"Who says I'm joking?"

"I do."

"Want me to prove you wrong?" His voice was a weapon of seduction.

"No."

"Liar."

"Arrogant chauvinist."

"That the best you can do? I would have thought that a woman like you could come up with a better insult than that. Come on, give it your best try."

"You're ridiculous." She turned and started walking away.

He was right beside her. "Ridiculous really doesn't cut it."

"I am *not* having this conversation with you."

"Yes, you are. I'm walking you home and we're talking. That's a conversation."

She stopped in her tracks again. "You are *not* walking me home."

"Yeah, I am."

"No."

"Yes."

"What is it with you?"

"What is it with you?" he countered.

"I asked you first."

He had to grin at her childish response.

So did she. Reluctantly.

They started walking again.

"So did RJ warn you off me?" Luke asked.

"I'm getting tired of people doing that," she said.

"Yeah, me, too."

"He accused me of being naive."

"The dog. Want me to beat him up for you?" Luke's expression was hopeful.

Hers was reprimanding. "You already asked me that, and I told you no."

"But that was before he said you were naive. And I only said I'd punch him before."

"I don't want you going anywhere near him."

"You sure?"

"Positive." Eager to change the subject, she said, "So tell me, how are the renovations going at Maguire's?"

"You've been there. How do you think they're going?"

"The hunter green looks nice on the walls toward the front. I'm not sure what you're doing with that one side wall in the back."

"Neither am I."

"You could always add tablecloths and some nice drapes to the décor. And maybe a brick fireplace. And some plants."

"Are you trying to turn the place into a fern bar?"

"Of course not. That's totally outdated. I was thinking more along the lines of something with an English country motif. Some chintz and . . ."

"Whoa, stop right there. I do *not* do chintz."

"You probably don't even know what it is."

"I don't have to know what it is to know that I don't do it. Or want it in Maguire's."

"Has anyone ever told you that you have a closed mind?"

"Not and lived to talk about it, no."

She hoped he was kidding about that. But what did she really know about him, as RJ had just pointed out? Not much.

"You said you were a Marine."

He nodded.

"You never said what you did when you left the Marine Corps."

"No, I didn't."

"So what did you do?"

"This and that." He took her hand in his.

"Why the big mystery about your past?"

"I have my reasons."

"And they are?"

"My business."

Stung by his words, she yanked her hand away.

"But if I told anyone, I'd tell you," he murmured, taking her hand back and threading his fingers through hers.

"Is that supposed to make me feel better?"

"Sex with me would make you feel better."

She smacked his arm with her free hand. "Stop that."

"You know that using that librarian voice on me only makes me want you more."

"I have nothing to say to that."

"Good." He grinned. "Remember, I don't like gabby women."

They walked in silence for a few moments. Darkness was falling earlier and earlier now as they headed into mid-November. The leafless branches of the trees along the way created dark silhouettes etched against the chromatic twilight sky. This was Julia's favorite time of day.

She stopped in front of her house. "Well, here we are."

"I'll walk you to your door."

"Why? No." She put her fingers back on his lips. "Never mind. Don't answer that."

He nibbled at her fingers.

She yanked them away, irritated that she'd allowed herself to fall for that again. You'd think the second time around her heart wouldn't skip so much. That couldn't be healthy.

She needed to regain some control here. Make it all sound like a tempest in a teapot. Now she sounded like Edith. As old as the hills.

"Are you afraid to be seen with me?" Luke said.

"Of course not." She managed to make her voice sound calm. "I've got to say it seems a lot of commotion over one little kiss."

Luke moved closer. "You think so?"

"Yes, I do." She refused to let him intimidate her.

"Hmmm." He slid his fingers between hers, warming her with his heat. "Let's make it two kisses then."

Without further ado, Luke kissed her, moving his hands and hers around to the small of her back so she was arched against him.

A part of her had wondered if that first kiss they'd so passionately shared had been a one-time deal, like a twister in Vermont or something. A rare occurrence that was unlikely to be repeated. That even if Luke did kiss her again, it wouldn't be as intensely awesome. It wouldn't be the same.

It wasn't. But it was just as good. Just as intensely awesome.

It was like discovering a new book by a favorite author, drawing you in and inviting you to share an entirely different story but with the same appeal as the first one.

Only a librarian would compare a life-altering kiss to a book, but then Julia had a special connection with books and she was developing a special connection with Luke.

Not just because he could do those magical moves with his talented tongue, although they did snatch her breath away and make her feel all feverish.

And not just because he nibbled his way right across her mouth, although she loved that.

Even the way he held her in his arms was unique. He had her tethered, which should have made her feel like the llamas she'd had in her backyard. But instead, he made her feel protected and adored as he worked his way from first base to second.

Julia was pressed against the storm door and he was pressed tight against her, his knee nudging hers apart. They were both wearing jeans, and the denim provided an evocative friction whenever he moved. Or she did.

Luke still had her hands cuffed, so she couldn't explore his body beneath the soft leather jacket and T-shirt he wore. But somehow her own coat had come undone and shimmied out of the way enough that she could feel the heat of his body against her breasts. The drag of her nipples against him as she shifted felt so good she did it again, and again.

Her moan of pleasure was incorporated into their kiss.

So was her startled gasp as the door behind her shifted.

"Hello, you two," her mother cheerfully greeted them. "Having fun?"

"We were," Luke replied, because Julia was clearly speechless.

"Good." Angel opened the screen door. "Come on inside. I just brewed some green tea and baked some cookies."

"What's that smell?" Julia asked, having just caught of a whiff of something . . . not quite right.

"The first batch of my yellow squash cookies didn't quite come out as planned. I overcooked them a bit."

"I'm going to have to take a raincheck on

those cookies," Luke said, taking a quick step backward.

"Coward," Julia muttered under her breath.

"I heard that," he replied.

"He doesn't do chintz or yellow squash cookies," Julia told Angel.

"You've got that right." An instant later, Luke was gone, leaving Julia with the memory of his kiss and the reminder that sexy bad boys never stuck around for very long.

Two days later, Julia sat at the table in her kitchen, enjoying the Saturday morning sunshine flooding in through the window. She'd just finished eating some fresh baked wheat toast and homemade strawberry jam Angel had purchased from the organic market. It didn't taste half bad.

Opening the *Serenity News*, she quickly flipped through the newspaper's pages, wanting to be sure they'd put in the notice about this month's programs at the library. Instead, she was distracted by the full-page ad photo of Sue Ellen Riley.

Below it was written:

Hi there, this is Sue Ellen Riley. Are you seeing things that aren't there? Then you should have your vision checked at Goodwin Eye Care Center.

"I don't believe this," Julia growled. "She got a job out of this?"

"Who did?" Angel asked as she entered the room.

"Sue Ellen Riley." Julia held up the paper for her mom to see.

"Let me put my reading glasses on first." Angel slid them into place. "Ah, that's Sue Ellen, isn't it?"

"Right." Julia slid her own reading glasses a bit farther up the bridge of her nose. "Do you believe that?"

"Believe what? That it's Sue Ellen?"

"That she's advertising for the vision center."

"At least she's leaving Lucy and Ricky alone. I miss those llamas, you know. Even though I do go visit them. You should see how they clown around sometimes. They're so funny."

Julia closed the paper. She didn't want to think about Sue Ellen or the llamas. She just wanted to enjoy her day off.

Angel had other plans. "Can you take Toni with you when you run your errands? I've got a yoga class, and Skye is doing a belly-dancing presentation over at the

Moose Lodge in Rock Creek." At Julia's look, Angel added, "Don't ask. It pays well. Everything will be fine. My centering exercise for today is outer peace."

Peace. Julia faded out as her mother went into detail about her plans for the upcoming yoga class. Peace. That was something Julia used to have. She remembered being able to eat what she wanted, do what she wanted, live as she wanted.

The sound of something crashing in the living room made Julia jump out of her chair and reminded her yet again how much her life had changed over the past few weeks. Her calm haven was now a chaotic commune.

Toni was the culprit, but there was no blood, which was always a good thing. She'd tried to climb the pile of oversized books and leap onto the couch, something she'd done before. The books toppled over and caused the noise they'd heard. Julia had already moved the larger tomes out of the room, but she was running out of places to hide things to make the house safe for the little girl.

"Toni, you're going with Julia this morning," Angel announced.

"No, I'm not!" For someone who never had the word applied to her, it was still

Toni's favorite reply.

"You're both going to have a wonderful time together," Angel continued.

"Let's go get you changed into some other clothes," Julia told her niece.

"No!" This time her voice rose two decibel levels.

"You can't wear the tutu outside. You've got to change."

"NO!" Toni added a foot stomp for emphasis.

"You're the one who showed her *The Nutcracker* ballet on TV," Angel pointed out.

Julia rolled her eyes. "I never meant for her to wear that tutu outside the house."

"She likes what she's wearing," Angel said.

Julia didn't like it, but there was no convincing Toni.

And so it was that Julia found herself in line at the bank, holding onto Toni's hand and trying to act as if it were perfectly natural for a four-year-old to be wearing an orange polka-dotted angora sweater, purple tutu, kitten-print flannel pj bottoms, and yellow Wellington boots that would make Paddington Bear proud. The broken tiara drunkenly perched on Toni's head completed the picture.

She could feel Mabel's eyes boring into

her back as she stood in line. Julia would have used the drive-thru but because Toni refused to get in the child seat in the car, she'd had to walk into town. Thankfully, Toni had held onto Julia's hand without protest.

In the line beside them was Julia's neighbor Val and her two kids, one of which was near Toni's age. But Val had kept her kids clear of Toni since she'd tried to bite her oldest boy, Danny. Julia still felt the need to apologize every time she saw Val, but because she'd already done that a dozen or two times, she figured enough was probably enough.

Of course, Val's little girl, Morgan, looked adorable in a fleecy pink coat and matching pants. No broken tiaras in that family.

Julia was relieved to leave the bank without incident and without Toni making any references to her vagina, or anyone else's. That relief waned when Toni declared, "I've gotta pee now."

Julia looked around. They were standing outside Maguire's.

"Now!" Toni started hopping from one boot to the other.

Julia hurried her inside the pub.

"We're not open," Luke began before looking up to see her.

"Sorry. Bathroom emergency."

Luke pointed to the ladies' room at the back.

Julia hurried Toni into the washroom and managed to get everything undone without incident, but just in the nick of time. Afterward, Toni was in no hurry to get off the toilet, and was balanced so precariously that Julia was sure she was going to fall in with a splash. Ten minutes later, Adele knocked at the door. "Everything okay in there?"

"Fine." Julia answered. There was only one toilet in the ladies' room, and she couldn't get Toni off it.

"Come on." Julia used her best coaxing voice, the one that convinced Ron Johnson to return the twenty overdue books he had held onto for six months. "Time to leave. You're done now, right?"

Toni nodded but made no move.

"Hey, who wants ice cream?" Julia asked.

"Olivia does."

"Who's that?"

"My invisible friend." Toni pointed to the corner of the bathroom. "She already peed."

"What a relief." This was the first Julia had heard of an invisible friend. She wondered if the name had come from the popular Olivia books she'd been reading Toni.

"Where's my ice cream?" Toni demanded

the instant they finally left the washroom.

"Chocolate or strawberry?" Adele asked.

"Oh, no, you don't have to do that," Julia quickly assured her.

Adele made a *forget it* motion with her hand. "I want to. So, honey, what flavor would you like?"

"Banana chocolate-chip cherry," Toni promptly replied.

"Chocolate will be fine," Julia said in a quiet aside to Adele.

"I'll add some cherries and bananas," Adele whispered back.

"You don't have to . . ." Julia began.

But Adele had already bustled back to the kitchen.

Luke remained behind the bar as if he didn't trust the kid.

"Wise move," Julia congratulated him.

"What?"

"Staying over there. Wise move. You don't want her . . ." Julia made a Jaws-like motion with her hand.

"I'm not afraid of kids," Luke stated.

"Of course you're not." Her voice mocked him.

"I just don't want to hang out with them."

"Aw, and here I was hoping she could help you pour drinks."

"Very funny," he growled. "What's she wearing?"

"A tiara."

"I meant that frilly thing around her waist."

"A tutu. Like a ballerina."

"Looks weird."

"No kidding."

"You let her out like that?"

"I didn't have much choice."

"You look good, though."

She glanced down at her jeans and red microfleece pullover. "I do?"

"Yeah."

Adele brought out two dishes of ice cream and a separate bowl of cherries, which Julia took custody of so Toni wouldn't gobble them all in one swallow.

"Where's the dish for Olivia?" Toni demanded.

"She wants to share your dish with you," Julia said.

"Okay."

Julia didn't even realize she was nibbling on a cherry until she heard Luke groan from across the room. She looked up to find him staring at her with lust in his heart, mind, and body.

She met his stare head-on, refusing to look away from the sexual heat he was aiming her way. He was making her feel all hot and squishy inside.

Not Hallmark-cards-sweet kind of squishy. Definitely *Sex and the City* squishy. Hot, moist, pulsing squishy.

Julia stared at the cherry, then at Luke, then at the cherry and remembered how many times he'd tempted her. This was her opportunity to turn the tables on him for a change.

She started with her tongue. He was a master at using his to make her burn with desire. She held the cherry by its stem and tilted her head back as she licked the edge of the delicious fruit.

Only after she'd tested every millimeter did she then dangle the cherry above her mouth before biting into it.

Then she took the next cherry and did the same, with a few more elaborate moves, plucking the stem from the cherry before setting it midway between her lips.

A second later, Luke was at her side, yanking her up out of the chair and tasting that cherry with her. His warm tongue swirled over hers and the fruit. His teeth nibbled the cherry and her bottom lip before sweeping inside her mouth.

"Yuck!" Toni declared. "Yuck, yuck, YUCK!!" She banged her spoon on the table for added emphasis.

"What's going on out here?" Adele demanded as she came from the kitchen.

"Nothing," Luke murmured, running his thumb over Julia's still-damp mouth, the mouth he'd just devoured. "I was just showing Julia how one of our specials should be . . . consumed."

Toni pointed her dripping spoon at Julia. "Girls have vaginas!"

Julia knew . . . and hers was aching for Luke, the last man on the planet she should be wanting to invite into her bed.

Chapter Ten

Luke glared at the letter from the video store he held in his hand. The DVD he'd checked out was overdue, and he'd been charged the cost onto his credit card. He'd only checked out one — the *Monty Python* thing — and handed it over to someone else. Clearly a mistake. He was making entirely too many of those since coming here.

"Do you know the mayor's kid?" he asked Adele.

"You mean Billy?"

"Yeah."

"Sure, I know him."

"Know where I can find him?"

"He hangs out at Cosmic Comics a lot."

"Thanks."

Adele looked up from the homemade soup she was creating on the huge commercial stove. "Why are you looking for him?"

"I thought I'd lead him into a lifetime of crime."

Adele just gave him a look.

"What?" he countered. "You're not buying that?"

"Not for one second."

"Why not? The rest of the town would."

"Not all of them. Not the librarian."

"She's informed me that she doesn't like to be known as the librarian. That she has a name. Julia."

"She'd be good for you," Adele stated.

"That's debatable. Plenty of people have warned her that I'm not good for her."

"They're wrong."

"Tell that to that sheriff you have a crush on."

"I have."

"He believe you?"

"That's still debatable," Adele admitted. "But I'm still working on him."

"Well, I can't stand around here chatting. I've got a kid to corrupt. A bad seed's work is never done."

It was Luke's first real foray into the comic book place down the street. When he'd originally met Algee, the store had been shut and he'd merely banged on the door but hadn't stepped inside.

The place was as colorful and lively as the guy who owned it. Posters of the X-Men, Batman, Spiderman, Superman, Captain America, and others marched along the top part of the walls. The rest of the space was covered with shelves and row after row of comic books. Among the crowded aisles were displays of everything from action figures to collector card sets to Pez dispensers in the shape of superheroes. Up front was the cash register beside a locked glass case with even more comic books. And standing guard over it all was Algee, looking as massive as the Incredible Hulk in the poster behind him.

"If you're looking for the fancy banker, you've come to the wrong place," Algee told him with a wide grin that showed off a flash of white teeth.

"No surprise there. This doesn't seem the kind of establishment that stuffed shirt would patronize, which puts it right at the top of my list."

"Glad to hear that. Considering the amount of money I've dropped at Maguire's eating there a couple times a week, it seems only fair that you come here and make a few purchases."

"Now you're sounding like a banker."

"No, just like a businessman."

"I didn't come here looking for a businessman. I'm looking for someone shorter . . . ah, there he is." Luke spotted Billy. "Hey, kid, where's that *Monty Python* DVD?"

"I took it back."

"That's not what the rental place says."

"They lie."

"Maybe. Or maybe you lie."

"Or maybe the kid just wanted to see you again and didn't know how to do that," Algee inserted.

Luke frowned at him. "What are you, a psychic now?"

Algee lifted his shoulders. "Just an educated guess."

"*Guess* being the operative word in that sentence." Luke returned his attention to Billy. "So, kid, you got anything to say here?"

"Why should I bother?" Billy jammed his hands into the pockets of his oversized pants. "You already know what you think."

"I do, do I?"

Billy nodded and glared at him.

"What's with the outfit?" Luke pointed at the hooded sweatshirt and baggy pants. "You trying to be a bad seed again?"

"You're not a bad seed," Billy scoffed, "you're just an adult."

Luke was highly insulted. "Hey, I've already warned you once about calling me that."

"Whatever."

"So you like reading comic books?"

"Maybe."

"Only the most intelligent members of our community read graphic novels, what you call comic books," Algee said.

"I've almost got the complete *Sandman* collection," Billy added.

Luke shrugged. "Never heard of him."

"Neophyte," Algee noted with a shake of his head and a shared look with Billy.

"Whatever happened to Spiderman or the X-Men?" Luke pointed up at their posters. "Besides having movies made about them, I mean. I've heard of them."

"They're still around," Algee said.

"Spidey's okay," Billy said.

"You two are apparently on a first-name basis, huh?" Luke mocked.

Billy just gave him one of those looks Luke used to give adults — still did sometimes. Basically it said *You are so lame.*

Being the subject instead of the offender was such a weird feeling for Luke that it rattled him and made him ask another dorky question. "You in high school yet?" Luke realized he had no idea how old the mayor's kid was. He was guessing somewhere between twelve and fourteen.

"No. Why do you want to know?" Billy's voice was suspicious.

"Just wondering if I need to go through your locker looking for that missing DVD."

"You'd need a warrant."

"Not if I was good at picking locks after hours."

Billy's eyes widened and then narrowed. "I don't keep anything in my locker."

"Why not?"

"Because the other kids break in and steal stuff. They think I'm a freakazoid."

"What makes them think that?"

"Who knows. I don't care. They don't read comics."

"Peons," Algee scoffed.

"I'm not peeing on them," Billy looked outraged at the idea.

"That's not what I meant. Never mind." Algee waved his hand. "Remember how other kids treated Peter Parker, aka Spiderman?"

Billy nodded. "Like a freakazoid."

"Seems to be a continuing theme," Luke noted. "Clark Kent wasn't exactly winning any awards for being smooth, either."

"My dad wanted me to be on the football team," Billy abruptly announced.

"So did mine," Luke said.

"I'm not good enough." Billy kicked his backpack.

"For what?"

"For the team."

Luke inclined his head toward the maligned backpack. "You try out for kicker?"

- "Kickers suck."

"Maybe. But they can win games."

"They were gonna put me on as a backup kicker, but only because I'm the mayor's kid."

"And that pissed you off."

"Wouldn't it piss you off?" Billy retorted.

"I'm not you, kid. Now about that DVD —"

"I returned it."

Luke just gave him a look, the same one Billy had given him, that said, *You're so lame.* Only Luke's held years of experience at dealing with cons.

"Maybe you meant to return it," Algee said. "Maybe you should check your backpack just in case it's still in there after all."

Billy stubbornly stuck out his chin. "Why should I?"

"Because you really don't want to piss me off," Luke said.

"You don't scare me."

"I'm not even trying," Luke retorted. "Not yet, anyway."

"You never even asked me how I liked it."

"Did you like it?"

"It sucked."

"Fine. Then you should be glad to get rid of it. Hand it over."

Billy bent down and yanked open his backpack, dug around a minute, and then pulled out a DVD. "Here."

Luke frowned down at it. "That isn't the *Monty Python* DVD."

"I *told* you I returned it. Did you even bother going to the rental place and seeing if they have it?"

No. Luke hadn't. But he didn't have to tell the kid that.

Billy read the answer on his face. "You already figured I was guilty," the kid said.

That accusation really struck home for Luke. How many times had the same thing happened to him growing up? People figuring he was guilty just because of his past.

"Stay here," Luke growled. "I'll be right back."

Luke was not in a good mood when he walked into the video rental store, and he was sure Mabel behind the counter picked up on that fact.

Ignoring her, he headed right for the shelf where he'd first found the *Monty Python* DVD. Sure enough, there it was.

He grabbed it and marched toward the front. "I got this letter saying a DVD I rented had never been returned, yet here it is, right on your shelves."

"Maybe we have more than one copy," Mabel said.

"Check it out on that computer of yours."

It took her forever.

"Well . . . ?" Luke was losing what little patience he had left.

"It appears we do only have one copy," Mabel reluctantly admitted.

"And it appears this is it, right?"

Mabel opened up the plastic container to verify his claim. "Yes, it does appear that way."

"Then it *appears* you made a mistake."

"The computer did."

"Fix it."

She did, issuing a credit to his credit card account.

Luke handed her the letter. "And write on there that this was an error and that the DVD was returned."

She did in a nearly illegible scrawl.

"Good. Thank you." Five minutes later he was back in Cosmic Comics. "Where's the kid?"

Algee pointed to the back of the store.

Billy ignored him as he approached, keeping his attention focused on the comic book he was studying.

"I was wrong. You were right. You did return it. I apologize," Luke said gruffly.

Billy remained silent.

"You hear me?" Luke's voice rose. "I said I was sorry, and I don't say that very often."

Still no response.

Only then did Luke notice the white wires going down from Billy's ears to the iPod hanging from his belt.

"Yo." Luke poked Billy's shoulder with his index finger.

Billy turned. "What?"

"I've been standing here apologizing to you for the past ten minutes, and you didn't even hear me."

"Yeah, I did. I didn't have it turned on." Billy pointed to his iPod.

Luke had to laugh. "You're evil, kid."

"Yeah, I know." Billy grinned. "Sweet, huh?"

"Yeah," Luke had to admit as he exchanged a high-five with the mayor's son. "Sweet."

"I'm telling you, I saw them in that awful comic book store," Mabel was telling Edith as she checked out the video of *Pride and Prejudice* with Colin Firth, a favorite of Edith's. "Luke Maguire and the mayor's son. Who knows what they sell in there?"

"They sell comic books," Edith said.

"Can't the town council do something about that?"

"No."

"You can't be saying you approve of that sort of thing."

"What sort of thing?"

"Well, comic books. He could be selling pornography for all we know."

"Oh, we'd know. We send in people to check things out."

"People?"

"The mayor's brother."

Mabel's carefully plucked and penciled eyebrows rose. "Phil the dentist reads comic books?"

"He's posing as a fan to keep an eye on the situation."

"Well, that's a relief."

"Don't you worry about a thing, Mabel." Edith patted her hand. "Your town council is hard at work for you and has everything under control."

"You don't have Luke Maguire under control."

"No. I fear that is an impossible task. But we're still working on it."

"It looks like he has a thing for the librarian."

Edith nodded. "I understand he's been spotted kissing her once or twice."

"Twice? I only know about the one time at the Wiener Races."

"Yes, that was quite a . . . situation.

Nothing Mr. Darcy would have done, making a scene like that."

"Who's Mr. Darcy? Does he work at the funeral home?"

"No, he's the hero in *Pride and Prejudice*." Edith tapped the video box.

"Oh. I never saw the movie."

"What about reading the book?"

"They made it into a book, too?"

"Never mind."

"Wait!" Mabel grabbed Edith's wrist to stop her from leaving. "What about the second kiss you were talking about?"

"Mrs. Selznick was taking her dog Terminator for a walk and claims she might have seen them on Julia's front porch."

"Them?"

"Julia and Luke."

"What were they doing?"

"Well, it was getting dark by then so she couldn't be sure, but it looked like they might have been kissing. Don't say you heard it from me, however."

"I won't. When did this happen?"

"A few days ago." Edith shook her head. "I thought Julia had more sense than that."

"Who's Julia? Is she in *Pride and Prejudice*, too?"

"No, Julia is the librarian," Edith said impatiently.

"Oh. Right. I knew that. Sometimes it's hard to keep up, though."

"Just remember, you didn't hear any of this from me."

"Got it."

Julia loved the holidays. She loved decorating the library with snowflakes and putting up the Christmas tree with book-shaped ornaments made by Friends of the Library.

And it wasn't just the festivities at work that warmed her heart. She loved the traditional lighting of the town Christmas tree in the town square and all the thousands of tiny white twinkling lights adorning the bare trees around the park and along Main Street. Serenity Falls was definitely in a festive mood this time of year.

She couldn't believe that the past two weeks had gone by so quickly. Now that the llamas were no longer in her backyard, her mom was spending more time on the road going to visit them. Angel and Skye had started their yoga and belly-dancing classes at Julia's house during the day, and those seemed to be going well.

Thanksgiving had gone smoothly. Toni hadn't bitten anyone, and the tofurkey had been . . . interesting.

Meanwhile, Luke hadn't contacted her once. He'd kissed her until her kneecaps melted and then disappeared.

Well, not disappeared. She knew he was at Maguire's. It wasn't as if he'd skipped town or anything.

He just hadn't seen her. Or kissed her.

Why not?

A gutsy woman would go over there and find out, not sit here at the library's reference desk, pushing around papers.

It wasn't as if Julia didn't have things to do. She did. Three issues of *Booklist* sat there waiting for her to go through them and make selection choices. And she had to check her e-mail to see if there had been any responses to the post she'd put on the Fiction-L listserv asking for read-alike recommendations for a reader who liked the *Mrs. Pollifax* mystery series. She also had to check on the status of those READ posters she'd ordered from the American Library Association online store. Plus there was a presentation on holiday quilting tomorrow night that she was supposed to get organized with additional reading material and handouts for those attending. And the holiday cookbook bookcart needed refilling.

But she couldn't seem to concentrate on any of that.

If she wasn't going to think about work, she should at least be thinking about Christmas lists and things she still had to do. There were holiday cards to address and mail. Cookies to mix and bake. Presents to buy and wrap.

Yet here she sat, restlessly pushing her rolling chair back and forth, staring out the window and thinking about Luke.

Her plan to punish herself with carrot sticks and bok choy every time he came to mind had worn thin when she'd gotten so badly in the hole that she had to abandon the idea or risk eating the two dreaded veggies every hour of every day for the next six months. That's how often she'd thought of him lately.

The man was clearly a bad influence on her. He distracted her. He tempted her. He got to her. He didn't like gabby women.

What was that about?

Who cared?

She did . . . and that was a problem.

Two weeks. Luke hated the fact that he knew exactly how many days it had been since he'd kissed Julia. He hated the fact that he hadn't kissed her again since then. Or gotten her between the sheets.

He especially hated that he was getting

twinges of something stupid like noble re-grets. What ever happened to bedding a woman and then forgetting about her? Getting horizontal, vertical, just doing it again and again . . . What was wrong with the two of them having a good time and then moving on?

"You've been cleaning that same glass for ten minutes now," Adele noted wryly.

"It was really dirty."

"Apparently."

He frowned at her. "Don't you have something important to do in the kitchen?"

"More important than harassing you? Not at the moment, no."

"And that's another thing. I thought you said a new menu was going to increase busi-ness."

"That's right."

"Then why is the place empty?"

"Maybe because it's only eleven in the morning and we don't open until noon."

"Oh. Right."

"That's okay." She patted his arm as if he were Billy's age. "I know you've got a lot on your mind."

"How do you know that?"

"Because you've been cleaning a lot of glasses and spending a lot of time doing it. Isn't that right, Tyler?"

"Leave me out of this," Tyler said from the other side of the room where he was eating a meal Adele had prepared for him. "Have you figured out what you want to do about that mural idea I suggested for the side wall in the back room?"

"Go ahead with it," Luke said absently, his gaze on the front window where he watched the people walking by. No sign of a belly-dancing librarian though.

"You sure?"

"Yeah, why not?"

"Because it's gonna cost you more money."

"How much?"

Tyler named a figure that made Luke choke.

"Just seeing if you were still paying attention," Tyler noted with a rare smile that was there and gone.

"Very funny," Luke growled. "I'm surrounded by a pair of comedians today."

"Not just today, but every day. Lucky you." Adele actually pinched his cheek before heading back to the kitchen.

"Yeah, lucky you," Tyler said.

Luke glared at him. "You pinch my cheek and you're a dead man."

"Same here," Tyler returned dryly. "So what did you want on this mural of yours?"

"A naked woman would be fine by me,"

he mockingly replied.

"Okay. Speaking of women . . ."

"Don't even bring up the librarian's name," Luke warned him.

"I wasn't going to. I was going to ask you about her mom, but never mind."

"No, go ahead. I don't mind handing out advice to other guys on how to please the ladies."

"Like you're an expert," Tyler scoffed.

"Well, I don't like to brag but . . ."

"You're having regrets."

"What?" Luke almost choked again. Did the guy have ESP or something?

"Me, too."

"You? What have *you* got to have regrets about?"

"Tons. How about you?"

"Ditto."

"Well, then."

"Yeah." Luke looked away. "Well then . . ."

"She's better off without me," Tyler abruptly stated.

"Who is?"

"Julia's mother."

"Why? She doesn't seem the type who'd be upset by your career choices or uh . . . unusual lifestyle. I mean it's not as if she's Suzie Homemaker herself."

"She's an angel."

"That's her name, yeah."

"No, I mean she's an *angel*. She sees the good in everyone. People like us, you and me, we don't. We know better."

"Yeah, we do," Luke said slowly, wondering what was going on with Tyler. What had gone on in his past?

"Glad you agree with me."

"You married?" Luke asked.

"Not anymore."

"You got a last name?"

"Yeah."

"Mind telling me what it is?"

"Yeah."

Tyler had insisted on being paid in cash, and Luke had had no problem with that. He knew cash left no paper trails. And he'd suspected that's why Tyler had wanted things that way.

But for the first time he wondered if there was something darker going on with the insomniac Rollerblader/handyman.

Which is why after Tyler left, Luke took the glass of water Tyler had used and wrapped it in a sheet of newspaper until he could get his hands on a fingerprinting kit. It wouldn't hurt to run Tyler's prints through the system and see what came up.

"If you tell me you've finished all your

Christmas shopping already, I'm going to have to kill you," Julia warned Pam as the two of them met outside the library after work.

"There are still one or two things I have to get."

"I hate you, you know that, right?"

"Absolutely." Pam grinned. "That's why we're such good friends."

"How have your December weddings been going?"

"So far, so good. We have two down and two yet to go."

Julia looked up at the feathery flakes of snow starting to fall. "Have you heard a weather report?"

"We're under a winter storm watch. Five to six inches of snow possible by morning."

"Which means we might have a white Christmas." So far they'd only been teased with a light dusting of snow earlier in the month which had long since melted.

Julia liked her Christmases to be white. Growing up on the West Coast, she hadn't had many snowy postcard holidays. Nothing traditional. Her mother often celebrated Winter Solstice with small handmade gifts and told her that Santa was taking advantage of the elves by not paying them decent wages or benefits.

They would usually attend a midnight Christmas Eve service, going to a different church and denomination each year — Baptist, Catholic, Lutheran, Episcopalian. At other times in the year they'd visited Buddhist temples and Jewish synagogues. Angel was an equal-opportunity believer.

"We better get going before the snow really piles up," Pam said.

Julia had already done some shopping online — ordering books, music, and a few educational toys from Amazon.com, and specialty yarn for her mom from an online knitting store.

She had no idea what to get for her sister Skye. Or for Pam.

"How are things going between you and Luke?" Pam asked.

Julia shrugged. "I haven't heard from him lately. We've both been busy with holiday preparations."

"What's he doing for Christmas?"

"I'm not sure."

"Ah, ladies." Walt walked up to them. "Good to see you both. Julia, I meant to tell you that after further consideration, the town council has decided to temporarily shelf the idea of the llamas as prognosticators."

"That's good."

"Otherwise, we're still on track with the

preparations for the Best Small Town judges."

"I've been meaning to ask you if they show up incognito or what?"

"They have a scheduled visit coming up in April, and they also have an unannounced visit before that. Of course, we already know that Serenity Falls is a great place to live and raise a family. Smart Americans are leaving the crowded metropolitan areas and moving to quiet, peaceful communities such as ours."

Since the mishap at the Wiener Races, things *had* been relatively quiet around town. That made Julia wonder when chaos was going to return — and which one of her family members would be the cause of it.

Luke looked up from his distributor's alcohol re-order form to find Skye sauntering into Maguire's. It was cold enough outside that she should be wearing a coat. Instead, she had what looked like a Peruvian blanket wrapped around her and a weird hat with flaps over her ears.

"We don't open for another ten minutes," he told her.

"Then you shouldn't leave the front door unlocked."

"You're right."

"But as I'm in here . . ." She paused and deftly settled onto a bar stool. "Angel wants you to come to Christmas dinner."

"Angel does? What about your sister?"

"What about her?"

"Never mind. Tell your mom thanks but no thanks."

"You don't understand. Saying 'no' is not an option."

"Why not? Is your mom some kind of New Age mob kingpin or something?"

"She's really looking forward to you and Tyler and Algee coming to dinner. You don't have other plans, do you?"

"No, but . . ."

"Good."

He glared at her. "Look, I don't do family dinners."

Skye shrugged. "Hey, we're not your usual family."

"Yeah, I noticed that."

"You've noticed my sister a lot, too. So just look on this as another chance to get in her good graces. Or get her in your bed."

"Yeah, you're definitely not your average family." He didn't know many sisters who'd try to get their sibling into bed with a guy.

"So you are coming to dinner?" Skye asked.

"No."

"How about this? How about we play a hand of poker for it?" She reached for a deck of cards someone had left at the end of the bar. "I win, you come and you get your buddies Tyler and Algee to come, too. You win, and I'll drop this."

Luke paused.

"Come on. You strike me as a gambling man."

Oh, he'd gambled plenty. Right down to his last dime and then some. That's why he was stuck here in Podunkville. Because he was broke.

That hadn't always been the case. He couldn't pinpoint the exact date when things had gone bad. He'd spent day after day mired in violence and tragedy in a job where one mistake would get you or others killed, losing himself bit by bit, blurring the lines that had once been so clear to him.

That's when he'd started gambling, not just with his life but with his money as well. By the time he realized how out of control he was, it was too late. He was broke, in debt up to his eyeballs.

He'd gotten help and walked away.

Luke stared down at the cards. They beckoned to him. Tempted him. Like that belly-dancing librarian sister of Skye's. "Just one hand?" he heard himself say.

Skye slipped off her silly hat and nodded. She looked like a radioactive porcupine with her brilliant neon-red hair spiked up. How much could she know about cards? This was a simple way to make her invitation go away — beat her at cards and get on with it.

"Okay, you're on."

Five minutes later he stared down at the four of a kind she had laid out on the bar in front of him.

"Great," Skye said cheerfully. "We'll see you at two on Christmas Day."

Watching her walk away, Luke had the unmistakable feeling he'd just been played by a pro.

Chapter Eleven

"You want me to do *what?!*" Tyler growled.

"Come on, don't make it sound like I'm asking you to strip naked in the middle of town or something," Luke replied.

"You might as well."

"It's just a meal. What's the big deal?"

"It's Christmas dinner."

Luke nodded. "Yeah, so?"

"So it's a big deal."

"Look, we have to go."

"Why?"

"Because Skye won the bet between us."

"Important word there. The bet was between *you* and Skye. Nothing to do with me."

"Yes, it is. You were included in the invitation."

"Why?"

"How should I know? Because Angel wants you there, I guess."

"She said that?"

"I haven't talked to Angel."

"What about Julia the librarian?"

"What about her?"

"Have you talked to her?"

"Not about this, no."

"Why not?"

"You're just full of questions, aren't you?" This time Luke was the one who growled. "Look, do you want to break Angel's heart by refusing her invitation?"

The look on Tyler's face answered that.

"Right, so I'll see you there at two on Christmas." Luke watched Tyler stomp out of Maguire's. One guest down, one left to go.

Algee's only concession to the holiday was a vintage aluminum tree with superhero ornaments hanging from it; superhero action figures placed around it, and red, white, and blue lights surrounding the window.

"Hey Big Al."

Algee responded with one of his huge smiles.

"I hope you're not doing anything Christmas day," Luke quickly continued, "because we've got an invitation we can't turn down. From Angel. For dinner. You can't say no."

"I wasn't going to."

"You weren't?"

Algee shook his head, the overhead lights gleaming on his bald head. "Sounds like fun."

"I wouldn't go that far," Luke muttered.

"You don't sound very excited about it. And why couldn't we turn down this invitation?"

"Because I lost a bet."

"Ah."

"What's that supposed to mean?" Luke demanded.

Algee shrugged. "Whatever you want it to mean."

"Don't you go sounding all New Age on me now."

"Yo, Luke!" The shout came from Billy as he entered the store. His pants were almost as wide as they were long and hung well below the waistband of his black underwear, which was clearly visible.

"Hey, I heard your dad is working on an ordinance banning the public display of underwear. That true?" Algee asked.

Billy shrugged. "Do I look like I care?"

"So what's up with the football jersey?" Luke asked. "I thought you weren't a fan."

"Football sucks," Billy declared with a hip-hop jab of his fingers. "Who names their team after a condom, anyway?"

Luke frowned. "What?"

"Rock Creek. They're the Trojans."

Algee tried to keep a straight face while Luke tried for once to impart some knowledge. "The original Trojans were fierce warriors from Troy."

Billy shrugged. "I don't care about history. Everyone already thinks I'm a freakazoid. Being a brain would only make things worse."

"So history and football suck. What do you like? Besides comic books."

Billy's face lit up. "Extreme snowboarding. When they get some good jo-jo going, the amplitude is awesome."

Luke shared a blank look with Algee, who had the nerve to grin at him.

"They show it on TV," Billy said. "You should have the screen at Maguire's show that instead of a lame football game."

"Yeah, I'm sure that would go over real well with the local patrons," Luke noted sarcastically. In a state boasting two NFL teams — the Steelers and the Eagles — football ruled.

"Maybe after the Super Bowl," Algee suggested. "Instead of arena football."

"I happen to like arena football," Luke said. "It's not as good as the real thing maybe . . ."

Billy laid a counseling hand on Luke's arm. "You need to be open to new experiences. You're in a rut."

Great. Now he was being counseled by

Mini-Me in droopy pants.

"You don't want your balls to the wall, do you?" Billy said.

"Who does?" Luke replied, trying to keep a straight face.

"Then don't wait until it's too late. Take my advice, Luke." Billy gave him a mano-a-mano look. "Live a little dangerously."

If only the kid knew exactly how dangerously Luke had lived the past few years. How he'd gotten hooked on the adrenaline rush of knowing you were going to die . . . and surviving. Only risk had made Luke feel alive. Which was a sure way to end up six feet under.

Oh, yeah, Luke had lived dangerously. The question was, could he live *without* the danger? The jury was still out on that one.

Luke waited two days before taking Tyler's indirect advice and going to speak to Julia. She was working at the library. He didn't get there much.

As luck would have it, the first person he ran into inside the doors was the town mayor.

"What are you doing here? Trying to get a library card?" Walt mocked.

"Maybe." Luke pinned him with a narrow-eyed stare of a man who'd been trained in deadly force. "You got a problem with that?"

"Well . . . I . . . uh . . ." Walt backed up and then caught himself and regrouped. "The library doesn't carry pornography, you know."

"One man's pornography is another's classic piece of literature. Why look, there's a poster with a list of books that people tried to ban. Hmmm, *The Catcher in the Rye*. Bad stuff, right? You trying to ban books at the library now, Walt? Want to set up a bonfire outside and burn a batch of them?"

"We don't allow bonfires within the city limits," Walt said.

"Can I help you with something?" Julia sounded a tad breathless, as if she might have raced across the library to prevent a fist fight between the two of them.

"Not unless you can get rid of this guy." Luke pointed to Walt.

"We don't need your kind around here," Walt retorted, his face turning that reddish purple some guy's did when they were about to blow a gasket.

"You've really got to work on that welcome wagon routine of yours, Mr. Mayor," Luke drawled mockingly.

"You . . . you!" Walt both sputtered and shouted.

"Now, now. No yelling in the library," Luke reprimanded him.

Walt's face turned even redder before he stormed out of the building, unable to speak.

"Enjoy that, did you?" Julia fixed him with admonishing look.

"Not as much as I enjoy watching you, kissing you." Luke saw her eyes darken as she nervously licked her lips. He was dying to taste her mouth. "Aren't you going to shush me?"

"No." But she did tug him around a corner and down a deserted aisle to the back corner of the library.

"Why not? We're in a library. The capital of shushdom."

"A library is an information center —" she heatedly began when he interrupted her.

"Yeah, yeah. Listen, did you know your mother wants us to come to Christmas dinner? Me, Tyler, and Algee."

Julia nodded cautiously.

"Why didn't you warn me?"

"She only told me this morning. She also told me you'd all accepted."

"Under duress."

"What do you mean?"

"I mean I lost a bet with your sister."

"What kind of bet?" she asked suspiciously.

"A hand of poker."

Julia laughed. "Never play poker with my sister. She always wins."

"She cheated?"

"No. She just wins."

"A New Age cardsharp. I suppose I should have expected as much from the sister of a belly-dancing librarian." He paused a beat. "So it's okay with you that we're coming for Christmas dinner?"

"Sure. Why wouldn't it be?"

"Because you might not be able to resist the urge to tear off my clothes and have your way with me."

"Not a chance."

"Then how about because I might not be able to resist wanting to tear off *your* clothes and have my way with *you?*"

"We won't be alone."

"In case you haven't noticed, that hasn't stopped me before."

"It will this time."

"You think so?" He smoothed a loose strand of her hair away from her face. She was wearing such sensible clothing — black pants and a blue sweater — that there was no excuse for him to want to strip her naked and nibble every inch of her soft, bare skin.

But he sure wanted to anyway. "Because?"

"Because I say so."

"That argument doesn't work well with me."

"No argument works well with you," she muttered. "You can be very stubborn."

He grinned. "Another thing you love about me."

"Hah!"

"Julia, do you need help back there?" a woman called out.

"No, Alice, I'm fine," she quickly called back.

"There are patrons waiting for you." The woman's voice was clearly disapproving.

"I've got to get back to work," Julia said.

"Don't let me stop you."

"I don't intend to," she informed him before walking away and leaving him to enjoy the sway of her hips as she did so.

Oh yeah, libraries were great. So were sexy librarians.

When Julia stopped in her tracks, he almost ran into her. Looking over her shoulder, he saw Angel standing there.

"I wanted to look through a few cookbooks to see if they spark any ideas for me," Angel told Julia.

"I don't think Walt has banned the cookbooks yet, so you're probably in luck," Luke said.

"Walt is banning books? We need to stop that immediately!" Angel was getting her protestor face on. "If you let these power-mongers have an inch, they'll take a mile!"

Luke nodded. "I hear you."

"Don't get her riled up," Julia warned him, elbowing him in the ribs.

"If someone is threatening to censor what the library carries, then we should all be riled up." Angel's voice rose. "Unless this is part of a bigger plot?"

Julia rolled her eyes. Her mother loved conspiracy theories.

"Does this have something to do with that corporation wanting to pollute the falls by bottling the water?" Angel demanded.

"I hadn't heard that one," Luke noted.

Angel nodded. "I've been doing some re-search on the Internet about it, but someone doesn't want us to know much about the project."

"I've heard a few rumors, but the bottom line is that the town of Serenity Falls owns the park," Julia pointed out. "So no one can ruin the waterfalls."

"Unless the town council votes to turn the park over to a private concern," Angel re-plied.

"Why would they do that? It certainly wouldn't help their Best Small Town in America cause. The judges pay attention to things like parks."

"And clean water? They should pay attention to that, too," Angel said.

"I'm sure they will." Julia used her best soothing voice. "Let me show you where the cookbooks are."

"I'll leave you two alone," Luke said.

Julia watched him walk away.

"He really has a great butt, doesn't he?" her mother noted with approval.

All Julia could do was nod and admire the denim-clad view. For once, she was in complete agreement with her mother.

Tyler's only concession to the holiday was the fact that his flannel shirt was red and black. Algee wore a blazer over his Superman T-shirt. They left Luke feeling like a dork for wearing a jacket and tie.

What did he know? He couldn't even remember the last time he'd eaten Christmas dinner with a family. Probably not since his mom had died when he was a kid. His dad certainly never bothered doing anything special.

The holidays were pretty much the same as any other day on his calendar lately. He'd often been working, pulling shifts for others in the bureau who had families needing their attention. He certainly hadn't been the only agent who'd done that. But he hadn't done it because he was married to the FBI the way some agents were.

No, he'd done it because he didn't want to stop working. Unless it was to start gambling.

Which is how he ended up here, with Algee and Tyler as his trusty sidekicks, ringing the doorbell of the tidy house on Cherry Lane.

They hadn't had a white Christmas, despite the weatherman's prediction of possible snow last night. The four inches they'd gotten a week ago had melted. Not that it was warm today. His leather coat wasn't effective. He'd forgotten how damn cold it could get around here.

He warmed up the instant he saw Julia, looking all curvy and sexy in a red dress that hugged her body in all the right places. A little more cleavage and a shorter hem, and it would have been perfect.

"Merry Christmas everyone!" she greeted them. "Come on in."

Algee shoved a bedraggled bouquet of white and red carnations at her along with a bag of presents. Only now was it occurring to Luke that maybe he should have gotten something for the rest of Julia's family.

After Julia proclaimed her thanks and hugged Algee, Luke tugged him aside. "Why didn't you tell me to bring stuff?"

"I'm not your assistant, man."

"No, you're a buddy. And buddies protect each other's backs."

"Which is why Adele put a gift certificate for dinner at Maguire's in your coat pocket for Skye and Angel. I'm assuming you weren't so dense you didn't get Julia something on your own."

"You assume correctly. What about Tyler?"

"What about him?"

"He know about this present protocol?"

"Tyler knows a lot more than he lets on."

Luke was coming to realize that. He still hadn't heard anything on that set of fingerprints he'd lifted from Tyler a few weeks ago. He'd have to get on that.

"Welcome, everyone," Angel greeted them. She was wearing a swirling purple velvet dress that matched the amethyst crystal she always wore around her neck.

As her mother led the group into the living room, Julia felt like a stranger in her own home.

Her mother had prepared the dinner —

bourbon brown sugar salmon, organic baby carrots, lemon angel-hair pasta with fresh snow peas, oven-roasted squash, sweet peppers, and yams. Not the traditional turkey fare maybe, but it all smelled really good.

Julia had tried to help out, but her mother has insisted on doing it all herself. So Julia had fussed with the holiday decorations and the table, making sure that each place setting was just right. Angel had insisted they get a live tree that could be planted in the backyard afterward, so it was on the small side but held a cute selection of wooden snowmen ornaments Julia had recently purchased. There was no chance she was unpacking the hand-blown German glass ornaments she normally had on her tree. Not with Toni around. As it was, her niece had already yanked one snowman's head off.

After getting everyone a drink, a special cranberry concoction Julia had made up, she tried to make conversation. Algee was the only one who really cooperated. Tyler looked ready to dash out the door any second, and Luke was eyeing her as if imagining her in bed.

"Come on, people, this isn't a funeral," Skye stated as she sauntered into the room, wearing an orange tank top and sequined royal blue sarong-style skirt that hung low enough on her hips to show off her navel ring. "I told you that you should have added alcohol to the drinks," she said to Julia.

"I want presents," Toni declared, wearing her customary lopsided tiara, tutu, and yellow Wellington boots. Today she'd replaced the kitten flannel pj's beneath the tutu with red and white polka-dotted ones.

Julia just knew that Morgan, the little girl next door, was probably wearing an adorable red velvet dress with dainty white stockings.

"Nice threads," Luke noted.

"You sucked Julia's face," Toni retorted. "On the mouth."

"Okay then," Julia said, her face turning bright red, brighter than her own red dress. "I'm just going to check on our meal."

"Dinner almost ready?" she asked her mother as she entered the kitchen.

"Yes. Why don't you get everyone gathered around the table."

That proved to be easier said than done when Toni decided she wanted to play tag around the table. But eventually Julia got everyone settled and helped get all the food on the table.

"If we could all join hands, please?" Angel said.

Julia was seated next to Luke, who brushed his thumb over her knuckles before insinuating his fingers through hers as if stealing gems from a safe.

"May we join our souls and energies together so we can experience our shared planetary presence." Angel was using her serious voice. "May today be a joyful celebration of our spiritual togetherness and entrained vibrations."

"Did she just say entrails?" Algee frantically whispered from Luke's other side. "Are we having entrails for dinner? I don't do entrails, man."

"Relax," Luke whispered back.

"Relax?" Algee's eyes widened. "You know what entrails are? Guts, man. They're guts!"

"Is there a problem?" Angel asked.

"I don't do guts, ma'am," Algee stated with the utmost politeness. "No offense intended."

"None taken," Angel assured him. "I don't do guts either. We eat fish, but otherwise we're vegetarians. Or most of us are," Angel added with a meaningful look in Julia's direction.

"She said *entrained* not *entrails*. Right?" Luke looked at Angel.

"Right. Entrained vibrations in regard

to specific vortexes of energy beyond present scientific experimentation or description."

Julia looked at the blank expressions on all three male faces around the table. "Right. Well then, let's eat, shall we?"

"Time for a celebration experience," Angel stated once the meal was over and the table cleared. "If you'll all join me in the living room, please."

"Celebration experience?" Algee repeated, clearly still a tad nervous from the earlier entrails scare. "What do you think that means?"

"Spin the bottle maybe?" Luke suggested with a look at Julia, who was on the other side of the room.

"You know if you Google 'sexy librarian,' you get boatloads of porn photos," Algee told him in a quiet aside.

Luke blinked. "What?"

"I'm just saying that librarians are hotter than I thought."

"Julia isn't a porn star."

"Of course not. At least I don't think so. Anyway, all I'm saying is that it's no surprise you're hooked on her. Apparently that image is a popular one."

"It's never affected me before."

"Been in contact with many librarians before?"

"No," Luke admitted.

"Well," Algee smacked him on the back with enough force to make a rhino grimace. "There you have it."

"If we could gather in a semi-circle, please," Angel requested. "I just wanted to share a moment with you all. A moment of joy. By telling you what brings me joy. Well, only telling you *one* of the things because there are thousands of things and then we'd be here all night. Then after I share my joy, we'll move on to the next person." Angel paused to draw in a calming breath. "My daughters bring me joy." She spoke reverently before returning to her normal voice again. "Okay, now you go next, Julia."

What could she say? That Pop-Tarts brought her joy? They did, but that seemed a little shallow after what her mother had just said. "The holidays bring me joy." That was true enough.

Angel nodded and then moved on to her next victim. "Okay, Algee you're up next."

"The first issue of *Superman*, volume 1, number 1, brings me joy. And mega-mega bucks if I ever wanted to sell it on eBay, which I wouldn't."

Again Angel nodded. "Luke?"

"A good beer."

"Tyler?"

"Peace and quiet."

"Skye?"

"Mixing things up."

"Toni? What brings you joy, honey?"

The four-year-old frowned a moment as if searching for the answer. Then she said, "A vagina."

Julia felt like sinking through the floor, but Angel just laughed. "They bring a lot of women joy. Women are the goddesses of the planet. We represent fertility and hope. Okay, now that we've all shared our feelings, I'll go make us some tea."

Once she left, Algee went to retrieve the bag of presents he'd brought. "I got your daughter a little something. I hope you don't mind," he said to Skye.

"Depends what you got her. If it's a sexist doll with an impossible body shape that will destroy her self-esteem and give her an eating disorder, then I do mind."

"It's a teddy bear." He handed it to her with caution.

"That's okay, as long as it wasn't made by child labor in some work camp overseas."

"It says it's made in the USA."

"Thank you, Algee, that was very sweet of you," Julia said on her sister's behalf.

"No problem."

"You should have gotten her a muzzle," Luke noted after Toni bit Algee's left ankle a few moments later.

"Aw, the kid likes me."

"That's why she tried to take a chomp out of you? Because she likes you?"

"Yeah. Isn't that sweet?"

"It's twisted, man. And so are you if think that rug rat is sweet. Right, Tyler?"

Looking around, Luke realized that Tyler had taken off for the kitchen with Angel. Smart man.

"You really don't have to help," Angel said as Tyler brought a load of glasses into the kitchen.

He just shrugged. So she said what she was really thinking, because since he'd first arrived, she'd sensed that he wasn't there willingly. "You didn't really want to be here, did you?"

"What makes you say that?"

"You do."

"What did I do?"

"You didn't say much."

"I never do."

"I realize that. But this time was different. Did my daughter talk you into coming?"

"No."

"Are you telling me the truth?"

"I swear it on your bourbon salmon, which was delicious."

Angel felt herself blushing for the first time in years. "You don't have to say that."

"I don't say things I don't mean."

"Most people do."

"I'm not most people."

"Neither am I."

"Something we both have in common."

"Yeah."

They shared a look. His eyes were windows to his soul, but he often kept the shades tightly shut, not allowing anyone in. But now, she got a glimpse of the man inside, the man behind the pain. What she saw made her catch her breath like a teenager. Was that desire? Was he feeling the connection, too?

Tyler suddenly looked away, as if afraid he may have revealed too much. "Uh, I got you something."

"You didn't have to do that. The invitation wasn't intended to make you feel you had to give me a gift. Just your presence is a gift to me. I like spending time with you. I hope you like spending time with me."

"You're a breath of fresh air for my soul."

Her heart sang. "I feel the same way."

"I'm not good for you," he said abruptly.

"There are things you don't know . . ."

She placed her hand on his arm. His flannel shirt was soft beneath her fingertips, his muscles strong. "I know all I need to know. I've seen your aura, and that tells me you're a man who's experienced deep pain that left you questioning everything. But at the core, your heart is pure."

"It's not."

"It is to me," she said simply.

"Here." Tyler shoved a small item wrapped in newspaper into her hands.

She opened it with the care of someone who'd received the most precious of gifts. It was a carved wooden llama.

"I do a little whittling in my spare time," he said.

"This is beautiful. You're very talented." Tyler shook his head, but she put her hand on his arm again and firmly said, "Yes, you are. This is a wonderful piece."

"I did two." He gave her another awkwardly wrapped item. "Because you have two llamas."

"Thank you so much. I really miss them, you know. Even though I visit them several times a week, I still miss them and I get all teary-eyed when I leave. Stupid, huh?"

"No. You're a woman who feels things deeply. It's one of the many things that makes you so special."

"My oldest daughter doesn't think so. She thinks I'm sappy and ditsy."

"She's wrong," he said simply.

"I don't know. There are a few times when I think it might be nice to have your emotions neatly under control instead of wearing your heart on your sleeve, right out there for the entire world to see."

"Have you done anything about that secret you were talking about when we spoke last time?" Tyler asked.

"Not yet. But I plan to. Very soon."

"I hope it goes well for you."

"Thanks. Me, too." Angel knew she'd need all the good karma she could get to make things go well.

An hour later Luke finally got Julia alone in the kitchen. "I'm actually a pretty good cook," she was saying. "Okay, maybe I don't have a huge repertoire, but I really can make a mean dish of Moroccan chicken thighs."

Luke was instantly consumed with thoughts of Julia's thighs parting for him as he drove into her again and again. Her creamy, trembling thighs . . .

"And then I finish the meal off with an awesome champagne cherry sorbet," she said.

He imagined pouring champagne over her luscious thighs and licking his way up to the sweetest cherry in the world.

"Stop . . . stop talking!" His voice was hoarse.

"Are you okay?" She studied him. "You sound funny. Are you sick? Do you think you have a fever?"

"Yeah, a fever for you," he growled, pinning her against the fridge door and kissing her.

The old dependable Maytag fridge hummed against Julia's bottom while hotheaded bad boy Luke throbbed against her front. His arousal was evident and became more so as he lifted her arms above her head and moved even closer.

Her breasts were pressed against his chest, but it wasn't enough. For either of them. Muttering breathlessly, she freed her hand to reach for his shirt.

Great minds must think alike, because Luke released her to reach for the neckline of her wrap-around dress and slip his hand inside, cupping her breast in the palm of his hand, brushing his thumb over her satin-covered nipple.

He could create such intense pleasure so quickly it almost scared her, but the heated bliss was too all-consuming to really register anything else. Like the fact that they were making out in her kitchen with a bunch of people in the next room — one of whom walked in on them mid-caress.

"Never mind me," Angel cheerfully stated. "I was just going to make some tea, but I'll come back later."

"There are too many people in your house," Luke growled.

"You think?" Julia leaned her forehead on his shoulder and tried to regain control of her trembling legs.

"Moms are such a mood killer." Luke's rough voice reflected his extreme frustration.

"They don't have to be," Angel called from the living room. "You two go right on as you were. Pretend I'm not here."

"Impossible." Julia knew. She'd already tried. Many times. There was just no pretending her family wasn't there. Or that she wasn't in danger of falling for Luke big time.

"Orgasm is our most certain way of interfacing with the divine," Angel stated as she and Skye and Julia gathered together on New Year's Eve.

Julia knew she had too much wine when she heard herself saying, "If the fate of the world depended on you having sex with

Tommy Lee or Ozzy Osbourne, would you do it?"

Skye laughed. "I would do it just for the comic relief."

"What about Jerry Springer?" Julia asked.

"Sure, if the fate of the world depended on it."

"Is there anyone *none* of us would do it with?" Julia demanded.

Skye shrugged. "I'm doing it with Jerry Springer and Tommy Lee. What does that say about me?"

"That you have no taste," Julia retorted.

"I don't like sweaty guys," Angel admitted.

"I don't mind sweaty if they smell good," Skye said. "What about you, Julia? You started this."

"I don't know what I was thinking," she muttered before pouring herself more wine.

"You were probably thinking about Luke, as you always are."

"Not always." Wine sloshed over the edge of Julia's glass as she protested.

"No, not every second. Sometimes you're reciting the Dewey Decimal System," Skye mocked her.

"Not when you're having an orgasm, though, right?" Angel said with a worried expression.

"Maybe she's never had an orgasm," Skye said.

Angel defended her oldest daughter. "Of course she has. Right?" She turned to Julia, who nodded and drank more wine.

"With a man?" Skye persisted. "Or just by yourself? Was a vibrator involved?"

Julia ignored her. "What about Bob Dylan?"

Angel blinked. "You had an orgasm with Bob Dylan?"

"No, would you do Bob Dylan?"

"You have to do Bob Dylan," Angel claimed. "Just as an homage. I mean, he's Bob Dylan."

"So it's true then?" Julia was definitely feeling a buzz now. More than that, she had to be edging toward downright drunk, or she'd never be continuing this conversation let alone start it in the first place. "There's *no one* that *none* of us would do it with?"

Angel had to think a minute, her forehead furled in concentration, before saying, "Walt."

"Walt," Julia immediately agreed.

"Right, like you'd do it with anyone," Skye said.

"And you'd do it with everyone," Julia retorted.

"Except Walt," Skye maintained. "I have my standards."

"This from a woman who'd do Tommy Lee and Jerry Springer."

"Only if the fate of the world depended on it."

"I just love it when we get together and talk girl talk," Angel said, hugging them both. "Female empowerment begins with sharing."

"I'm not sharing Tommy Lee," Skye said before looking down at her oversized watch. "I've got to go, or I'll be late for the party in Rock Creek." She was gone a moment later. Nobody made faster exits than Skye.

Angel took another gulp of wine before speaking. "I vowed there was something I was going to do before this year ended. It's not an easy thing for me, and I've been putting it off much too long as it is. But I really thought I was doing the right thing. Now I'm not so sure."

Julia tried to keep up. "Is this about the llamas? I'm sure they're doing well in their new digs."

"They are doing well, but this isn't about Ricky and Lucy. It's about you."

"Me?"

Angel nodded.

"What about me?"

"I thought I'd have a good way to say it by now," Angel fretted. "I kept waiting for spiritual illumination, but it never really came."

"If this is about my eating habits . . ." Julia began.

"It's not."

"My lifestyle . . ."

Angel waved her hand. "Not that either."

"Then what?"

"Your father."

Julia blinked. "What about him?"

"He's not dead."

"What are you talking about? You told me they found his body and buried it in the jungle of Colombia."

"That's what happened. He died fighting for what he believed in."

"Then I don't understand what you're trying to say here."

"Well, the thing is . . . you see . . . the truth is . . . uh . . . he . . . uh . . . he wasn't actually your biological father."

Chapter Twelve

Julia heard Angel's words, but she couldn't make sense out of them. She watched her mother's mouth move, but she couldn't really process what Angel was saying. Julia's mind had suddenly turned into Teflon. Nothing was sticking.

A chill swept over her, erasing the warmth the wine had provided. Wrapping her arms around her middle, she scrambled to regain control.

Note to self: Focus, focus, focus.

Finally she found some words. "Not . . . not my biological father?"

Angel shook her head.

She summoned up anger. The emotional heat felt better than the arctic neverland she'd been zapped into seconds earlier. "Is this some kind of a joke?"

"Of course not!"

"You're telling me that you lied to me all these years? That the man you told me was my father never really was?"

Angel slowly nodded.

"Why? I don't understand." The more

Julia spoke, the more upset she got. "Why would you lie to me all these years? You, of all people! A person who always claimed to base their life on the truth!"

Angel reached out to touch her, but Julia pulled away. "I did it for you."

"Did what for me? Lie? Why? What's wrong with my real father? Was he a drug dealer? Is he in jail?"

"Of course not!"

"Then what's wrong with him? Is he still alive?"

"Yes, he's alive, and he's a corporate capitalist pig."

"Then why did you get together with him in the first place?"

"I didn't know who he was at first. We were at a party —"

"Great," Julia interrupted. "So you had sex with some stranger you just picked up one night at a party? How do you know I'm his and not someone else's?"

"There was no one else."

"How long were you two together?"

"A month or so. We shared an Ethics class as UCLA."

"Who is he?"

Angel nervously plucked at the fuzzy red sweater she was wearing. "His name was Adam."

"Adam what?"

"That's all you need to know."

"Does he know about me?"

Angel shook her head.

"Why not?" Julia demanded.

"I never told him."

Julia felt curiously numb. The disbelieving chill and the heated anger had both vanished. Now it all felt surreal.

Up and down the block people were preparing for the New Year, their televisions tuned to the impending Times Square celebration. But here . . . inside her home . . . her carefully created sanctuary . . . Julia sat on her comfy couch, disintegrating into tiny pieces.

She remembered a scene in her kitchen with Skye saying, *I can't believe we're sisters.* If Angel was telling the truth, then Skye was Julia's half sister. They shared the same mother but different fathers.

How could her mother have lied to her? The woman who based her life on the cosmic truth had perpetrated the largest lie possible. Julia's stomach clenched.

"Talk to me, Julia. Tell me what you're feeling," Angel begged. "Don't keep it all bottled up inside."

"Why are you telling me this now?"

"Because the guilt was too much for me to continue."

"So you did it to make yourself feel better. Nice of you to think how I might feel about it." Julia's sarcasm was clear.

"I did worry about that. It kept me up nights. I told Tyler —"

"He knows about this?"

"No, of course not. He only knows that I had a secret and that I was concerned about revealing it to you."

"Does anyone else know? Does Skye know?" Julia could read the answer on her mom's face. It was the final blow. "You told her before you told me? That we have different fathers? How could you do that to me?"

Julia couldn't breathe. She had to get away or suffocate. She jumped up, relieved that her shaking legs still supported her after emotionally having the rug torn out from under her.

"Julia, wait . . ." Angel put out her hand.

But Julia sidestepped her, dashing toward the foyer where she grabbed a coat, slid into a pair of shoes, and ran out the front door.

Luke stood outside in the alley behind Maguire's and inhaled the cold air. Adele would have his hide for taking off during the busy New Year's Eve festivities, but he didn't care. Too many bad memories were hanging around the edge of his consciousness tonight, taunting him like old bullies. Bullies like his dad.

The belt, the voice, the back of his hamlike hand. All were weapons to be used against Luke. And he'd used them often.

Had his father been right? Doubt rose in his throat like a bad meal. Had he deserved the beatings? Maybe he was just a screwup who couldn't do anything right.

Maybe that was why he always walked away — from the Marines, from the FBI. Because he was a loser.

Luke started pacing. He hated thinking about this stuff. He'd been through enough fires by now to have burned those negative voices out of his head, the ones in his father's bellowing voice.

Returning here had brought it all back, even though he fought to keep the images away. You'd think that painting Maguire's would clean the slate, but it had only camouflaged it.

What a way to celebrate New Year's Eve. Instead of seducing the sexy belly-dancing librarian, he was pouring drinks for other happy couples.

Not that he and Julia were a couple . . . happy or otherwise.

Wham! Luke grabbed hold of the person

who had just blindsided him and almost knocked them both on their butts.

He knew it was Julia the instant he touched her. Had she come racing to his side, ready to jump into bed with him? Wishful thinking maybe . . . but . . .

Then he saw the tears on her face. "Are you okay?"

"No." Julia gulped and hiccuped.

"What happened? What's the matter?"

She just shook her head, tears continuing to run down her face as the sound of people celebrating the New Year echoed in the alley. *Five, four, three, two, one . . . Happy New Year!*

"Come here." He tugged her into his arms. "Did someone hurt you?"

She nodded.

"Who?" His voice was grim. "Do you know who it was? Were you attacked? Should I call the police?"

"It was Angel."

"Angel attacked you?"

Julia shook her head.

"You two had a fight?" Luke rubbed circles around her back in a way that was meant to be reassuring. "Not a good way to start off a new year, huh?"

"I don't cry," Julia mumbled against his shoulder.

"Of course you don't."

"I mean it," she said fiercely. "I *never* cry."

"Me, neither. Another thing we have in common, huh?"

She lifted her hands to wipe the dampness from her cheeks, but his fingers were there before hers. "It'll be okay." His voice was roughly reassuring.

Looking up at him, so close she could see the individual dark eyelashes circling his vivid blue eyes, Julia knew what she had to do.

She slid her hands up to his face, cupping his cheeks and tugging him down so she could kiss him.

The moment their lips met, the passion was once again all-consuming. There was no room to think about the bombshell Angel had dropped on her. No time to fret over that fact that she'd never been a pretty cryer and that her nose probably resembled Rudolph the Red-Nosed Reindeer by now.

No, there was only this heated moment. His tongue parting her lips, her tongue greeting his . . . tangling, tasting, tempting.

Desire escalated rapidly. Luke yanked her into the shadows of the alleyway and up against the wall, his thigh between her legs, her hands under his shirt. Neither was properly dressed for the snowy weather. Neither cared.

His mouth continued to consume hers while her tongue danced with his. In the distance she could hear revelers inside Maguire's, but mostly she heard the pounding of her own heart and felt the throbbing need to have him with her, within her.

"Make love to me," she murmured against his lips.

Shaking his head, Luke reluctantly pulled away. "Ask me again when you're not hysterical."

"I am *not* hysterical. And even if I was, since when have you had a thing against having sex with hysterical women?"

"Oh, so you figured with my reputation I'd have sex with anyone, right?" He sounded aggravated now.

"You said you wanted to have sex with me. You've told me that more than once. Or was it just a line?"

"No."

"Then you only wanted to have sex with me providing I didn't want to have sex with *you*."

"You *always* wanted to have sex with me."

"That is so not true."

"And that is so a lie," he mocked her.

"Go to hell!" Totally humiliated by now, she spun away from him.

"Trust me, I know hell well," Luke said even as he caught her in his arms.

"Let me go!" She was so angry she couldn't even see straight. Plus all that wine she'd consumed earlier was clouding her thinking. Which was good. She didn't want to think.

"You're not going anywhere until you tell me what's going on."

"Forget it!"

"As much as I'd like to, I won't be able to. Which is why you're coming upstairs with me and having some coffee and . . ."

"No way!"

"We can do this the easy way or the hard way. Your call."

She struggled to free herself.

"Okay, you chose the hard way. Fine by me." The next thing Julia knew, he had her slung over his shoulder in a fireman's lift. She hung onto handfuls of his soft leather jacket as she found herself staring at his sexy butt. She didn't have much choice. It was right there in front of her nose.

"Put me down!"

"Keep it down back there. You don't want the entire town to see you this way, do you?"

The wine she'd consumed and the stress

were catching up to her, making head spin. Or maybe it was all the blood rushing to her head. Either way, she was woozy.

Her sudden stillness made him suspicious. "You're not gonna hurl or anything are you?"

She didn't answer, which made him hurry up the back stairs to the apartment over Maguire's. He returned her to her feet with surprising care and gentleness. "Are you okay?"

Tears threatened again, and she struggled to hold them back. "I already told you before that I wasn't."

"Come on, you'll feel better after you've had some coffee."

She only came inside and took the seat on the couch he offered her because her legs were suddenly too wobbly to hold her up. He had a mug in her hand in fifteen seconds flat.

"Talk to me," he ordered.

"You told me you don't like gabby women."

"You told me you didn't care."

"I don't."

"Then talk to me."

She stared down at the swirl of milk he'd added to her coffee but hadn't bothered stirring and remembered how her mother learned how to read tea leaves from a Greek neighbor many years ago. What was that woman's name? Helena? Athena? something-ena.

Keeping her eyes on her coffee she said, "Have you ever felt like your life is suddenly not what you thought it was? That it just unravelled and totally fell apart? That it was all based on a lie?"

"Yeah." More of his life was based on a lie than not. Luke had trained in everything from mobile surveillance to high-risk building entries, but he had no experience in how to deal with a woman like Julia.

Or maybe he did. In interrogation training he'd learned that human beings give off all kinds of indicators. Body language. Eye movement. At one point, he'd been good at getting people to tell him what he wanted to know. At one point, he'd had a gut-deep confidence in his abilities. He needed to get that back.

"What did you and Angel argue about?" he asked.

"We didn't argue. She dropped a bombshell on me. Turns out my father isn't who I though he was."

Because Luke would have taken the news that his father wasn't really Tommy Maguire as good news, he wasn't sure how to react to this. Julia didn't appear to view it as good news in her case. So he let her do all the talking, glad that he hadn't had to use much prompting to get her to confide in him.

"I always felt like I didn't fit in with the rest of my family. I guess now I know the reason why." She took an unsteady sip of coffee. "I never liked the footloose lifestyle we had. Even so, I put up with all the moves. I didn't complain about not going to my senior prom because we left the state a week before. I never said anything about always being the kid with the kooky family. But this . . . this is too much."

"Did she tell you who your real father is?"

Julia shook her head. "Just that he was a corporate capitalist monster."

"Well, that narrows the list, doesn't it?"

"She met him at a party in the seventies. She did say they shared an Ethics class at UCLA. And that his name was Adam."

"How old are you?"

She blinked. "Why should I tell you that?"

"Because maybe we can figure out who this guy is. If you want that, I mean. By going back and figuring out what year they shared that class and then looking at the records . . ."

"Can that be done?"

"I've got some friends who could do it, yeah."

She eyed him suspiciously. "What kind of friends?"

"Why do you care?"

"I don't want to do anything illegal or get into trouble or get you or them into trouble."

"That's a long list of what you *don't* want. Now tell me what you *do* want."

She'd tried to tell him that she wanted *him* down in the alley, but he'd turned her away.

"Do you want to track down your father or not?" he said.

"I don't know. I only discovered all this an hour ago. I need some time for it to sink in."

"Yeah, I guess that makes sense."

"I don't understand why she lied to me all these years. Angel always made such a big deal out of living an honest life. Of being in touch with your inner self, no deception. Yet here she'd been hiding a huge part of my life from me. Was my father so bad that she was afraid of him?"

"What did she say about that?"

"I only asked if he was a drug dealer or in jail and she said 'no.' "

When Luke's cell phone rang, he was going to ignore it until he saw the caller ID number. He answered.

"Luke, this is Angel." Her voice was breathless and agitated. "I'm looking for Julia. Have you seen her?"

"Yes, Angel, she's here." When Luke motioned as if to hand the phone over, Julia vehemently shook her head.

"Tell her I don't want to talk to her," Julia said.

"You don't have to tell me." Angel sounded very polite. And very relieved to have located her daughter. "I heard her and I understand. She needs space. Tell her I get that. And that I'll be waiting for her whenever she's ready."

"Your mom said she'll be waiting for you whenever you're ready," Luke repeated after disconnecting the call and turning off his cell.

Another wild thought popped into Julia's head. "What if she's not really my mother? What if *everything* was a lie, not just that part of my parenthood?"

"A DNA test would give you the answer to that, but you look a lot like her."

"I do not."

"Sure you do. You've both got that thing going on with your eyes."

"What thing?"

He tipped up her chin with his fingertip. "That green hazel thing."

"She starts riots."

He brushed his thumb over her cheek. "So could you if you wanted to."

"I don't. All I wanted was some peace and quiet, and instead I get llamas in my backyard, my mother telling me my father isn't who I thought he was, and you . . ."

"Yeah? And me?"

"Getting nuns to help me out."

"And that bothers you, huh? That I had Sister Mary come to your aid?"

"You said you did it because you wanted to have sex with me."

"That's right."

She set down her coffee and stood, feeling the need to move around. Or even better, to hit something. The punching bag was nearby so she gave it an open-handed smack. "But you just told me no."

"Not true. I told you that I don't take advantage of women who've had too much to drink."

"You said I was hysterical."

"That, too."

"That why you brought me up here? To sober me up? Or to teach me more boxing moves?" She paused to peel off her coat and soft fleece hoodie.

"What are you doing?"

"It's hot in here."

She stood before him, wearing a black tank top that molded to her breasts and made his mouth water. Her pants hugged her hips, leaving a tantalizing strip of creamy skin just beneath her navel.

She moved closer to him, sliding the leather jacket off his shoulders. "Show me what you've got."

"You first."

"Okay." She stepped away and kicked off her shoes.

The next thing he knew, she was undulating her hips in a way that brought his body to full alert. His belly-dancing librarian was putting on a show for him, moving to a beat only she could hear, starting slowly and then moving faster. Desire shot through his veins like quicksilver. Closing her eyes, she lifted her arms, dancing with a feminine mystery as old as time itself.

Suddenly she stopped, and when she opened her eyes, they were damp with the threat of tears. "My mother taught me those moves."

"Oh, baby, I'm sorry."

No one had called Julia "baby" before. Not that she'd ever wanted them to. She wasn't a "baby" kind of person. She was an old soul at the age of four.

But hearing Luke say that to her made her heart unexpectedly melt. For just one moment, the idea of someone else taking care of her was overwhelmingly powerful.

He took her in his arms and patted her back in soothing circular motions. Then he paused. "You're not wearing a bra."

He slid his hand beneath her tank top as if to verify his comment. While there, his fingertips curved around her side and brushed the sides of her bare breasts. The soft light from the single lamp in the room created shadows on his face, but it didn't hide the fact that he wanted her.

She stared at him.

He stared at her.

She circled her fingers around his arms and lowered them. Then she slid her fingers to his wrists, lifting his hands and guiding them beneath her tank top to cup her breasts. His calloused palms were warm against her skin.

Julia closed her eyes as supreme pleasure coursed through her. She licked her lips as he slowly and oh-so-lightly brushed the pad of his thumbs over the very tip of her nipples.

Her back bowed, arching her hips against his. Now his fingertips were splayed around her side, holding her upright as he explored her with his thumbs, trailing circles and abstract designs.

Using his tongue, he licked his way from the corner of her mouth, teasing her but not kissing her, down to her jaw, to her earlobe, to the underside of her jaw.

She tilted her head back to allow him more freedom and was rewarded with an erotic nibble along the cord in her neck. He paused to bathe the hollow at the base of her throat while he slowly shifted her tank top.

His hands now covered her breasts entirely, keeping them warm until he lowered his head to seduce her with the erotic curl of his tongue. Rough and wet, hot and wild.

She almost came right then and there.

Awash with a fierce need, her knees buckled and she stumbled, landing on his low bed, which she didn't even realize was there until that moment. He came with her, and she kept him close by wrapping her legs around his hips.

His shirt was in the way so she got rid of it, ripping half his buttons in the process and not caring. Her tank top flew across the room as his fingers deftly undid her jeans and removed them.

"Daisy panties," he noted with a satisfied growl.

He sounded as if he couldn't have been

happier if she'd been wearing a tiny thong.

She couldn't have been happier when he slid his hand beneath the floral cotton underwear. Finding her wet silky folds, he delved into her feminine dampness. His moves left her gasping his name as shards of bliss shot through her. Seconds later, her panties were gone and his lips were boldly transporting her to a level of pleasure she'd never attained before.

Tiny ripples of elation continued to pulse through her body as Luke yanked off his jeans and put on a condom. Then he entered her in one powerful thrust, raising her hips so she could take him into her very depths. With a brazen cry of satisfaction, she closed around him, moving as he instructed, adding some touches of her own.

He surged in and out, deeper and deeper, the silken friction building into an ecstasy that went beyond sensation. She'd never felt more alive, never been so rocked to the core, never ascended to such dizzying peaks.

Her climax came with a divinely wicked fierceness and the knowledge that if this was being bad, she didn't want to be good.

Julia woke shortly after dawn to find Luke sitting in bed, the sheets pooled around his bare hips as he stared down at her. He'd turned off the light at some point, but she could still see him in the shadowy room.

Who speaks first in a situation like this, she wondered.

Luke answered that silent question by abruptly saying, "You're sorry. You think I took advantage of you."

She stretched lazily. "You suck at being a mind-reader. The sex was incredible, though."

He frowned at hearing her reduce what they'd just shared to just sex.

"You do this often?" he demanded.

"Get drunk and seduce a man? No, not really."

"You didn't seduce me."

"Of course, I did." She ran her finger down his bare arm. "You were trying to be polite and noble."

He snorted.

"Well, you were. And I made you break your cardinal rule about having sex with hysterical women."

She'd done it again. Reduced it to sex. He should be relieved, not aggravated.

"You were upset. You wanted a distraction." He made it sound like an accusation. What was up with that?

"I wanted you. You wanted me. We cured that itch."

"You think so? Then why do I still want to do this?" He urged her legs apart. "And this . . ." He brushed his thumb against her clitoris. Instant surges of delight shot through her.

"I can't imagine." Her voice was unsteady.

"I can. Imagine. Plenty. You. Doing this." He placed her hands on him, around his velvety heat. "Me. Doing this." He placed his hands on her, sliding one finger and then two into her damp core.

"Mmmmm." She pulled him to her.

Luke barely had time to put on another condom before he once again thrust into her, his entry smooth and swift, a sliding rush that was both wondrous and welcome.

The next time she awoke, it was morning and she smelled bacon. She opened her eyes to find Luke standing in the dining area of the room, putting plates on a pine table there.

"You made breakfast." She sounded stunned.

He shrugged awkwardly, his broad shoulders bare, a pair of jeans hanging low on his hips. "It's no big deal. Just bacon, scrambled eggs, and toast."

Julia wanted food. But she was naked under the sheets and wasn't about to parade nude across the room. So she yanked the sheets around her, toga style, and headed for the food.

"Mmmm, good," she mumbled around her first bite. She was starving. "You're good. Very, very good."

"As a cook, you mean?" he teased her, offering her another slice of perfectly prepared bacon by holding it in front of her mouth.

"Mmmm." She bit into the bacon. "That, too."

"So you thought I was a good lover?"

"You were great. But you already know that."

"So were you. But you already know that," he repeated with a wicked grin.

She blushed. "I really had no idea. I mean it's never been like that for me before . . ."

"Like what?"

"Like flying into the sun. Thank you." She leaned closer to kiss him — intending it to be short and sweet but ending up being long and leisurely.

"You're thanking me for what specifically?" he murmured.

"For everything. For understanding."

"Mmmm." He nibbled on her fingertips.

"And for that move . . . what did you call it?"

"Butterfly whiplash."

"Mmmm."

He peeled the sheet from her body. "Maybe I should demonstrate it for you again, so you'll remember this time."

Julia never realized that making love in a chair could be so awesome, but Luke grabbed a condom and showed her just how to make the most of their position . . . with her on his lap and him lodged deep within her.

Later that afternoon, Julia sat at Luke's dining table and tried to make sense out of her life. Recognizing that she might need some time alone and that she wasn't ready to face her mom yet, Luke had gone over to Algee's to watch the football game.

The minute Julia was alone, she realized that solitary meditation might not be all it was cracked up to be. But by then Luke had left and calling him back would only make her look like more of an idiot.

Note to self: Get a plan. Fast.

Julia found a pad of paper and a pen and started writing.

Options:
1) Move elsewhere in the country.
   Too much trouble.

Would need new job. Like it here.
2) Move elsewhere in Serenity Falls.
   *Get an apartment and leave Angel
      et al in house.*
   *Town would talk, and too expensive
      anyway.*
3) Kick my family out.

That one definitely had appeal, but what kind of person would that make her?

A smart chick with backbone.

And one without compassion.

4) Move in with Pam.
   *She only has a small one-bedroom
      place, so that isn't really practical.*
5) Move in with Luke.

Julia immediately crossed that line out. Where had that thought come from?

The man kept his bed and a punching bag in his living room.

And a couch. One that looked like something from the brand-new IKEA catalog, now that she thought about it.

She couldn't see Luke thumbing through home furnishing catalogs, though.

She could see him telling Adele to order him a couch like he'd order a pizza.

It was obvious to her that this was not a

man who put down roots. Despite having ordered a new couch. And a bed, too, now that she looked at it.

What did she really know about him? He'd been in town two months now, and she still had no idea what he'd done in the twelve years he'd been away from Serenity Falls.

Sure, he'd let it slip that he'd been in the Marines. But that was it.

What else did she know?

That he was an awesome kisser. That he knew just where and when to touch her. That he hadn't taken advantage of her last night despite the fact that she'd wanted him to. But that he had allowed her to seduce him and had given her incredible pleasure in return.

That he looked great in black leather and jeans on the back of a Harley. That she wanted to be there with him, riding off for a wild weekend of hot sex.

And that was so *not* like her. She wasn't the type of woman to get sidetracked by a bad-boy image.

But there was more to Luke. At Christmas dinner, she'd seen the way he interacted with Tyler and Algee. All three of the town's outcasts had drawn together like companions-at-arms. And he'd been thrilled with the Harley-Davidson book she'd gotten him for Christmas. He'd clearly put some thought into the presents he'd gotten her — a silver dachshund and a silver hot dog charm on a lovely chunky silver bracelet. And a set of daisy underwear — from prim briefs to outrageous thongs.

Yes, he was cocky.

Yes, he was exasperating.

Yes, she was falling in love with him.

And yes, she knew that wasn't a very smart move.

Julia stared down at the pad she'd filled with her neat notes and tidy handwriting.

Lots of words, but still no plan. Not a good thing.

Chapter Thirteen

"Are you okay?" Angel asked the instant Julia walked in the door later that afternoon. Her mother's hands fluttered as if they were doves that wanted to land on Julia but were afraid to. "I've been worried sick about you."

"I can't talk to you yet." Julia thought she could. That's why she'd come home. Well, maybe not the primary reason — that was because this was her house and she'd left it with only the clothes on her back. Plus, she couldn't hide out at Luke's, making love with him forever — as tempting as that might be. Or sit at his dining table like a wimp making useless lists.

She'd thought she'd regained enough control to come home and deal with her mother. She was wrong.

Note to self: Not ready yet. Definitely not ready yet.

"You're angry." Angel's hands came together in a wringing motion. "I understand that. You feel I betrayed you."

"Please don't tell me how I feel."

"Okay, then *you* tell me how you feel."

"I just told you I can't talk to you right now."

"I know." Angel nodded. "I should listen. You need time. Your aura is disrupted."

"Do not talk to me about reading auras. I'm sick of hearing about things that aren't true!"

"Auras are true."

"This from a woman who lied to me my entire life about who my father really was!"

"I explained."

"Yes, that you'd already told Skye before you told me. I'm the family joke." Julia's voice shattered with the humiliation and pain she still felt inside.

"No, you're not! Don't say that."

"Why not? That's how you and Skye view me. As the stupid, sensible one who doesn't know how to have fun. As the good girl. Well, that's changed."

"Oh, honey." Angel shook her head and looked at her with such sad, sad eyes. "I hope you didn't do anything you'll regret."

"This from the woman who last night was mocking my ability to have an orgasm?"

"I wasn't mocking."

"Well, for your information, I do not recite the Dewey Decimal System when I come. I'm sure that will reassure you."

Angel hung her head. "We were wrong to tease you. How can I make it up to you?"

"By telling me my father's name," Julia immediately said.

"I can't do that."

"You mean you *won't* do that."

Angel wrung her hands again, her narrow face displaying her agitation. "You don't understand."

"You've got that right. I *don't* understand. If you weren't going to tell me the entire story, the entire truth, then why tell me anything at all? Why not leave me in blissful ignorance? Didn't you stop to think how this news might affect me? Or were you too wrapped up in your own guilt to care about that?"

"I did care. I do care. That's why I was so conflicted about telling you."

"Oh, but the runes told you to do it now, is that it? Or the tarot cards? Or tea leaves?"

Angel stood her ground, her colorful Indian cotton skirt flowing around her ankles. "Mock me all you want, but that doesn't change the fact that the time had come to tell you."

"Fact?" Julia scoffed. "You don't deal with facts. You deal with fiction. And what did you actually tell me? Only enough to upset me."

"That wasn't my intention."

"Then what was your intention? Tell me, because I still don't get it. Did you want to disrupt my life? Make me doubt who I am? Turn my entire world upside down?" Julia fought back the tears to no avail. "Well, congratulations. Mission accomplished. Are you happy now?"

"No." Angel looked as if she were about to cry as well. "I'm not happy. I deeply regret hurting you. I made a mistake."

"So now I'm a mistake?"

"No!" Angel vehemently denied. "I meant it was a mistake not to tell you earlier."

"Yes, it was." When her mother made no further comment, Julia said, "I'm going upstairs to take a shower."

As she walked away, Julia noted that this wasn't the way she'd expected to start the New Year — with an awesome lover, a deceitful mother, and a mystery-man father.

Luke's motto of "expect the unexpected" was turning out to be the story of her life.

"You're whistling, man," Algee told Luke. "What's up with that? You never whistle."

Luke reached for a tortilla chip. "Hey, I'm just watching a football game."

"Since when are you a fan of a college bowl game?"

"You know I like football."

"I know you've got the look of a man who got laid last night."

Luke glared at him.

Algee shrugged. "Fine. You want to limit the conversation to football, I can do that. Far be it from me to intrude where I'm not wanted."

"I'm not into locker-room bragging about the women I may or may not have been with."

"Neither am I. My momma raised me better than that."

"You never talk about your family."

"You don't either," Algee pointed out.

"I've got reasons."

"My momma raised me on her own in the projects in Chicago. My daddy took off right after I was born. She made sure I stayed out of trouble and got a good education, courtesy of the United States Navy."

"Ah, so you were a squid."

"Yeah, and I figure you must have been a jarhead, right?"

Luke nodded. "The few, the proud, the Marines."

"There's always been something crazy about jarheads," Algee stated.

"On the contrary. There's something crazy about squids, cooped up in a boat all day, away from all the action."

"Totally inaccurate. And it's a ship, not a boat. Hey, that was out of bounds!" Algee yelled at the screen, almost upsetting the huge bowl of popcorn he'd made in the process. "Are you blind? That catch was totally out of bounds! Did you see that?" he asked Luke.

"I was reaching for a nacho."

"That's the problem with life, man. It happens while you're getting distracted by a nacho."

"Uh-huh."

"I mean look how that librarian got to you. Like a stealth weapon, she flew right under your defenses."

"You trying to write a romance novel or something?"

Algee tugged on the diamond stud earring he'd gotten since the last time they were together. "I've read a few. Some of 'em aren't bad."

Luke held up his hands as if warding off evil cooties. "Don't give me any."

"Why? Because you're living the studly life?"

"A gentleman never kisses and tells."

"And we know what a perfect gentleman you are," Algee scoffed.

"Hey, I was polite to those nuns," Luke

reminded him. "Even moved furniture for them."

"Yeah, right. A prince among men, that's you."

Luke threw a tortilla chip at him. "Just watch the game."

"I will. But you better watch yourself, or you'll be married and settled down before you know what hit you."

"Not in this lifetime," Luke stated emphatically.

"Julia!" Bang, bang, bang on her bedroom door. "Read to me!" Toni shouted.

She reluctantly undid the lock.

"Here." Toni shoved the book Julia had gotten her for Christmas at her. "Read to me."

Julia looked down at the title. *Are You My Momma, Llama?*

The story, about wondering who your parent was, struck a little too close to home for her at the moment. "How about I read you something else?" Julia suggested. "One of the *Olivia* stories or . . ."

"No, I want this one!" Toni pointed to the book for extra emphasis, her tiny finger tapping the cover, before she climbed up onto Julia's bed.

Toni had removed her Wellington boots in

the house, which was a good thing. And she wasn't wearing her tiara today. In fact, she was dressed rather normally for a change and was even wearing the top with the kitty on it Julia had gotten her a few weeks ago.

Looking at her little niece, who was rather adorable sitting on her bed, Julia suddenly wondered what it would be like to have a child of her own. Sitting beside Toni, Julia felt her heart melt when the normally mischievous child suddenly leaned her head against her and hugged her.

"I missed you today," Toni told her.

Julia was stunned. "You did?"

Toni nodded.

"But you don't miss me when I go to work at the library, do you?"

"Sometimes."

"You never told me so."

"I never told you about the kitten I want, either. I asked Santa, even though he doesn't pay his elves. But my kitten didn't come." She lifted her head and stared at Julia with such big sorrowful eyes that Julia wanted to rush right out and get her a kitten immediately.

The intensity of her emotions gripped Julia by the throat and left her momentarily speechless.

Toni had no such trouble. "Maybe the

Easter bunny will bring my kitten. The Easter bunny doesn't have elves. Danny next door says there is no Easter bunny, but I don't believe him. He's a capitalist pig."

The ultimate insult. Skye and Angel had taught her well. But Angel claimed that Julia's father was a capitalist pig.

"Do you believe in the Easter bunny?" Toni demanded.

Julia didn't know what to say. "I don't know."

"That's okay." Toni patted her cheek reassuringly. "You know lots of other stuff. You're smart."

"You think so?"

Toni nodded. "You can even read the big words."

Julia might be able to do that, but she sure couldn't make sense out of the mess her life was in right now.

Gazing down at Toni, Julia wondered — if she had a child with Luke, would she lie and not tell him?

So many questions, so few answers.

Angel sat beneath the big pine tree in the town square . . . as close to it as she could get on the bench beside it. There was snow on the ground, so she'd had to make do with the bench.

Angel remembered how as a child Julia had always wanted snow during the holiday season. She used to draw picture after picture of snowflakes. She was fascinated with the white stuff.

Angel stared up at the pine tree. They were supposed to interact with the human energy in a cleansing way, drawing off negative emotions. Especially guilt.

And Angel was certainly feeling plenty of that. Guilt. Eating away at her. She'd hurt her daughter. Hurt her deeply.

Was Julia right? Had she been selfish to tell her?

"Happy New Year," Tyler said quietly.

She hadn't even heard him approach.

"Mind if I join you?" He pointed to the bench.

She waited until he sat beside her before blurting out, "You know that secret I had? It didn't work out."

"What didn't?"

"Telling the truth. Julia hates me now."

"I doubt that."

"You shouldn't. I'm telling you the truth." Angel paused to smile with sad self-mockery. "I always prided myself on telling the truth, on living a truthful life. My daughter knew that, and I think it made this all harder for her to accept."

"Whatever you two argued about, you'll make it up."

Angel shook her head. "I don't think so. I hurt her to the soul of her being."

"I can't imagine you hurting anyone."

"I try not to, but in this case . . ." She wiped away a tear. "I haven't been a good mother to her. I should have done better. Should have told her the truth about her father."

"What do you mean?"

"I mean that I just told my oldest daughter that the man she thought was her father wasn't really. He died in South America when she was nine."

"Her father?"

"No, the man she *thought* was her father. Her biological father is still alive."

"Who is he?"

"You have a strange look on your face. Are you worried I'm going to tell you that you have a daughter, that you're her father?"

"Trust me, I would have remembered if you and I had met before."

"Really?"

"Absolutely."

"That's nice of you to say. You're not Julia's father, although I wouldn't mind if you were. That would be convenient, huh? Julia knows you, likes you. But maybe it wouldn't have been convenient for you. Maybe you already have kids."

Tyler didn't say anything.

"Anyway, her father isn't someone like you. I wish he were, but he's not."

"What's wrong with him?"

"He's a corporate capitalist. Rich, of course."

"And you've kept his daughter from him all these years because of that?"

Angel wrapped her arms around herself defensively. "He would have been a bad influence on her. He cheated on me and walked away from our relationship without ever looking back."

"Who is he?"

Angel shook her head. "I don't want to say, because I don't want her to know."

"But you know?"

"Yes, although I haven't had contact with him in thirty years. But I did see his picture in the paper recently."

"How recently?"

"Right before I came here in October."

"Why was he in the paper?"

"He was closing some big deal, merging two companies together and putting lots of people out of work. He's my worst nightmare."

"Why?"

"Because he has the money to take my daughter away from me."

"Doesn't he have a family of his own?"

She shook her head. "He's been married twice but has no kids."

"Julia is an adult. Why would he try to take her from you?"

"You're asking me logical questions, and I don't deal well with logic." Her voice reflected her agitation. "I'm telling you how I *feel*, okay?"

"Okay."

"I don't want her knowing who he is," Angel continued. "I should never have said anything. She was right when she said I was only telling her now to get rid of some of the guilt I was feeling. That I didn't think about how she'd feel with all this dumped on her. I shouldn't have come here in the first place." Angel jumped up from the bench. "Maybe I should leave. She's going to want me to leave." She looked around. "But where would I go?"

"Calm down." Tyler tugged her back down onto the bench. "Don't make assumptions."

"Maybe if I were a better mother . . . Wait, I could do that. I could become more the kind of mother she always wanted. Maybe that would make it up to her."

"What are you talking about now?"

"More conservative. More normal. I could do that. How hard can it be? I could wear khakis and polo shirts with little logos and get my fingernails manicured. I could fit in instead of always standing out. Don't you think?"

"You're a free spirit. You were meant to stand out."

"Not if it hurts my daughter," Angel said fiercely. "I've already hurt her enough. I've got to make it up to her somehow."

"Maybe the best way to do that is to tell her the name of her father."

"No." She nervously fingered her hand-knit scarf. "That's the one thing I *can't* do."

"She's going to find out on her own."

"How can she do that? I didn't tell her much, just his first name."

"And where you met?"

"At a party. That's nothing . . ." Her voice trailed off. "I may have mentioned us taking an Ethics class together at UCLA."

"That could give her a lead."

"What can I do?"

"Tell her everything."

"No, I can't. I'm too much of a coward to do that. He'll take her away, show her that world and —"

"She's not a kid anymore. She's capable of

making her own decisions."

"I know she is. She'd love him more than me," Angel whispered.

"She doesn't even know him."

"But she's like him in small ways. Planning ahead. Never letting go and letting fate take you where it will."

"Most people are that way."

"I know. But I didn't raise Julia to be *most people*. I raised her to be my daughter. *Mine,*" Angel said fiercely, "and no one else's!"

"The time may have come for you to share."

"He'll hurt her. I know he will. I've seen it in the runes, in the tarot cards, in every medium I've used."

"Maybe you're seeing what you want to see."

"Why would I want to see my daughter hurt?"

"Because it gives you a good reason to keep her from her father."

"I don't need more reasons. I need to think like Julia. I need to have a plan. I need to become the mother she's always wanted."

"You think transforming yourself into June Cleaver is going to solve your problems?"

"No, but it certainly can't hurt."

"Lies hurt."

"So does the truth," Angel noted sadly.

★ ★ ★

Julia had never really understood that reference to ignoring the elephant in the middle of the room until now. For the past week, Angel had been acting as if nothing had changed. No, that wasn't true. She was trying to be on her best behavior. She'd traded in her colorful billowing clothes for tailored khaki pants and bland tops. But she refused to give Julia the information she wanted — the name of her father.

The rift between them meant Julia spent a lot of time away from home, either at Luke's or at work or at Pam's. Today she and Pam were venturing out for another of their Saturday antiquing expeditions.

Pam was bent over a glass display case with a selection of 1950s clip earrings. Julia had yet to tell her about the bombshell her mother had dropped on her on New Year's Eve. She wasn't exactly sure why. The time just wasn't right yet. For now, other than her family, Luke was the only one who knew.

Julia also hadn't talked to Pam about Luke. Pam had been busy preparing for a new batch of weddings, so their conversation had focused on that when they'd been together the past week.

"See something you like?" the shop owner asked.

Pam shook her head. "Just looking."

This particular antique mall was filled with quilts, baskets, primitive furniture, stained glass, pottery, and trunks, but their jewelry was the reason Pam liked this spot.

"You seem unusually quiet today," Pam said as they wandered around the rest of the booths, searching for treasures. "Everything okay with you and Luke?"

Julia nodded.

"Ah, so you're no longer denying that there *is* something going on between the two of you."

Julia ran her fingers over the smooth patina of an oak student chair. "This is nice."

"Julia . . ." Pam complained.

"What?"

"You. Luke. Details?"

"It's been . . . good." The sex had been awesome. She and Luke had spent most nights together, making love. They'd been discreet. Most mornings she was back in her own house with no one aside from her own family the wiser.

"Good, huh?"

Julia grinned and nodded. "Mind-blowing."

Pam picked up on that instantly. "You mean you two have . . . ?"

Julia nodded again.

"Wow."

"Yeah, wow."

Julia had to tell someone about her feelings for Luke, and she certainly wasn't going to confide in her family.

"Why didn't you say anything before this?" Pam demanded.

"I wasn't sure how you'd take the news."

"Are you happy?"

Julia nodded.

"Then I'm happy for you." Pam paused a moment before adding, "Has he told you how long he plans on staying in town?"

"What do you mean?" Julia set down the vintage wooden sign she'd been looking at.

"Just that the town has a pool going as to when he's going to sell Maguire's."

"Sell it? Why would he do that?"

"Because he's always hated Serenity Falls."

"In the past, maybe."

"He's told you he plans on staying?"

"We haven't really talked about it," Julia admitted.

"You might want to." Pam gave her a worried look. "Before you get in too deep."

It was already too late for that, Julia knew. But she kept an outwardly calm expression as she checked out an oak post top. "What do you think about using this as a paperweight?"

"That would work. But what about Luke?"

"What about him?"

"Where do you see this relationship with him going?"

"I have no idea."

"Doesn't that scare you?"

Julia nodded. "Freaks me out totally."

"Really? You don't look freaked out."

"You have no idea."

"Because you won't tell me."

"Because I can't."

"He won't let you?"

"No, of course not. I meant it's not easy for me to talk about personal stuff."

"I had noticed that about you."

"Yeah, well I guess it comes from my upbringing. My mother always wore her emotions like a huge neon sign around her neck. And my sister has no discretion at all. She says whatever comes into her mind, no matter what it is or whom she's speaking to."

"How have you been getting along with your family?"

"We're having some . . . problems at the moment."

"You want to talk about it?"

Julia shook her head.

"You can talk to me, you know. Anything you said would go no further."

"I know that." Telling her about Luke had been hard enough. Confiding that she didn't even know her father's name was too much for Julia to handle at the moment.

"I mean, I realize that a lot of people in Serenity Falls talk and gossip. It's one of the perils of living in a small town. Everyone knowing everyone else's business."

"I've noticed that."

"But I wouldn't betray your confidence in any way." Pam's expression was serious. "I certainly won't tell anyone about things between you and Luke."

"I appreciate that."

Pam gave her a hug and then asked, "Hey, are you ready for lunch?"

Julia nodded. "Absolutely. Only this time I'm going to order something different."

"You are?"

"Yes. I've turned over a new leaf. I'm tired of being so predictable. No more boring good girl. A new Julia has come to town, so Serenity Falls had better watch out."

"Sounds like I should get you one of those Danger: Rowdy Librarian T-shirts," Pam noted with a grin.

Julia grinned right back at her. "Maybe you should."

"Tyler." Luke confronted the handyman

336

at Maguire's, where he was repairing a sticky door to the men's room. "Let's talk."

Tyler eyed him suspiciously. "What for?"

Luke couldn't blame him. Talking wasn't Luke's favorite pastime. He'd rather chew nails than make polite conversation. But he didn't plan on discussing the weather with Tyler.

"You said you wanted a naked woman," Tyler reminded him.

Luke frowned. "What?"

Tyler pointed to the mural he'd been sporadically working on for the past few weeks. It was an abstract, and Luke really hadn't been paying that much attention to it.

"You told me you wanted a naked woman on the mural," Tyler said. "I asked. You answered."

"This isn't about the mural."

"It's not?"

"No. It's about you."

"What about me?" was the question a normal person would ask. But Tyler didn't say a word. Instead, his expression closed down and his eyes went cold.

Luke said, "I know about your life back in Chicago."

"And I know about yours with the FBI," Tyler shot back unexpectedly. "Guess that makes us even."

337

Chapter Fourteen

"No, it does not make us even," Luke growled. "Where do you get off sniffing around in my past?"

"I could ask the same thing of you."

"I wanted to be sure you weren't a pervert or an escaped convict or something."

"Same here."

"Well, hell." Luke pivoted and marched over to the bar, where he grabbed a bottle of Jack Daniel's. It was Monday, and Maguire's was closed. He poured himself a generous shot and another for Tyler. "To keeping the past in the past," Luke toasted him.

"Where it should be," Tyler added.

Luke let the strong spirits hit his gut before he had to ask, "Don't you find it hard leaving that life behind?"

"What life? I lived for my job. Prosecutor of the year on the fast track to success. Until that last case."

Luke knew what case it was, but he wasn't going to be the one to bring up the details. "And after that you just walked away?"

"Burnt out. Still am."

"But a hell of a painter," Luke noted with a grin.

Tyler's smile was slower but equally mocking. "Yeah."

They paused to drink the remainder of their Jack Daniel's. "I'm not the only one who walked away," Tyler said. "So did you."

"Yeah."

"So when did you lift my prints?"

"A few weeks ago. They were behind at the lab, so I didn't get the intel back until today. How about you?"

"Oh, I sent in your prints the first week you were in town. Got the results within forty-eight hours."

"You've got better connections than I do."

"I don't use them often. I try to leave that world behind."

"Yeah, I hear you."

Luke wanted to leave it behind, too. In the beginning, there had been the adrenaline rush of shouldering through a door, gun drawn, all set to save the world. He'd worked all-night stakeouts, sat on wiretaps, and maneuvered the FBI's paperwork jungle with ease. But as time went on and his undercover work increased, he'd eventually lost himself.

There hadn't been just one incident like in Tyler's case. No, it had been a cumulative thing, until Luke had woken one morning and known he couldn't go on. Broke, battered, and bruised from a bar fight the night before, he'd gotten out before it was too late, before he got someone killed.

The citations he'd gotten during his time in the FBI didn't really matter, because the bottom line was that he'd failed in the end. Something his old man had always told him he excelled at.

So here he was, stuck in Maguire's, talking to another guy who'd burnt out and dropped out. "Listen, Tyler, you know Angel pretty well, right?"

Tyler looked suspicious. "What's that supposed to mean?"

"Did she tell you about the situation between her and Julia?"

"She might have."

"Discreet to the end, huh? Your legal training is showing."

Tyler made no comment.

"Julia wants to track down her real father," Luke said.

"And you're helping her."

Luke just shrugged, neither denying nor confirming it. "Did Angel tell you who Julia's father is?"

"No. And even if she did, I wouldn't betray her confidence by telling anyone else."

"Yeah, I figured that's what you'd say, but it was worth a shot."

"I'm surprised you're getting involved in this. I thought your modus operandi was to play the loner and keep out of other people's business."

"That works pretty well for you."

"I get by."

"So do I."

"Except where Julia is concerned. Algee says she's your kryptonite."

"My weakness, yeah, I know. He's taken great pleasure in telling me that, too."

"What are you going to do about it? About her?"

"I don't make many plans these days."

"Understood."

"What are you going to do about Angel?"

"Like you said, I don't make many plans these days, either. Change of subject. That mural I'm doing . . . you get any complaints?"

"The art critic from the *New York Times* said it had a certain amateurish quality, but what does he know?" Luke retorted.

"Yeah, right. I meant from Walt."

"What does our illustrious mayor have to do with anything?"

"He wants to control everything in this town."

"No surprise there."

"Walt won't be happy you're putting a mural of a nude on your walls."

"It's not like it's a layout from *Playboy*, although now that I think of it, that might have been a good idea . . ." Luke grinned at the very concept. "We could have run a wet T-shirt contest to find the right model for it."

"Yeah, right. You're gonna be in enough hot water as it is."

Luke shrugged. "Nothing new for me."

"I heard that Walt may be planning to bring it up in next month's town meeting."

"The mural?"

"Among other things."

"Do I look like I care?" Luke retorted.

"He's very anal about this Best Small Town thing."

"That's the understatement of the year," Luke noted. "But enough chit-chat. Time to get back to work. I've got something called accounts payable to work out, and you've got a door to fix."

A week later, Luke looked up from the bar to find Angel standing there, a white apron around her waist like the other Maguire's servers wore. "I need two Flirtinis and two Samuel Adams on tap."

Luke frowned. "For you?" That was a lot

of alcohol for one female to consume at once.

Angel laughed. "No, of course not. For tables five and nine."

"What are you doing here?" he asked suspiciously.

"Helping you out. I heard you were short-staffed with two of your servers coming down with the flu. So I thought I'd step in and see what it's like being a server. I haven't done something like this since my college days, you know."

"Excuse me." A guy at a nearby table waved in their direction. "I didn't order this. I ordered the pot roast."

"I know you did," Angel replied, "but the halibut is much better for your arteries."

"I don't like fish."

"You just haven't had it prepared correctly. Our cook does an excellent job —"

"Yeah, she does," the guy interrupted her. "On pot roast. Which is what I want."

"Fine." Angel yanked the plate off the table and marched into the kitchen. A few moments later she returned and just about tossed the meal on the table before him. "There. Eat it and die."

"Okay then . . ." Luke hurried out from behind the bar. "I really think you've done enough here for one day, Angel."

He untied the apron from around her

middle and handed her the coat she had hanging on the coat rack in the corner. He knew it was hers because it was strange and fuzzy. "You go on home. I can handle things here."

"But you really need my help, Luke."

He shook his head. "I can manage. *Really.*"

"Yes, but I wanted to talk to you about Julia."

"I'm still waiting for a dessert menu," another diner pointed out.

"Sugar is poison," Angel told them before returning her attention to Luke. "You two are intimate now . . ."

"Whoa." Luke held up his hand. "I am *not* having this conversation with you."

"You're an experienced man. Surely you can't be embarrassed about sex?"

Luke looked at the roomful of diners, all of whom were suddenly staring at them with rapt attention. "What? You don't have anything better to do than eavesdrop?"

As a group they said, "Nope."

"Eat your dinners," Luke growled at them even as he took Angel by the elbow and led her toward the back. "Look, I don't have time for this right now."

"I know that. You've still got two Flirtinis and two Samuel Adams to get for tables five

344

and nine. Here, let me help. I can bartend if you want . . ."

"No!" At her hurt expression, he softened his voice just a bit. "No, thanks."

"I really don't see how you'll be able to manage without my help tonight, Luke."

"I'll make it through somehow."

"But we'll talk soon about Julia, right? I've given her time to settle down, but she's still extremely angry with me."

"Yeah, I got that."

"She told you everything?"

"She told me enough."

At that point, Julia walked into Maguire's. She stopped in her tracks when she saw her mom talking to him.

"What's going on?" Julia demanded.

"Your mother just stopped by to say hi."

"And to help him out," Angel added. "He's got two servers out with the flu."

"I told her I really don't need her help." Luke sent urgent visual messages to Julia, which she apparently picked up because she said, "That's right. I can help Luke. You don't have to stay, Angel."

Angel's shoulders seemed to sag at her daughter's words. "Oh. Well, I guess I'll go back to the house then."

Luke waited until she'd left before telling Julia, "She was informing the customers that the pot roast would kill them and that sugar is poison."

"You're lucky that's all she did."

"She also made the announcement that you and Luke are intimate," Adele said even as she slapped two plates of today's special — the pot roast — into Luke's startled hands. "Here, take these to table twelve. The one in the corner," she added.

"She told them we're intimate?" Julia looked around in dismay. "You're kidding, right?"

"Nope," the diners said en masse.

"Eat!" Luke growled. This time he meant business.

Maguire's was filled with the clatter of dozens of forks being picked up and conversations resumed.

Luke nodded his approval. "Okay then."

Julia put her hands to her flushed cheeks. "It's not okay."

"Uh, that's our dinner you've got there," an older man in the corner table reminded Luke.

"Stay here," Luke told her before marching over and depositing the two plates on the table with an irritated clatter that made the ice cubes in their drinks rattle against their glasses.

"Do you have any salt substitute . . . ?" The man's voice trailed off at the hardened expression on Luke's face. "Ah, never mind."

"Wise move. Enjoy your meal." Luke marched back to Julia's side. "Why isn't it okay that people know about us? Are you ashamed of me?"

His question startled her. So did the defensive look in his eyes. "No, of course not."

"What's the problem then?"

"I'm just not used to being the center of attention this way."

Luke turned to glare at the room over his shoulder. "Are you looking at her again? Stop staring. Didn't anyone ever tell you people that's rude?"

"Luke." Julia tugged on his arm. *"Luke!"*

He finally turned back to her. "What?"

"You're right. I don't care if everyone here knows. Hear that everyone?" she called out to them. She was tired of always being the good girl who did the right thing, who went out of her way to please other people and meet their expectations of her. "I don't care!"

"Listen," the woman at a nearby table said, "all I care about is getting dessert. So stop the floor show and get me a menu, would you please?"

Julia grabbed a dessert menu from the bin at the end of the bar and took it right over.

Seeing that the diners in the room were still watching her every move, she gave them her best librarian stare and took a page out of Luke's book. "Eat!" she told them.

They did.

"This has got to stop." Skye stated, her hands on her hips above her low-rider jeans. She'd confronted Julia first thing Sunday morning, which was unusual, because Skye was not a morning person.

So finding her in the kitchen, waiting, had already raised alarm bells within Julia.

"What are you talking about?" Julia replied.

"This thing with you and Angel. She's trying to please you by going respectable."

"Fat chance of that," Julia scoffed.

"She's got a job."

"You mean selling her scarves and hats on consignment at Bonnie's Boutique? I heard about that already."

"I mean a job at Aunt Sally's Pancake House. The one by the interstate. She has to wear a uniform complete with a frilly cap and feed people bacon. Do you know how difficult that is for her? But she's doing it for you."

"What are you talking about? I never asked her to feed people bacon."

"She's trying to be respectable. She's been looking for a so-called normal job to make you proud of her. After working at Maguire's for thirty minutes, she figured she could make it as a waitress."

"That's her choice."

"No, it's not. She's trying to fit into this anal town to please you."

Julia's patience snapped. "If you don't like it here, you should leave."

"I am. I rented a place over in Rock Creek. Toni and I are already packed."

Julia was stunned. "Is Angel going with you?"

"No. She refused. She says you need her."

"I need her to tell me the name of my real father. She told you the truth before she told me. Do you have any idea how that makes me feel?"

"Get over it. Seriously."

"This from someone who still holds a grudge over the fact that I lost some stupid cassette of yours years ago —"

"It was a bootleg Nirvana!"

"See?"

"I see all right," Skye retorted. "I see that you're trying to make Angel pay by ruining her life. She's even agreed to date that dorky dentist."

"What? Why?"

"Hello? Haven't you heard a word I've said? To please you."

"How would dating Phil the dentist please me?"

"He's respectable, isn't he?"

Julia nodded. "Eminently."

"Unlike the man she really likes. Tyler."

"I never told her she couldn't date Tyler."

Skye rolled her eyes. "She doesn't want to date him. She wants to get down and dirty with him. The way you are doing with Luke."

"My relationship with Luke is none of your business," Julia shot back.

"It's apparently the entire town's business. They all know about it."

"I don't care."

"Then you shouldn't care that I'm talking about it. After all, I'm your sister —"

"Half sister."

"Oh yeah, I knew we'd get around to that eventually. You know what I think? I think the news about your father really satisfied you on some level. Because now you have a logical explanation for why you're so different from me. Why you were always the good sister and I was the bad one."

"You like getting into trouble. You said yourself on Christmas that you like stirring things up."

"That's right."

"Like shoplifting."

"I wondered how long it would take you to get around to that. I was a rebellious teenager."

"What did you have to be rebellious about? You never had rules you had to obey."

"Sure we did. Be nice. Don't harm the earth."

"I meant things like a curfew."

"We didn't grow up in a state of marshal law, that's right."

"So I repeat my earlier question, what did you have to be rebellious about?"

"I was pushing the boundaries."

"Yeah, that's one way of saying it. Being a petty thief is another."

"Hey, there was nothing petty about what I did. I only took things from places that could afford it."

"Like that's an excuse?"

"I only got caught once."

"That was all it took." Something about Skye's expression made her add, "You're not still stealing, are you?"

"Why?" Skye drawled. "Do you want to check the silverware, be sure I didn't take any spoons?"

"I meant from stores. You're not doing that anymore, right?"

Skye was silent.

"Right?" Julia repeated.

"I may have taken one or two things recently that were made in child labor camps to bring attention to that cause."

"How recently? Since you've been in Serenity Falls?"

Skye nodded.

Julia panicked. "Take it back. Right now."

"Yeah, right."

"I mean it!"

"I can't. I sent the stuff to the media with a press release about the conditions in those child labor camps."

Julia closed her eyes, imagining the police or the FBI pulling up in front of her house at any moment to handcuff Skye and haul her away.

"Why do you do such stupid things? Don't you realize that your daughter could be taken from you if you get caught and prosecuted?"

"That will never happen."

"You can't know that."

"You always think the worst of me."

"And you always prove me right," Julia retorted.

"Admit it, you were *pleased* to hear that we're only half sisters."

"I'm pleased that you're getting your own place. Where will you be living in Rock Creek?"

"I thought I'd take a bed in Sister Mary's shelter for the homeless." At Julia's horrified look, she added, "Why not? That's what you expect from me, right? Not that I might actually have rented a nice two-bedroom place with character."

"With character? Does that mean it's falling apart?"

"There you go again. You think I'm going to have Toni eating lead paint chips for her afternoon snack? I know you don't think I'm a good mother."

"I never said that. I said you don't discipline your daughter, but I never said you were a bad mother. I know you love her."

"We're going," Toni said as she trailed down the stairs with her favorite blanket in hand. Taking Julia's hand in her small one, she tugged on it. "Come with us."

"I can't." Julia got down to Toni's level so they were eye to eye. "But I'll come visit you if your mommy lets me."

"I'm not the one with restrictions," Skye said.

"Gram is staying with you," Toni said.

Julia raised an eyebrow. Angel had never been known as Gram before.

"Yeah, she told Toni to call her Gram. It's more traditional, more respectable, more like something out of the *Donna Reed Show*. I am going to miss your cable TV," Skye remarked belatedly.

Julia felt badly, as if she were tossing her

family out onto the street. "You're sure this place in Rock Creek is nice?"

"No, it's a cockroach-infested hellhole," Skye retorted in irritation.

"What's a hellhole?" Toni asked.

"A place filled with negative energy," Skye replied.

Toni looked from one adult to the other. "Is this a hellhole?"

"Depends who you ask," Skye muttered before gathering her daughter in her arms. "Come on, pumpkin. Time to go."

Julia stood. "Did you pack her books?"

Skye nodded. "They're already in the van."

"What about child-proofing the cabinets and drawers in the kitchen and bathroom of the new place?"

"Algee already agreed to install them this afternoon."

Julia wrapped her arms around her middle, chilled all of a sudden. "I wish you'd given me more warning . . ."

"What for? You've wanted us gone since the second we got here."

"That's not true . . ."

"Yes, it is. Don't bother lying."

Julia blinked back the sting of tears. "Angel lied for thirty years." Great. She felt like a wimp for saying that. And sounded like one, too. She hated that.

"Right. She did. And you're going to make her pay for every one of them, aren't you? Well, forgive me if I can't sit around and watch you do that. I've told Angel how I feel. And now I've told you."

"So you're just walking away, is that it? Walking away is something you're real good at isn't it? Whenever things get rough, you take a hike."

"I didn't take a hike when I found myself pregnant and alone," Skye countered.

"You had Angel to help you. You were never alone."

"And you were?"

"Yes."

"Your own choice. You could have stayed . . ."

"I don't belong."

"Your choice," Skye repeated before walking out.

Julia blinked away the tears as Toni waved to her over her mother's shoulder. "Bye bye, don't cry, my mommy's name is Skye."

"Skye's left," Julia told Angel when she got home later that evening. Her mother wasn't wearing a waitress uniform. "She told me you're working at Aunt Sally's Pancake House."

"That's right. That's where I was today.

And I knew Skye was leaving."

Yet another example of how close Angel and Skye were. Julia tried not to be hurt. "She said she asked you to go with her."

"You need me more than she does."

"I *need* you to tell me the name of my father."

"I've explained about that."

"I'm going to find out sooner or later. Luke is helping me track him down, you know. It's only a matter of time."

"Maybe by then you and I will have reached an understanding."

Julia's patience, already worn thin by Skye earlier in the day, started to fray once more. "Do you really think that wearing a frilly uniform at the pancake house and dating Phil the dentist is going to bring you and me closer together?"

"I'm trying to be a good mother to you."

"I'm an adult."

Angel reached out to touch her cheek. "You were an adult even when you were Toni's age. An old soul. I just want you to be happy, and I'm glad that you and Luke are together."

"Because he's reckless?"

"Because he cares for you. I can see it in his eyes. But he's a man with a lot of secrets. I can see that in his aura."

"Tyler is a man with a lot of secrets. Can

you see that in his aura, too?"

"I see a great deal of pain in his aura."

"You like him."

Angel shook her head. "He's not respectable. I'm into respectable now."

Julia rolled her eyes. "Oh, please."

"What? I can fit in here. Really I can! You just haven't seen that side of me. But I can do it. I'm going to prove that to you."

"It won't make a difference," she warned Angel.

"It will. You'll see. Just give it a chance. Give us a chance."

Julia sadly shook her head. "How can I do that when you still won't be truthful with me? When you still don't trust me with the whole truth? If you really want to be a good mother, then tell me my father's name."

"I can't do that, but I will show you how respectable I can be. I'll fit in here. You'll see. I got a normal job. I'm dating a normal man. I'm even wearing conservative clothes. No more wild ways. I *will* fit in," she fiercely repeated. "You'll see."

What Julia saw was Angel, once again refusing to listen to what Julia was saying.

Julia sat at a table sipping the whipped cream from her hot cocoa as Luke locked up at Maguire's. He'd already told her there was no news yet on the search for her father. No one named Adam was officially registered in that Ethics class, which complicated things. "How's the mural going?"

"Come take a look for yourself." Luke held out his hand to her. "Bring your hot cocoa if you want."

As they entered the room at the back, she paused beside the pool table. "You know, I've never understood the game of pool."

"Really? It's simple." Luke took her cup from her and put his hands on her waist, lifting her to the edge of the massive felt-covered table.

Startled, she braced her hands on his shoulders for balance. "What are you doing?"

"Educating you about the game. Some people are finesse players who use fancy moves . . ."

He slid his hands up her legs, which were bare above her knee-high boots and beneath her black skirt.

"Fancy moves, huh?"

"Mmm-hmm." Trailing his fingers along the edge of her panties, he asked, "Want to learn more?"

"Absolutely."

He slipped his fingers beneath the elastic to tempt her before tugging them out of his way completely. Her skirt was shoved up around her hips as he gently tipped her back until she was lying on the table. All the while he seduced her with his fingertips.

"See what I mean about finesse moves?"

"Mmmmm."

He opened her legs like a book, pressing her knees apart before bending down to read her with his wickedly talented mouth. He gently overcame her initial reservations, showing her how much gratification could be had. He was a masterful instructor, tutoring her step by step until Julia was totally steeped in desire, almost drugged by the intense need.

He took his time, building her anticipation, lifting her from one delicious plane of erotic sensuality to the next. She didn't realize he'd taken a swipe of whipped cream from her cup of hot cocoa until she felt the coolness on her overheated and ultra-sensitive skin. Her gasp of surprise was quickly followed by a moan of delight as he lapped at her like a huge jungle tiger.

Each time she thought she couldn't feel more, he did something new to make her mind and body melt. Each time Luke's rough tongue rubbed and licked her clitoris, she flew apart in his arms — not once, not twice, but time after time.

Finally lifting his head, he looked down at her flushed face. "But me, I'm more of a straight shooter." He undid his jeans and shoved them and his briefs out of his way. She eagerly sat up to help him roll on a condom from his jeans pocket. Then he tugged her closer. "Yeah, I'm more of a straight shooter to get the balls in the hole." One thrust and he was deep inside her.

Excited and totally aroused again, she grabbed a pool stick with one hand.

"You gonna hit me over the head with that?" Luke growled, holding still within her, filling her.

"No." She slid the stick behind his back and took a tight grip on both ends with each hand. Using the stick, she tugged him even closer. "I'm going to use it to keep you doing exactly what you're doing."

"Exactly?" He flexed. "You mean you don't want me experimenting? Faster?" He pumped two, three times. "Slower?" He pulled out almost completely and then smoothly slid back in.

"Yes, *oh yes!*"

Julia dropped the pool stick and clenched her hands against his bare muscular butt.

He gripped her bottom, parting her cheeks and taking her to another planet as he yanked her closer.

He rocked her back and forth, timing his movements, building their pleasure to a point of almost painful ecstasy.

She came with a powerful orgasm that clenched and released, clenched and released, over and over again — rolling over her like a drumbeat, vibrating throughout her entire body from her womb to her fingertips.

It took several minutes before either one had enough breath to speak or energy to move. "Do you get the appeal of pool now?" Luke murmured.

"Mmmm." She trailed her fingers over his bare hip. "But you may have to show me again, demonstrate a few of those finesse plays again versus the straight-shooter method. I can't seem to decide which I prefer."

"Well, we can't leave you undecided now, can we?" Luke tugged her closer, yanking off her skirt and panties entirely and tossing them out of his way. "Remember, it's all about ways to sink the ball in the hole . . ."

That exhilarating, darkly seductive night was one Julia would always remember . . . forever etched in the very depths of her consciousness.

Chapter Fifteen

Julia sat in the guest's chair in the library director's office, proud of the fact that she wasn't squirming in discomfort. Not that the chair was that uncomfortable, but the disapproving stare Frasier was giving her didn't make for the best of mornings. "I understand there was an . . . incident at Maguire's recently involving you and Mr. Maguire."

The pool table? Julia tried not to panic. How could anyone know? They'd been alone. The doors to Maguire's had been locked, and there were no windows in the back room.

How did they know she'd been wickedly wanton? Was it written on her face? A giant "S" for Scarlet woman . . . for Sensually Saturated and Sexually Satisfied woman? Or a giant "W" for Wanton?

"Supposedly it took place during the dinner hour."

No way! Like she'd make love in front of a crowd. Julia might be loosening up, but she wasn't crazy.

"You uh," Frasier cleared his throat. "You are alleged to have informed the diners that you and Luke were . . . uh . . ."

Julia heaved a huge internal sigh of relief and then resumed her position of strength. No squirming.

"Yes?" For once, she didn't step forward to make things more comfortable.

"Well, that you two were . . . seeing each other."

"Is there a law against that?"

"No." Frasier was the one who squirmed in his high-backed chair. "Of course not. It's just that Alice said you both caused a scene at Maguire's, and she worried about it reflecting badly on the library as a result."

"Alice wasn't there."

"No, but a friend of hers was."

Julia decided it was time to stop beating around the bush. "Frasier, are you happy with my work here at the library?"

He was clearly taken aback by her question. "Of course I am. The patrons all love you. We've got more people coming in making interlibrary loan requests, book requests, more interest from the community than ever before."

"And I welcome that interest. *Except* where it comes to my personal life."

"Yes, well, this is a small town. It's diffi-

363

cult to avoid gossip. Naturally, Alice is concerned —"

She stopped him right there. "Do you realize how intimidated most of the staff is by Alice? She terrorizes people. You know this kick she's on about the uniforms for library staff? Everyone hates the idea of being forced to wear green polo shirts every day."

"Green is our mayor's favorite color . . ."

"Then let him wear the shirt!" Julia was really getting aggravated now.

Frasier removed his glasses and rubbed them clean with a tissue. "Well, I thought the staff might prefer not having to worry about what to wear to work every day . . ."

"Did you ask them?"

"That was Alice's job."

Julia just gave him a look.

"Okay, point taken," Frasier admitted. "No one is going to cross Alice." He replaced his glasses and gave her a perceptive look. "Except for you."

"Alice and I tend to have a different viewpoint on things."

"I had noticed that." Frasier's voice was dry. "Can you at least try not to rock the boat for the next few weeks? Rumor has it that the BST committee may be visiting incognito very soon."

"BST?"

"Best Small Town."

"Right."

"And it wouldn't do for them to find the town librarian in Maguire's declaring details of her personal love life in front of everyone."

"Especially when that love life involves the town's rebel, right?"

Frasier nodded. "Well, there is that, yes. Just think about what I've said, okay?"

No, it wasn't okay with her. None of this was. Alice, the green shirts, the gossiping, the lies her mother told her.

Julia was getting fed up.

She'd always been kind and agreeable, steady and thoughtful. Ask anyone. Julia had never been one to rock the boat.

But now she wanted to stir things up, to steer that boat in a new direction.

"I don't need to think about it, Frasier. I haven't done anything to deserve this interrogation about my personal life, and frankly I resent it. I've done everything possible to give one hundred and ten percent to this library, but if that's not enough for you . . ."

Frasier looked panicked. "It is enough. I know Alice is difficult. Believe me, I know."

"Then please keep her off my back and out of my personal life. Just think about what I've said, okay?" She deliberately repeated his earlier words back at him.

As she walked out of Frasier's office, she was amazed at herself and what she'd just done.

I am a wronged librarian, hear me roar.

Thankfully, things got better after that, turning into one of those memorable days that made her glad she'd chosen this career path. She was working the desk, dealing directly with patrons, one of her favorite things to do anyway.

Julia dealt with one question after another — information on the most popular baby names, the best route for touring the Cinque Terre in Italy, ways to select the best digital camera, how to get rid of spider mites. A hassled mom with a toddler wanted a book dealing with potty-training. Carla from the bank wanted a book on coping with menopause. Lena from the post office wanted a self-help book with a cure for "the need to please."

Mystery buff and Anglophile Edith the high school teacher was having the "devil of a day" and wanted an armful of cozy mysteries. She also warned Julia that she'd assigned a term paper on the Restoration period in English history, so there would be a run on those books. Edith looked like she might be tempted to warn Julia about Luke again but wisely decided against it.

After Edith came Tanya, who worked in Phil the dentist's office as his receptionist and was always in a hurry. She followed the smash-and-grab method of pulling science-fiction paperbacks from the rack, as well as a few new releases that Julia quickly handed her as she raced by. Tanya then rushed them to the circulation desk, where she'd been known to check out the same book more than once by mistake. "I hate it when I do that," she'd told Julia a few weeks ago. "I'll start reading it and two pages in I'll realize I read it before and it wasn't all that great the first time around." But Tanya had yet to find a way to slow down enough to change her library experience.

More questions came in rapid succession from other patrons, until by the end of the day Julia felt like a knowledge-brimming goddess of wisdom and information. She should have been wearing that T-shirt Patty had gotten her after the last ALA conference — LIBRARIANS MAY NOT KNOW EVERYTHING . . . BUT THEY KNOW WHERE TO FIND IT.

Oh yes, Julia was definitely feeling the power.

So you'd think she'd be able to find information about her own father. But no such luck, despite checking out books with titles like *Missing Persons*. Luke's friends hadn't had any luck tracking down her father yet, either. No one named Adam had officially registered for that Ethics class, but he might have audited the class or gone under someone else's name for some reason.

The bottom line was that newly revised Julia wasn't giving in, and she wasn't giving up.

"You want to do what?" Algee blinked at him, the overhead lights at Cosmic Comics reflecting off his cleanly shaven head as well as his diamond stud earring.

"You accuse me of being sappy, and I'm gonna have to punch you," Luke warned him.

"As if I'd ever do such a thing. I think it's a sweet Valentine's Day idea."

Luke glared at him.

"Well, it is."

"Forget I said anything," Luke growled, glad the store was empty.

"Come on, man. Can't you take a joke?"

"No."

"Okay, fine. Be that way. Hi there," Algee greeted a customer aged ten or thereabouts who'd just walked in. "Can I help you?"

"Yeah. Is Batman an orphan?"

Once that was cleared up, and the kid bought twenty bucks' worth of comics, Algee returned his attention to Luke. "I think it's cute that you want to do something like that for Julia."

"Cute?" Luke growled.

Algee's dark eyes twinkled. "Adorable?"

Luke wore his war face, the one that made grown men tremble with fear. It made Algee grin with glee.

"Forget I said anything," Luke ordered.

"No way. I can help you out. You're planning to do this Monday night, when Maguire's is shut, right?"

"That was the plan, yeah."

"That'll work. You're gonna need visual bling-bling."

"Huh?"

"Decorations."

"I can manage on my own," Luke said.

"Manage, maybe. But excel at pulling off an incredibly memorable occasion?" Algee made a rocking motion with his hand that indicated the answer to that question was doubtful.

"What are you now, a party planner?"

Algee fixed him with a stare. "Do you want my help or not?"

Luke made the same rocking motion with his hand.

His friend was not offended, his thoughts clearly already on possibilities for the event. "You're gonna surprise her with this, though, right?"

"Yeah."

"That's good."

"I'm so glad you approve," Luke drawled.

"Hey, you came to me for help."

"A momentary lapse in judgment on my part."

"Ha-ha." Algee slapped him on the back with a force that would have made most men stumble.

"I should have asked Adele," Luke muttered.

"She's doing the cooking for this event, right?"

"Uh, I guess."

"You didn't think of food, did you?" Algee shook his head. "I'm telling you, that's why you need my help with this project. The devil is in the details."

"Fine. You can help. But lay off the *cute* or *sweet* adjectives when referring to me."

"You got it. So what have you done about the music?"

"Not much yet."

"Man, you're hopeless, you know that?"

"I don't have much experience with this kind of stuff."

"You need a theme."

Luke frowned. "A theme?"

"Yeah. I'll be in charge of that, too."

"A Harley theme would be good," Luke suggested.

Algee stared at him with pity. "Hopeless, man. You're just hopeless. But never fear. Big Al is here."

Julia had no idea what Luke was up to, but she knew he was up to something. She'd catch him conversing quietly with Adele, and they'd stop the minute they saw her. Or Luke and Algee would be off whispering and then deny they were doing anything other than talking about sports.

Valentine's Day was coming up, and Luke had invited her to dinner at Maguire's — just the two of them on Monday night when the place was closed. A romantic evening she'd never forget, he'd promised her — which made her wonder if he had plans involving more pool lessons in the back room.

"Wear something special," he'd told her.

Did that mean Victoria Secret thong and a Wonderbra? Exotic lingerie?

Wanting further clarification, she'd asked, "Special?"

"Your best dress."

"Okay." She didn't really have one, but

she quickly went out and bought a stunning little black number. Well, it wasn't that little. It covered her nicely, the hem of the skirt falling demurely to her knees. But the material draped across her body the way really expensive outfits managed to do without looking tacky. The wrap-around bodice showed just the right amount of cleavage, and the antique Victorian garnet necklace and drop earrings she wore added a nice touch, as did the velvet cape she added.

She was surprised when Luke picked her up in a black Lincoln Town Car, looking sexy in the dark suit he'd worn for Christmas.

"I borrowed the car from Algee," Luke explained as he held open the passenger door for her. "I couldn't really pick you up with the Harley. It's too cold."

Before starting the car, he said, "You look beautiful."

"Thanks." She felt as nervous as a teenager during the short drive to Maguire's.

Just as they were about to enter the pub, Luke told her, "Close your eyes."

"Why?"

He gave her a look.

"I won't be able to see if my eyes are closed," she explained.

"I'll guide you in. Now close them and keep them shut. No peeking." He walked her inside, keeping his arm around her waist as he removed her velvet cape. "Okay. Now open them."

She did. Her jaw dropped. "What is this?"

"Welcome to your senior prom." Luke slid a wrist corsage of white carnations over her wrist as the sound of Vanessa Williams singing "Save the Best for Last" filled the room. "Algee informed me that proms have a theme, so we went with 'Paint the Town Red.'"

"You sure did." The dining room at Maguire's had been completely transformed. They were standing beneath a ten-foot-high red-and-gold corrugated star that welcomed them to the magical room where twinkle lights added extra sparkle. Starry gossamer banners soared from the floor to the ceiling, creating a starry-night effect. Red cardboard lamp posts created a walkway to a spotlit table in front of a backdrop of a city skyline.

Julia was totally overcome. "Is this what your prom at Serenity Falls High looked like?"

Luke shrugged. "I never went. I didn't have the money or the inclination. I hated that kind of pep-rally, school-spirit classmate crap."

She turned to face him. "If you hated it so

much, then why . . . ?"

"Because I thought you'd like it. You sounded so sad when you said you'd missed your prom because you moved."

"I did always wonder what it would be like," she admitted.

"Now you'll know."

"I can't believe you did all this."

Frankly, Luke couldn't believe it either. He'd thought a little crepe paper tossed around would do the trick. Instead, this had turned into a huge production, and he'd gone along with it all.

Why? Why had he done all this? Julia was supposed to be a distraction. She wasn't supposed to drive *him* to distraction.

He couldn't even use the excuse that he'd done this to get her into bed with him. They'd already had sex. A lot of sex. Awesome sex. It only made him want her more, not less.

That left Luke feeling very unsettled when he let himself think about it, which wasn't very often. He had a lifelong track record of ignoring stuff he didn't want to deal with. Why change now?

A sudden flash of light from his left had Luke going on automatic pilot, reverting to his law enforcement days. Some things you never forgot. Like not standing in an open doorway because the back light frames you as a perfect target.

In an instant he had the offender in a choke hold, back against the bar.

"Yo, man, chill out!" Algee gasped.

Luke immediately set him free.

"If I'd known you had such an aversion to having your picture taken, I wouldn't have done it," Algee said.

"Sorry about that," Luke muttered. "You startled me."

"Ditto."

The flash had come from a Polaroid camera, not a weapon.

"Here." Algee handed him the now almost fully developed photo. "Don't you kids look cute."

Algee had taken the shot right before Luke had reacted, so he didn't look like a maniac on the attack. But he did look like a guy falling for a girl who was gazing at him with stars in her eyes. Or maybe that was the flash?

"I can't believe all these flowers," Julia was saying.

"Algee told Pam about this and she donated them," Luke absently replied, still uncomfortable with what the photo in his hand showed.

"Pam knew? She didn't say a word."

"She wasn't supposed to. This was all meant to be a big surprise."

"Normally I don't like surprises," Julia admitted, "but this . . . this is . . . I don't know what to say."

"Then don't say anything." Luke dropped the picture on the table and took her hand. "Just dance with me."

"Luke has assured me that he doesn't look like a frog in a blender when he dances, so you should be okay," Algee reassured Julia.

Luke glared at him in exasperation. "Don't you have someplace else you have to be?"

"No, not really."

"I can't believe you went to all this trouble," Julia said.

"I was glad to do it," Algee replied.

"She was talking to me," Luke said.

"He was glad to do it, too," Algee quickly added. "It was his idea to begin with. Even if he didn't have a clue. The man was going to go with a Harley theme." Algee just shook his head. "Then he was going to go with a glitter ball and some crepe paper. I expanded on that theme somewhat."

"Quite a bit. I'm stunned. Is this what your prom was like, Algee?" she asked.

"I didn't go."

"Only because he'd asked two girls and they both found out and dumped him," Luke inserted.

Algee shrugged. "What can I say? I find it hard to say no to a pretty face."

"Maybe you should have an event at Maguire's for everyone who missed their prom," Julia suggested with the excitement of someone who'd just had a lightbulb moment. "Then you could use the decorations again."

"How did this supposedly romantic evening turn into a business discussion? Come on, let's dance. They're playing our song." He wasn't really listening to the music, he just wanted her in his arms.

Julia grinned. " 'I'm Too Sexy' is our song?"

"I had no idea you were a Right Said Fred fan, Luke," Algee noted from his position near the bar.

"I don't need an audience here," Luke growled.

"You mean I can't stay and make fun of the way a white boy dances?" Algee looked crushed.

"Affirmative, squid."

"Roger that, jarhead."

"Am I missing something here?" Julia asked, confused by their conversation.

"Algee was just leaving," Luke said.

The big guy had no sooner walked out the door than Adele joined them from the kitchen. "Pretty fancy stuff, huh?"

Julia nodded. "It's incredible."

"Wait until you eat the dinner I've prepared for you two. It's ready now if you are."

"I guess we can dance later," Luke said, holding a chair out for Julia.

They dined on filet mignon, baby asparagus, and Adele's famous sweet potato fries, which Luke hand fed her. Dessert was a melt-in-your-mouth chocolate mousse accompanied by a bowl of cherries.

Luke took great pleasure in placing a cherry between her lips and then kissing her, nibbling on her and the fruit. She felt it was only fair to reciprocate. Meanwhile, the music from her high school years continued with Elton John's "The One."

"We never did get that dance," Luke murmured once the cherries were all gone. "Come on." He gently tugged her to her feet and into his arms.

At seventeen, Julia never imagined she'd ever be dancing with a hottie like Luke. The first time she heard "Take My Breath Away" by Berlin, she hadn't envisioned being held like this — so close to Luke that she could feel every breath he took. Even then, it wasn't close enough.

Adele cleared her throat. "Uh, I'm leaving now. Just thought I'd let you know."

"Thanks, Adele, for the delicious meal," Julia said without leaving Luke's arms.

"I'm glad you enjoyed it. Good night."

"Our chaperon is gone," Luke whispered against Julia's temple. "Want to make out?"

"Make out?"

"Mmmm. You know how to make out, don't you?"

"Put your lips together and blow?"

He cracked up. "I've turned you into a wanton woman."

"Are you complaining?"

"No way."

"Good."

"I just want this night to be special for you."

"It already is," she whispered.

"Then maybe we should continue this upstairs . . ." He swept her off her feet and lifted her in his arms to carry her upstairs. He had to lean down so she could open the apartment door, then he pretended to almost drop her, making her clutch her arms around his neck even tighter.

"I've gotta say, the view from here is great," he noted as he carried her inside.

"Are you looking down my dress?"

"Guilty as charged." He set her on her feet next to his bed.

"Maybe you should take a closer look," she suggested.

"Maybe I should."

Luke took his time with her, celebrating each moment as if it were the first. The first time he'd kissed her collarbone. The first time he'd nibbled on her earlobe. The first time he'd tickled the roof of her mouth with his tongue.

His hands moved to her dress, slowly undoing the ties that held the wrap-around bodice together. He unwrapped her as if she were the most precious and valuable of gifts. Where before they'd often tossed their clothes out of the way, now they lived in the moment, building the anticipation step by step. He slid the dress off one shoulder, kissing every inch of skin as he revealed it.

She responded by undoing his tie and slowly sliding it . . . bit by bit . . . out from under his shirt collar.

Luke slid her dress off the other shoulder as their mutual slow-motion striptease continued. Now every inch of bare skin revealed on that side had to have equal attention, his mouth caressing the rounded tip of her shoulder.

Julia unbuttoned his top shirt button and

slipped her index finger beneath to trace his collarbone with the tip of her nail.

He moved to her lacy black bra.

She undid more of his shirt buttons.

He toyed with the bra's front fastening, trailing his fingers along the edge of her lingerie.

She tugged the shirt from the waistband of his pants.

He lowered his head and kissed his way from the hollow of her throat down to the shadowy valley between her breasts.

She shoved his shirt off one shoulder.

He placed his open mouth directly over her lace-covered nipple.

She moaned with pleasure and threaded her fingers through his dark, silky hair.

He moved to her other breast and treated it with equal reverence.

She held him tight.

He undid her bra.

She shimmied out of it.

He lowered her dress past her hips until it fell in a silken heap on the floor.

She finally removed his shirt and undid the zipper on his trousers.

He murmured his appreciation of her thigh-high stockings and black satin bikini underwear.

She showed her appreciation of his

arousal by reaching inside his black cotton briefs to hold his velvety hard sex in her hand.

Luke traced his fingertip along the edge of her tiny panties, teasing her, stroking her near her core but never quite touching her there.

Julia trembled under the sweet torture and ran her fingertips along his throbbing length.

"Enough!" he growled, tumbling her back onto his bed.

Shoes were kicked off. His pants yanked off by them both. A condom rolled on with his guidance and her seductive help.

By now Julia's need for him was at a fever pitch. Every nerve in her body was at a heightened state and hypersensitive. He trailed his fingers up her inner thigh, removing her underwear as if unlocking the secrets of the world. He cupped her feminine mound, the palm of his hand creating a rhythmic pressure that made her burn inside.

"Now," she said.

"Now what?" He exquisitely tortured her, his skillful fingers brushing the crisp curls guarding her silken folds. "This?" He slipped one finger inside. "Or this?" He seduced her with two fingers now.

"No, this." She rolled him onto his back and sat atop him, using one hand to guide him to her and then easing down until the entire throbbing length of him was buried deep deep within her.

Their bodies slipped into a steady rhythm as she rocked on top of him and he met her thrust for thrust. Yes, the passion was intense. Yes, the pleasure was powerful.

But there was more. Julia felt more than just the physical connection with Luke. She felt bound to him heart and soul. Her hand was braced on his chest, where she could feel the thundering beat of his heart. Staring down at his face from this position, she marveled at the emotion in his mysterious eyes. At the raw passion etched on his face.

And when she finally came, she experienced the kind of remarkable seventh-chakra orgasm she'd only read about — the ultimate union of male and female energy.

Not because Luke was such an extraordinary lover, although he was. But because she loved him.

Exhausted, she collapsed beside him and cuddled close, murmuring the words against his shoulder before drifting off to sleep.

Luke froze. Had she just said she loved him?

He should have seen this coming. He should have done something to prevent it. Because she was in love with a man who didn't exist. He wasn't the man she thought he was. She looked at him with such faith and happiness, and he didn't have the heart to hurt her by telling her the truth.

Which meant he was as bad as Angel was, deceiving Julia in the name of protecting her. Not from danger, but from reality.

Maybe he'd just imagined she'd said the words. Maybe he was looking for trouble where none existed.

He'd take a wait-and-see position. He didn't want to examine his own emotions too closely, let alone hers. Doing that only complicated things.

If he were a better man, he'd walk away. But he couldn't do that. Not yet.

Chapter Sixteen

"This meeting is called to order," Walt proclaimed.

The March town meeting was held the fourth Tuesday night of the month in the courthouse, a white-columned building with an imposing brick facade. The room was unusually crowded this evening.

Normally Julia would rather eat Angel's awful yellow squash cookies than attend one of these things, but she'd gotten an official-looking notice in the mail advising her to be here tonight. So she'd come. And brought Pam with her for moral support.

Luke had come, too. He'd also gotten a notice and claimed he didn't want to miss the floor show.

The only empty seats left by the time they got there were in the front row. Luke actually brought a box of popcorn with him and leaned back in his chair as if he were attending a movie.

"Is it true that you're going to ban people showing their underwear in public?" The question came from Julia's neighbor Val.

"Blue-footed boobies don't wear underwear." Mr. Soames, who'd been quiet lately and hadn't visited the library much over the winter, was apparently back in his customary form.

"Don't put that in the official minutes," Walt instructed Edith. "I didn't recognize Mr. Soames . . ."

"What do you mean you don't recognize me?" the octogenarian demanded. "I've known you since before you were born."

"That's not actually possible," Walt replied.

"You never could see the big picture," Mr. Soames retorted.

"Maybe Walt needs to go over to the Goodwin Eye Care Center and get his vision tested like Sue Ellen did," someone in the back row suggested.

"Who said that?" Walt demanded in irritation.

Julia's neighbor Val raised her hand.

"You said that?" Walt's face showed his disbelief.

"No, I just wanted to point out that you never answered my question. About the underwear issue."

"It's obviously a good idea," Alice stood to inform everyone. "I've already discussed it with our U.S. Representative when I visited her in Washington, D.C., a few months back. The way some people are dressing these days, it's simply outrageous."

Alice was looking at Julia as she said that last word, even though Julia had never shown a centimeter of her underwear in public . . .

Wait, there was that one time when she'd worn the Bo Peep costume and Luke had carried her home.

But surely if Alice had spotted her then, she'd have said something before now.

"Your nephew, the mayor's son, wears clothing that shows the elastic band of his underwear," Mr. Soames of all people pointed out. "It even has some name on it. I don't need to have *my* vision tested," the old man added with a cackle.

"We don't have time for further discussion on this issue at the moment," Walt decided. "We'll shelve it for future discussion."

"Where do you plan on shelving it?" Mr. Soames demanded. "In the library? Because I heard a rumor that you were threatening to burn books there, Mr. Mayor. Is that true?"

Walt paused to give Luke a dirty look before replying. "Of course it's not true. It's a vicious lie, and if you'll tell me who said such a thing, I'll make sure they're punished."

"It was your son."

"Oh. Well, moving on . . ."

"Billy and I both enjoy extreme snowboarding, you know. We were really stoked about the world Superpipe last month."

Walt cleared his throat, clearly at a loss as to how to handle Mr. Soames. "Yes, well, as I said, moving on to the next item on the agenda tonight. It has come to our attention that a business or businesses were being run out of a private home in an area zoned as residential. The residence in question is located on Cherry Lane. 160 Cherry Lane, to be precise."

Pam elbowed Julia. "Hey, that's your address."

Julia stood up. "That's my house."

Walt nodded. "I believe it is."

"Are you talking about the llamas? You told me to keep them because you wanted to get on the *Late Show*. And because you wanted them as prognosticators."

"No, I'm not talking about the llamas."

"Good, because they're not living with me any longer and haven't been for a long time now."

Walt nodded again. "So I've heard."

"Then what are you talking about?"

"A school being run out of your home."

"A school?" Julia repeated, at a total loss.

"That's right." Walt tugged his reading glasses down from the top of his head where he'd shoved them and consulted his ever-ready clipboard of notes. "A yoga school and a belly-dancing school."

"There's no school."

"No?" He stared at her over the rim of his glasses. "It's my understanding that yoga and belly-dancing lessons were being offered."

"Well, yes they were, but . . ."

"And that a fee was involved?"

"In some cases, perhaps . . ."

"Then that's a business," Walt stated.

"No, it's not."

"Yes, it is."

To Julia's surprise, Mrs. Selznick came to her rescue. "Then what about your sister, Walt, doing manicures in her home? Or Mabel giving perms in her living room? Or you, Edith, giving piano lessons at home?"

"She has a point," Edith reluctantly admitted.

"Those yoga lessons were great," Dora Abernathy from the corner of Cherry Lane declared. "They really helped my arthritis."

"So did the belly-dancing," Sue Ellen stood up to say. "Helped my physical condition, I mean. Of course, I'm much too young to have arthritis yet." She paused to preen a moment. "My doctor says I've never been in better shape. And I've got new glasses, too," she added. "The Eye Care Center is running a two-for-one sale now through the end of the month, so be sure to check it out."

"The yoga lessons lowered my blood pressure," Patty from the library stated.

"Mine, too," Frasier the library director raised his hand to join to crowd.

"Both the belly-dancing and the yoga helped with my lower back pain." Laurie from the library added her two cents' worth.

"I think perhaps we'd better drop this item from the agenda," Edith suggested with a stern look at Walt. "It wasn't on my copy to begin with."

"Fine. Let's move on to complaint against the business establishment known as Maguire's. We are all in agreement that this is a business, correct?" The five members of the town council all nodded. "Then the complaint concerns the lascivious illustration on the premises."

"Hey, I took down that bikini babe calendar from Joe's Garage a long time ago," Luke said.

"We're not talking about a calendar.

We're talking about the mural you had commissioned."

"I don't know that *commissioned* is the right word to use . . ."

"Whatever word you used, you told Tyler to paint it and he did."

"Who told you that?"

"It's a logical assumption to make."

"Hey, I never claimed to be logical," Luke said.

"You're saying you don't have a mural on your wall?"

"No, I'm not saying that."

"Then what are you saying?"

"That I think this entire thing is ridiculous."

"Fine." Walt's voice reflected his increasing aggravation. "Duly noted. Put in the record that Luke Maguire refused to take the situation seriously."

"What situation?" Luke said.

"The situation involving the mural of a naked woman."

"She's not naked."

"Of course she is."

Luke raised an eyebrow. "Well, if *you* see her as being naked . . ."

"What do you mean?"

"She looks clothed to me. It's a modern abstract interpretation of the female form."

"A naked female form," Walt retorted.

"Are you sure you want to bring up these matters tonight?" Edith asked nervously. "What if someone from the BST committee is here undercover?"

"I checked everyone at the door when they came in, and Mabel is stationed there now."

"Locking us in, are you? Talk about a captive audience," Luke said.

"Mock all you want, but the bottom line here, Luke, is that you'll have to remove that mural or be closed down."

"It's a mural. It's painted on the wall. Unless you're telling me you want me to rip out the wall?"

"No, we're not unreasonable. You can have it painted over."

"Gee, that's real generous of you, Walt. I suppose you want me to paint it green like everything else in this town."

"Green is the official village color," Walt reminded him. "The board voted on it last year."

"I didn't know that," Mabel said. "I don't really care for green. I like blue much better."

"It brings out the color of my eyes, so I certainly like blue better," Sue Ellen said.

"Me, too!" Dora stated. "In fact, I'm

painting my green door blue as soon as I can. I'm sick of green." She stood and turned to the seated audience. "How many of you prefer blue to green?" A majority of hands popped up.

"Wait a second!" Walt protested.

"I voted nay on the green issue if you recall," Edith said. "It's all there in the meeting minutes."

"Who reads those?" Walt scoffed.

"I did," Tyler said from the back of the room. "And it appears you've got some legal discrepancies."

"This from the town handyman." Walt's voice was dismissive. "Have you been watching *Court TV* or something?"

"Or something," Tyler said. "It appears that you didn't have a quorum in several of your meetings and that you failed to notify the townspeople of the complete voting agenda. I can itemize the other problems as well, if you'd like. I've made a list."

Walt impatiently tapped on his clipboard. "This is ridiculous."

"Here." Tyler walked to the front of the room to hand over a printed sheet of paper to each town council member. "And here's a copy for the town attorney, your brother Phil."

"I thought Phil was a dentist," Dora said.

"He went to law school before dental school," Walt said defensively.

"I didn't realize he was our town attorney," Dora said. "What happened to old Mr. Weinstein?"

"He retired to Arizona two years ago."

"He did? I wondered why I hadn't seen him around town lately. But your brother?" Dora shook her head. "That doesn't sound right somehow."

"I voted nay on that one, too," Edith quickly stated. "But I was outvoted by everyone else."

"Let's not get distracted by these wild insinuations," RJ said. "Your town council has always worked hard to represent the best interests of the community."

"Really?" Luke noted. "Is that why you've entered secret negotiations with Kemp Enterprises to sell them rights to bottle water from the waterfalls?"

The audience gasped.

"But those falls belong to all of us," Val said.

"And any profit made from them would go into the town funds to help lower taxes," RJ replied.

"Wait a minute, I never authorized that," Walt said. "How can we be one of the Best Small Towns in America if we don't have the waterfalls?"

"Come on, it's just a tiny waterfall. We're not talking Niagara Falls here, folks." RJ tossed them his most congenial smile, but it didn't have much effect.

The residents of Serenity Falls, at least those present, were looking seriously pissed off.

Luke couldn't have been happier.

Well, yeah, he could have. But this unexpected turn of events made him smile. Having RJ on the hot seat for a change was satisfying. Not nearly as satisfying as hitting him would have been when he'd given Julia a hard time, but still . . .

"Serenity Falls is *not* for sale," Walt stated.

"That's right," Edith agreed.

"Absolutely," the Hinkler brothers said. They'd been on the town council since Nixon was president. They ran the local funeral home and had never really forgiven Luke for shooting out some of the lights from their sign.

"What happened to closing down Maguire's because of the pornographic mural?" RJ demanded.

"That was before we heard you might be closing down the falls," Mabel replied. "That's more important. Besides, that woman didn't look that naked to me."

"You were in Maguire's?" Alice sounded horrified. "You saw the mural?"

Mabel shrugged. "I had a hankering for some of Adele's delicious sweet potato fries. No one makes them like she does, you know. Edith was there with me."

Edith gasped and made quieting motions with her hands, which Mabel totally ignored.

"She also had a hankering for those fries," Mabel rambled on. "And some English ale, she called it. You know how she is about that limey stuff."

Edith looked like she might faint. "It was only one small glass," she protested.

"That's right," Mabel agreed. "I'm not saying she's a drunk like Alice's husband is. Anyway, I think we should shelve this topic, too, because someone's trying to open the door and get in here. We certainly wouldn't want outsiders hearing our dirty laundry."

"Or seeing it, either," Mr. Soames added. "For the record, I vote no on that underwear thing. I say, if you've got it, flaunt it. That's what the blue-footed boobies do."

"So you understand my dilemma, right?"

Lucy the llama nodded and nudged Angel for another piece of banana.

Angel gave it to her while continuing her

conversation with the animal. "I mean, if she's going to find out who her father is anyway, then maybe it would be best if I was the one to tell her. Tyler made a point of warning me that Luke was close to getting the information. No, I'm not seeing him. I mean, obviously I did see him or he couldn't have spoken to me. But it wasn't deliberate. I mean, I was just out sitting next to that pine tree I was telling you about the last time I visited you. Anyway, with the warmer weather now, Tyler has resumed his Rollerblading ways. He couldn't sleep and neither could I. So we chatted briefly. But that doesn't mean anything is going to happen. I won't let it. I'm determined to be an all-American mom to Julia."

Lucy looked perplexed.

"Yes, I realize she's thirty," Angel said. "An adult. But I never was a serious mom to her. I mean, I never fit the mold, you know? So I'm proving a point to her — that I can be normal. I've had that awful job at the pancake house for weeks now. Yes, I know it's bad karma to call the job awful. Instead, I should consider it a mere cosmic hiccup and a learning experience. But I get home and have to take a shower immediately to get the bacon smell out of my hair. But I haven't said a word to any of the patrons there about clogging their arteries. I've kept perfectly silent. And I've dated that guy Phil several times now. I confess, I do like his sense of humor, but there is absolutely no chemistry there. You know what I mean?"

Lucy nodded.

"Anyway, thanks for listening. I didn't mean to be unloading all this on you. I know you've got enough on your llama plate, what with trying to get pregnant and all. I don't want you to feel pressured. I hope you're settling in okay here? You and Ricky seem happy enough. But I sure do miss you both. Anyway, wish me luck tonight. I'm going to screw up my courage and give Julia what she's wanted for weeks. The name of her biological father."

Julia was having one of those days. The kind librarians write about in online blogs. Nothing was going right. All the copy machines on the premises had gone on the blink. The new teenage library clerk had mishelved three bookcarts' worth of books who knew where. The library's computer system was down for an hour, then up for ten minutes, down another hour, up five minutes, down two hours.

And then there was Luke. Julia was worried that she might have slipped up and revealed that she loved him that night last month when he'd created a prom experience for her.

The thing was, she couldn't be sure if she'd just dreamt that or not. Her memory was hazy. Her mind and body had been so saturated with total satisfaction from making love to him. There was a chance she'd murmured the words before dozing off. Or maybe not.

She had yet to figure out what really happened. What she'd really said.

It wasn't as if she could just casually say, *You know I dreamt I told you I loved you, but that didn't really happen did it?* It would be like saying the words all over again and then he'd know.

Luke hadn't said the words to her. She couldn't say them to him. Not yet. She wasn't like Skye, blurting out every word that came into her brain. At least, she usually wasn't that way. But since she'd started sleeping with Luke, Julia had changed a lot of her old ways.

Still . . . telling him she loved him could be disastrous. Maybe he loved her. When he did things like create that prom for her, she believed he did.

Or maybe he didn't.

She was trying so hard to just live in the

moment instead of having a plan. And all the while, she kept silently questioning herself and who she was because of the fact that she had an unknown father out there somewhere.

And now, to top off her weird day, her mother walked into the library. "Are you coming home right after work?"

Noting the way her mother was nervously tugging on the bland beige windbreaker she wore, Julia became suspicious. "Why?"

"I . . . uh . . . have that information you've wanted for a long time. The name. But I can't talk to you about it here."

"No," Julia immediately agreed, her stomach shot through with butterflies the size of T-Rexes. "Not here. I'll come home right after work. Or I can leave a few minutes early. Now, in fact. Now is a good time." She didn't want her mother chickening out and changing her mind about revealing her father's name. "Just wait a minute while I get my things."

Julia told Patty that she had to leave early. "After a day like today, I don't blame you. Go ahead," Patty said. "We'll cover for you."

Ten minutes later, Julia and Angel were sitting in Julia's living room. Her mother was still as nervous as a cat in a room full of rocking chairs. "Would you like some tea?"

Angel began before answering the question herself. "No, of course not. You just want one thing. The name. Oh, I uh . . . I got you this . . ." Angel reached around the corner of the couch to grab a box of Pop-Tarts. "I know they're your comfort food."

"You think I'm going to need comforting after I hear this news?"

"I don't know about you, but I sure will," Angel said. She coughed nervously.

"Maybe you should make some tea for yourself. Or I could do it," Julia said.

"Would you? That's sweet of you, but I can do it." They both ended up heading for the kitchen. "You've been working all day."

"So have you." Julia put the kettle on the stove while Angel reached for her stash of tea bags and a mug.

"I only worked this morning. From five to noon. Then I went to visit the llamas. It's so peaceful out there, driving along narrow country lanes behind clip-clopping black buggies driven by farmers wearing wide-rimmed black hats. And all the farms are so pristinely kept. It's just such a serene land-scape that it soothes the soul."

They both were silent until the kettle boiled. Once Angel had her tea and Julia her trusty Pop-Tart, they headed back to the living room couch. Julia was surprised to notice that her mother sat very primly, ankles daintily crossed instead of her usual flowing, free style. And she was wearing khaki, as she did just about every day now, along with a white shirt. Gone were the colorful skirts in Indian cotton, the flowing tunics, the bells on her toe rings, the toe rings themselves.

As if reading her mind, Angel said, "I hope you've noticed the changes I've made over the past weeks. I've gone completely respectable. I've gotten a job, a normal job. And I'm seeing a normal man, very respectable. I'm dressing conservatively to fit right in with everyone else in town. I stopped writing letters to the editor of the *Serenity News* about the terrible effect on children's health of having soda machines in the school cafeterias and how they should be replaced with fresh fruit stands. I also stopped writing letters about saving the Arctic Reserve from greedy oil companies, about protecting animal rights, about . . ."

"I never asked you to do any of that," Julia interrupted her to say. "I only asked for one thing . . ."

"I know. You want the name of your biological father." Angel took a deep breath. "Tyler thinks I should tell you."

Her words stung. Angel was still talking to

others about Julia, and it hurt that she appeared to value their opinion more than hers. "Did you ask Phil the dentist, too?"

"Of course not!"

"I thought you weren't seeing Tyler."

"I'm not. I ran into him one night in the park when he was Rollerblading and I was . . . never mind." Angel wasn't about to tell her that she'd been trying to soak up energy from a pine tree. "Anyway, Tyler merely said that I should tell you everything."

"He's right."

"I know that now. But it isn't easy." Angel took several calming sips of tea while surreptitiously trying to study her daughter and gage her mood. Julia was sitting at the edge of the couch, turned toward Angel with anticipation. She was nervously nibbling on the Pop-Tart. Angel had hoped that giving her the junk food had earned her brownie points.

Angel took a deep breath in an attempt to encourage more life-force energy to flow through her lungs and entire body. She needed to view this event not as a terrifying ordeal, but instead as a speed bump on the path to mystic illumination.

Outside, the earlier threat of drizzle had turned into a steady downpour. The ping of raindrops hitting the windows created a strangely soothing sound effect for Angel.

The time had come. She was in a calm state of consciousness now.

"Your father's name is Adam . . ." Angel began, and then the fear returned ten-fold. "Stop that. You need to let go of your negative thought flow," she muttered to herself.

"His name is Adam . . ." Julia repeated. "Adam what?"

"Adam . . . Adam . . . K . . . K . . ."

"Adam Kaka?"

Angel shook her head and took a gulp of tea. The warm liquid helped relax her frozen vocal cords. Words came out in a rush. "Before I tell you, you have to swear to me that you'll listen to the entire story, to everything I have to tell you about him."

"I promise." Julia didn't like to see her mother so upset. That wasn't her intent. It never had been.

"He's ruthless, you know. Adam Kemp. That's his name. He makes Donald Trump look like a wimp. I knew if he ever found out about you, he'd take you from me. He had the money and the power to do that. I had to protect you. So I didn't tell you. I thought I'd tell you when you were eighteen, but you'd just started college and I didn't want to upset you. So I pushed the deadline back to twenty-one, but you were frazzled with graduate school by then. And after that I just felt so guilty that I couldn't work up the nerve to tell you until now. That was wrong of me."

"Adam Kemp?" Julia repeated. "My biological father is . . . Adam Kemp?"

Angel nodded.

"But he's . . ."

"Rich. Yes, I warned you about that. I didn't realize he was rich when I first took up with him, of course. I already told you that. And he wasn't as wealthy then as he probably is now."

"He was on a recent cover of *Forbes*. He's quadrupled his family's net worth. Actually, it said his family was almost broke, that they'd invested unwisely, and would have been lost without him. That he'd actually broken off and started a company of his own, which is hugely successful. He's got a new book coming out. The library has it on order."

"You already sound like you're impressed with him. Keep in mind that this man has bought dozens of companies and then laid off workers, putting thousands of people out of work. Is that something you think is a good thing?"

"Of course not. I'm just . . ."

"Stunned, confused, dismayed, and dazed?"

"Yeah, I guess."

"Me, too. I think maybe we should break out the alcohol now," Angel said. "What do you think?"

"Good idea," Julia agreed.

Luke frowned at the sound of something hitting his apartment window. Was it hailing outside? He thought the earlier rain had stopped.

Abandoning the punching bag he'd been working out with, he moved to the window and opened it, only to quickly sidestep a handful of small stones. "What the hell?"

"Luke? It's me."

"Me who?" he asked, even though he knew the answer.

"The belly-dancing librarian."

"What's the secret code word?"

"Straight shooter." She started climbing the metal fire escape.

"What are you doing?"

"I need to talk to you."

"So call me. You don't have to resort to gravel morse code against my window pane."

"My cell phone was dead." Julia climbed in the window.

"You could have used a regular phone. It's almost midnight."

"I know. I'm not drunk."

He held her as she swayed. "Of course you're not."

"No, really. I only had one glass of wine. It's more like shock. Angel told me who my father is tonight. Told me his name. Adam —"

"Kemp. Yeah, I know."

"You know? And you didn't tell me?" She punched his arm with enough force to make him say "Hey!"

"Don't *hey* me," she angrily retorted. "If you knew, why didn't you tell me?"

"I only found out tonight."

"Swear to me. I mean it. Swear to me on . . . on your Harley. May you never ride another Harley in your entire life if you lie. Go ahead, say it."

"May I never ride another Harley if I lie."

"You left out the *in your entire life* part. Say it again."

He did so, his voice filled with exasperation.

"I'm sorry." She cupped his face with her hands. "Just don't ever lie to me, okay? I can take the truth, but I can't take any more lies. Promise me."

"I promise." Even as he said the words, Luke wondered if he even remembered how to tell the truth — and nothing but the truth — anymore.

Chapter Seventeen

Angel nervously adjusted the fuzzy knit scarf around her neck and eyed the people in the line ahead of her. She was trying to look on all of this as a life-enhancing exercise, but she was finding it difficult. After all, she was standing in a Philadelphia bookstore where Adam Kemp was signing his latest book *MONEY, MONEY!* this evening.

Angel had read about his appearance in the newspaper a few weeks ago. Since then, she'd tried to come up with the right way to tell Adam that he had a daughter. Julia had no idea what Angel intended to do.

The bottom line was that it wasn't fair for Julia to shoulder the burden of telling Adam what had occurred. If there was any wrath to be faced from the mega-billionaire, Angel planned on facing it herself and shielding her daughter.

Trying to avoid a panic attack, Angel practiced a few deep-breathing techniques and distracted herself by studying Adam's aura as he sat at the table signing books. Lots of red and brown going on — no surprise there, considering red indicated strong energy and brown represented industry and organization.

As for the man himself, he'd aged well. His hair was expensively cut and streaked with silver. His face had an expression of power and confidence while his hazel eyes looked at those around him as if sizing them up and finding most of them lacking.

"Name?" the harried bookstore clerk barked at her.

"I, uh, Angel."

The clerk wrote it down and moved to the next person in line.

Only three people ahead of her now. Then two. One who talked a bit and wanted mortgage advice. "Read my book," Adam replied with a salesman's laugh.

"Next," another clerk ordered, motioning Angel forward.

This was it. Do or die. "Ethics class, UCLA, you, me, we had sex. We have a daughter. Do the DNA. We need to talk."

Adam stared at her blankly for a moment while she hurriedly drew another breath.

"Security!" the bookstore clerk called out.

"No," Adam said, staring closely at Angel. "I know her."

She was frankly surprised that he remembered her all these years later. True, she hadn't really changed all that much. Her hair was as curly and long as it was then, still parted down the center, still the same brown color. "I'm sorry to barge in on your booksigning, but I had to speak to you and this is important."

Adam motioned over a lackey in a suit, an employee of his obviously. "Have her wait in the limo."

Angel eyed Adam suspiciously. Maybe that was some kind of code line that really meant "Get rid of this nutcase, pronto!"

"I can wait here," Angel said. "I'll just stand over there, out of the way —"

But the suited man was already escorting her out. If he tried to get rid of her instead of putting her in a limo, she was going to stage a sit-in.

It wouldn't be the first time. She'd dressed accordingly, wearing jeans and a thick sweater. After all, it was April and the weather could turn fickle — it was seventy yesterday but right now it was only in the low forties.

"This way please," the lackey said, leading her to a stretch limo.

As he held the door open for her, Angel abruptly wondered if Adam had any mob connections. Weren't they always driving off trouble-makers in limos, never to be seen again?

Maybe she should have told someone where she was going, what she planned on doing. What if she disappeared, never to be heard from again?

Who would teach Toni to read auras? Or tarot cards? And what about the llamas? Who would pay for their care? Would Julia sell the animals on the Internet? Would she break them up and sell them to different people? Ricky and Lucy were a couple. What if Lucy was pregnant? The baby would never know its father. Ricky would be a good father llama. He had heart. Unlike Adam Kemp. He probably wouldn't think twice about making Angel disappear. She should have discussed all these things with Julia. She'd know what to do. She always did.

Luckily, Angel didn't have time to conjure up any other wild scenarios in her head because Adam joined her.

The lackey handed him a sheaf of papers, a few of which Adam signed and handed back, and the others he studied before looking at her. The lackey, meanwhile, got out and sat in the front of the limo with the driver, leaving Adam alone with her.

"So, Angel, you've been a busy girl, I see."

411

Adam indicated the papers he held in his hands. "Which daughter is the one you're claiming is mine? Julia or Skye?"

Her jaw dropped. "How do you know their names?"

"Come on," he chided her. "Surely you don't think you're the first woman to accuse me of being the father of their child?"

"I never bothered thinking about it."

"Seems you do a lot of that. Not bothering to think things through. A tofu hot dog stand in Fairbanks, Alaska?" He raised an eyebrow at her. "Come on. What were you thinking?"

"Hey, they eat caribou meat up there. Who knew they'd turn up their noses at tofu?"

"Market research could have told you that. But getting back to this daughter thing —"

"She's not a *thing*," Angel said indignantly. "She's a wonderful person."

"After my money, no doubt."

"She doesn't want your money, you ass! She's a librarian. She wants information."

"To blackmail me with?"

"No!"

"So *you're* the one who wants money. I've already had you investigated." He impatiently tapped the papers with his finger.

"But it's only been a few minutes —"

"I pay people to be the best and be quick about it. The information is preliminary but enlightening. Getting back to your finances, it's not like you're rolling in the green stuff."

"Hey, you were the one who made money your god, not me. I can do without solid gold faucets, believe me." She'd read something about that in an article about him.

"What about paying the rent?" Adam retorted. "Can do you do without that?"

"I don't need your money. The only thing I need from you is for you to behave like a halfway decent human being for a change. Be kind to our daughter. Give her time, not money. Let her get to know you. Maybe once she does, she'll realize what an ass you are and will write you off and kick you out of her life."

"I'm not in her life."

"She wants you to be."

Adam rubbed his forehead. "Why didn't you tell me about her all those years ago?"

"What would you have done if I had told you?"

"I don't know. You never gave me the chance to find out."

"I'm giving you the chance now. The chance to get to know your daughter. It's a gift beyond value. *She's* a gift beyond value. Don't blow this."

"I'm going to need those DNA tests for verification. The only reason I didn't let them toss you out of that store is because there's a chance she could be my daughter. Shortly after our time together, I had a medical situation that left me unable to have children. So any woman who tried to claim she had my child after a relationship with me after that date was lying. But you . . . this could be possible."

"I'm sorry you couldn't have any more children." Her voice softened.

His face hardened. "You try and sell that story to anyone or repeat it to anyone, and I'll sue the pants off you."

"I can keep a secret."

"Obviously. You kept my daughter from me for what . . . thirty years now. The only child I'd ever have!"

She could tell he was getting riled up. Part of her couldn't blame him. The other part wanted to protect Julia from his anger. "Blame me, not my daughter."

Adam quickly got himself under control again. "I'll arrange for that DNA test immediately, and we'll go from there."

"Go where?" Angel asked.

"We'll see." Adam's cell phone rang. He spoke for a few minutes and then the limo smoothly pulled over. "My driver will take you wherever you need to go."

"My VW is parked back by the bookstore. You know, you really should be conserving gasoline by using a more fuel-efficient vehicle. How many miles per gallon does this thing get?"

"I have no idea."

Angel quickly got out of the limo. "Well, you should think about these things now. You're a parent. You should work to preserve this planet for your children and grandchildren. So I'll walk back to the bookstore instead of having your driver waste the gasoline to take me there."

"Suit yourself. You always have."

As she watched him walk away, she wasn't sure if he'd just insulted her or given her a compliment.

Julia started her day bright and early with a swab test to confirm her DNA was the same as Adam Kemp's, the twelfth richest man in America. She still couldn't believe her mother had taken things into her own hands and gone off to see him at a booksigning, of all things, to tell him about her.

When Julia had asked what his reaction was to the news that he had a daughter, all

Angel had said was that he was surprised but pleased. Then she'd gone into the whole "who wouldn't want you for a daughter" spiel. Which told Julia nothing at all.

"Today's the big day," Patty greeted her as Julia walked in the library's staff entrance at the back of the building.

For a second, Julia's heart stopped. "Big day?" Did Patty know about the DNA test? How? Sure Alice was good at ferreting out info and gossip, but even so . . .

"The Best Small Towns judging committee is making their official visit to the library today," Patty said. "You didn't forget, did you?"

Julia had. "Of course not," she fibbed.

"They're supposed to be here in a few minutes. At least we've got good weather today. The daffodils are up around the front entrance. Those few days of unusually warm weather we had really made things pop around here. Even the star magnolias are blooming. I just hope we don't get a frost to kill everything now that it's come out. The tender shoots might not survive that."

Tender shoots. That's how Julia felt at the moment. Like a tender shoot . . . all vulnerable and easily damaged by any coldness aimed her way by her as-yet-unfamiliar father.

Note to self: Get over it.

She couldn't afford to let her emotions be so easily affected, to wear them on her sleeve. She needed to hold back, put up some protective walls, and see for herself what Adam was like before making any further judgment calls.

Of course, she'd spent the early dawn hours researching him on the Internet. Nothing she'd found had reassured her that he had a warm and fuzzy side.

"I'm so excited about all this," Patty was saying. "I didn't think I would be, but I am. How about you?"

"I'm excited, too."

"What do you think our chances are?"

"I have no idea," Julia replied, eager to return to work where she could bury herself in familiarity.

An hour later, Frasier brought a group of people over to the reference desk. A wild thought streaked through Julia's head. Could they tell she was the illegitimate daughter of a multibillionaire? Her outfit sure didn't show it. The black tailored pants and pink sweater set didn't scream haute couture. But at least she wasn't wearing a green polo shirt with the library logo on it. She'd managed to nix that idea, despite Alice's best efforts to ram it through.

Frasier made the introductions, but she didn't really register their names. All she noted was that there were four judges, two women, two men. "This is Julia Wright, our reference librarian."

"Didn't I see you on the news?" one of the woman judges asked her.

Julia almost freaked. Had the news come out about her relationship with Adam Kemp already? How had that happened?

"I know," the woman continued. "It had to do with those llamas, right?"

Julia nodded and resumed breathing again. The llamas. Right. She really did need to stop obsessing about her father and focus on the matter at hand here.

"Doesn't your mother knit those fabulous berets and scarves they sell in a shop here in town?" another woman asked. "I bought a set when I was visiting undercover a few weeks ago. She really does beautiful work."

"Thank you. I'll tell her."

"Are you a longtime resident of Serenity Falls, Julia?" This question came from the older male judge.

"I've been here more than three years."

"What made you select this town over any other?"

She told them the same thing she'd told Luke all those months ago. "I fell in love

418

with it the first time I saw it, nestled in these beautiful wooded hills. It seemed too good to be true."

"And is it?"

"No."

"What would you say is the town's biggest asset?"

"There are too many for me to list just one. But a top five list would include, in random order, the town square; the downtown area with its mix of colonial, federal, and Victorian buildings; the waterfalls; the public library; and of course the friendly people who live here."

"Well said. And the town's biggest drawback?"

The people who live here. But she couldn't really say that.

Alice. But that was another answer she couldn't use. Then it finally came to her.

"No good Thai take-out," Julia replied with a grin. "I sometimes miss that."

"Thank you for speaking with us," the judge said, pausing to shake her hand. "We really appreciate it. By the way, how are those llamas doing?"

"Just fine."

"Good, glad to hear it."

As he walked away with the judges, Frasier gave her a thumbs-up sign behind his back. That or he had an itch between his shoulder blades. She couldn't be sure which. Just as she couldn't be sure what she would do or say when she finally came face to face with her father.

After work, Julia headed to Maguire's to fill Luke in on the latest. He had one of the servers take over his bartending duties and took Julia upstairs so they could talk privately.

"My mother went to see Adam Kemp at a booksigning in Philadelphia yesterday evening and confronted him."

"She did what? Do you have any idea how risky that was?"

"I didn't know she was going to do it." Julia sat on the couch a second before bouncing up and pacing the room. "What do you mean, risky?"

"He could have sicced security on her for one thing."

"It wouldn't be the first time that's happened."

"We're not talking about letting the lobsters go free at a restaurant. We're talking about a powerful guy here. He's got a lot of connections. Adam Kemp has a reputation for being ruthless, doing whatever it takes to get whatever he wants. He isn't above cutting a corner or two to keep things profitable."

"Yes, I gathered that much when I was researching him on the Internet earlier today. But enough about me." Even thinking about it made her edgy. "The Best Small Towns judges visited the library today. Did they come to Maguire's, too?"

"Yeah, they stopped by for a minute or two. Asked me what my favorite thing was in this town. I said you. Then they asked me my least favorite thing."

"And you said?"

"Everything else in town. They seemed to think I was kidding, so I let them go on thinking that. They had some of Adele's sweet potato fries and left. They never did get to see the magnificent mural in the pool room."

"That mural isn't why I think that room is magnificent," Julia noted with a sassy grin.

Luke raised a dark eyebrow. "No?"

"No."

"Then why do you have fond memories of that room?"

"You don't remember?" she murmured, moving closer to seductively walk her fingertips down his chest. "You were there."

"Really?" He looped his arms around her waist and tugged her close. "I was present?"

421

"You were more than just present. You were extremely . . . active. And very educational. Downright illuminating, in fact."

"Really?"

"Absolutely." She peeled off his T-shirt and reached for his jeans zipper. "Maybe I should refresh your memory a bit?"

"I don't have a pool table up here."

"I think we can improvise, don't you?" She shoved him backward onto the bed.

"Affirmative."

She straddled his hips and stared down at him with deliberate doubt. "You're sure a straight-shooter like you can improvise?"

He clearly believed actions spoke louder than words, because he had her naked and was embedded deep within her seconds later. He then proceeded to show her how much he could improvise, muffling her scream of pleasure with his mouth.

Luke was wiping down the bar when Walt walked into Maguire's the next day, shortly after noon. It was the first time the mayor had stopped by since Luke had returned to Serenity Falls six months ago.

"I've asked RJ to resign," he abruptly informed Luke.

"If you're asking me if I want to take his place on the town council, the answer is no."

"That's not why I'm here."

"No? Then did you come to see the mural for yourself?"

"No. I came here to thank you for letting me know about RJ's dealings regarding the waterfalls. I had no idea. I do wish you'd told me privately instead of in front of the entire town at the last meeting —"

"The entire town wasn't there," Luke stated.

"You know what I mean."

"We haven't exactly been on close speaking terms."

"No, I realize that. You and Billy appear to have hit it off, though." Walt sounded a bit resentful of that fact.

Luke shrugged. "I just showed an interest in his life. Do you have any idea of what sort of things he likes? It sure as hell isn't football."

"Is that right? What makes you an expert on kids?"

"I'm not. But I know what it takes to be a bad seed, and I see that happening with Billy. So just talk to your kid, mayor. You might be surprised what you learn."

"Your father would never have painted Maguire's red."

"Exactly."

"So you did it to get back at him."

423

"I did it because I wanted to."

"And you always do what you want, no matter who it hurts? You know people are talking about you and Julia."

"People are always talking about something in this town." Luke refused to feel guilty. Julia hadn't said she loved him again. They were just two consenting adults having great sex.

Telling himself that somehow no longer convinced him it was true. The sex was great. But something else was going on here and that freaked him out. He'd never been with a woman who made him feel the way she did. Making love to her wasn't enough. He wanted to protect her, to take care of her.

When he'd first seen her standing by the library's pond in her Bo Peep costume, he'd never anticipated that she'd have this kind of effect on him. She made him wish he was some sort of superhero from one of those comic books Algee sold. The kind that could make good on his promises.

Not that he'd made any to her. Not aloud anyway. But she was still basically a picket-fence kind of female, despite her new good-girl-gone-bad persona. And he was still a rolling stone.

He was her way of thumbing her nose at

propriety. He'd painted Maguire's red as a gesture of rebellion. Going to bed with him was her gesture of rebellion.

Luke didn't even realize that Walt had left the building, that's how consumed he'd been with his own thoughts about Julia.

Maybe Algee was right. Maybe Julia was Luke's weakness.

Or maybe he was hers.

"Are you nervous?" Pam asked Julia as they waited at one of Philadelphia's top-notch eateries for Adam Kemp to show up.

Julia nodded. "I think I ate half a bottle of Tums last night. Thanks for coming with me," she added.

"No thanks are necessary. I think Luke was a bit ticked off that you wouldn't let him come."

"I didn't want him punching Adam if he said something wrong."

"I may not have as mean a right hook as Luke, but I took some tae kwon do lessons at the Park District last year. So if you need protecting . . ."

Julia laughed at the image of her petite and perky friend taking on Adam. "I'll keep that in mind if I need backup."

"There he is." Pam pointed to the silver-haired man walking in the entrance. The maître d' rushed over to him, greeting him with marked deference and quickly escorting him to their table.

"Which one of you is my supposed daughter?" Adam Kemp stood there looking from Julia to Pam and back again. "You." He pointed to Julia. "It's you."

"So I've been told."

Adam frowned. "You don't sound like you believe it."

"Neither do you."

"Something we both have in common." Adam took a seat. "Well, ladies, what are you having? The prime rib here is excellent. Really one of the very best in the country. It's not every day a man hears he has a daughter. Lunch is on me."

"You make it sound like this is just another business deal."

"How do you want me to sound?"

"I don't know. More human."

"I can assure you, I'm very human."

"Weren't you surprised to find out you had a grown daughter? This is my friend Pam, by the way. Not that you asked."

Adam nodded his acknowledgment of the introduction and then answered Julia's question. "Yes, I was surprised. But life is a constantly evolving situation. You make adjustments or you fail."

"A constantly evolving situation? You sound like Angel."

"Your mother and I really have little in common."

"So I've been told."

"She raised you to be like her, I suppose."

He was only with her a few minutes and already he sounded disappointed in her. Julia tried not to be upset, but this entire conversation was extremely unsettling for her. Apparently not for him, however. "You suppose wrong. She raised me to think for myself."

"I hear you're a librarian."

"That's right."

"In a regular library?"

What did he think? That she worked in a nudist library? "Serenity Falls Public Library."

"Serenity Falls, huh? One of my subsidiaries was investigating a business opportunity there. But the deal fell through."

Great. Her father had been involved with trying to ruin the town's scenic pride and joy — the waterfalls. She'd forgotten that incident at the town meeting but now recalled that Luke had said Kemp Enterprises had talked with RJ about the project.

But right now, Adam sat across the table from her, looking entirely too much like the

PR photo on the back of his book. She wanted to shake that bedrock confidence of his. "Angel says you're ruthless."

He was totally unfazed. "She says you're interested in information. What do you want to know about me?"

"What do you want to know about me?" she countered, playing for time.

"I already know a great deal about you. I had you investigated. There's a file on my desk with all the details."

"Then why ask me what library I worked at?"

Adam shrugged. "I didn't recall all the details."

"Right." His answer stung. "A little detail like a daughter might get in the way of your big-business decisions."

"Not really. I try to keep my personal life separate from my professional life."

"How tidy. I really can't picture you and my mother as a couple."

"We got together. It was nice and then it was over. End of story. Now let's order."

He did so for both Julia and Pam.

Then he asked Julia, "Do you have your mother's aversion to wealth?"

His question caught her off-guard and without a quick answer.

"Money is better than poverty, if only for

financial reasons. That's a Woody Allen quote, but it's true," he continued. "If I'd known about you when you were a child, you wouldn't have wanted for anything. I'd have made sure of that. You would have gone to the best boarding schools, gotten the best education, had the best opportunities."

He used the word *best* a lot. She noticed that when reading his book, which she'd picked up at a local bookstore the day before. That and the words *take control*. He'd used those a lot in the book as well. Take control of your subordinates. Take control of your life.

Julia had always liked control, but since meeting Luke, she'd learned that losing control could bring more happiness than she'd thought possible.

"I take my responsibilities seriously," Adam added.

Julia always had as well. But listening to him go on about the need to deliver successful results in life left her feeling very unsettled. Because that list of things Adam had said he could have given her were all material things. But maybe that's all he had to offer. Too bad it wasn't anything she really valued.

"Hey, sexy, want a ride?"

Julia turned at the sound of Luke's voice. She hadn't imagined it. He was there. Leaning against his big, bad Harley. Wearing those black jeans and T-shirt he'd had on when he'd first roared into Serenity Falls. Only now he was outside the restaurant in Philadelphia. Adam had already left. Julia had taken some time to compose herself in the ladies' room afterward, unsure why she'd gotten all teary-eyed. Lack of sleep, stress, disappointment — there were lots of possible reasons. "What are you doing here?"

"You really are gonna have to stop asking me that."

"Luke's here," Julia told Pam, who'd just come through the revolving door and joined them.

"I see that. It's okay if you want to go back with him," Pam said.

And so it was that Julia found herself on the back of Luke's Harley, her arms wrapped around his waist, her skirt hitched up above her knees, her legs pressed against his, her cheek pressed against his warm back.

She loved this man with every fiber of her being. He'd come all the way to Philadelphia and waited for her just to be certain she was okay. Surely that meant he felt something for her?

As they rode home, Julia closed her eyes and imagined the two of them together forever. Luke running Maguire's and grumbling about Adele's bossiness. Her becoming library director and firing Alice. Them having children who'd grow up safely in Serenity Falls, enjoying everything that was good about living in a small town. A boy with Luke's blue eyes and a girl with her own hazel eyes. Their daughter would be able to wrap Luke around her little finger.

They'd buy a bigger house. He'd teach their son to throw a football. She'd read to their children. So would he. Their home would be filled with love and laughter and books and happiness.

Julia's earlier dissatisfaction with today's first meeting with her father was replaced with the warm glow of her love for Luke. It didn't matter who her father was. That was her past. Her future was with Luke.

As they roared into Serenity Falls, Julia felt such a sense of homecoming. This was where she belonged. Here, in this peaceful town with Luke.

Which was why she blinked at the brand-new For Sale sign clearly displayed in front of Maguire's when they pulled up.

"Look, someone put up a sign by mistake," Julia said.

That's when Luke said the words that shattered her dreams. "It's not a mistake."

Chapter Eighteen

Julia reached out for something stable to hold onto. The only thing handy was one of the city's quaint iron lampposts with a cheerful *Welcome Spring* banner fluttering from the top.

Her legs had been trembling since she'd gotten off the Harley — not because of the ride, but because of Luke's words. Maybe she hadn't heard him correctly. "What do you mean?"

"I want to dump this place. You knew I never liked it here. I've been in limbo waiting it out. I had to stay or lose the money . . ."

"So this is all about the money?"

"Yeah, it's about the money," he drawled. "Not all of us discover out of the blue that we're related to billionaires."

Luke saw the hurt take hold in her eyes and it killed him. But it was time he faced facts here. He was a broke, burnt-out former FBI agent. He was no great catch by any stretch of the imagination. And not a white-picket-fence, putting-down-roots, buying-a-Berkalounger kinda guy.

He wasn't doing her any favors by letting her build a dream world around him. He was not hero material. She could do so much better. He had to make her see that, for her own good. And so he continued on in the same vein. "I never said I'd stay here. You knew that. The terms of my father's will were simple. To inherit this place, I had to stay six months. Well, honey, it's been six months to the day." He was deliberately blunt.

Seeing the tears she blinked away tore him up inside. So did the pain and confusion in her voice.

"Why did you come get me in Philadelphia? Why not just let me come back and find the sign on my own? Or were you deliberately trying to rub my nose in it?"

Going to get her had been a mistake. He'd been worried about her. And the truth was that Luke had told his lawyer when he'd first heard about the will and its terms to put the place on the market the minute the six months was over with. The For Sale sign hadn't been there when he'd left earlier that day.

But it was a "sign" indicating it was time he moved on. Luke had gotten in much too deep here, much deeper than he'd expected.

Maybe if her dad had been a laid-off plumber or something, maybe then he'd think differently. Maybe not. He'd never been good at commitment. Had never learned to trust the concept of long-term plans.

Until now. Until Julia.

But that didn't change the fact that his life was still a mess while hers was taking off. Adam Kemp could give her things Luke couldn't. And Serenity Falls could give her the stability she'd always wanted.

How could he compete with a billionaire and a contender for Best Small Town in America?

What could he offer her? A life on the road? She had grown roots here, loved it here, had family here.

He'd never answered her last question, but she didn't seem to notice. Instead she said, "I thought you'd changed."

Her words hit him the wrong way. "Big mistake."

"I see that now. Why didn't you say anything to me before this? You never told me you were going to sell. Didn't you think I deserved to know?"

"I'm really not good at this relationship stuff."

It was nice, and then it was over. Julia remembered her father saying that about him and Angel. And now here she was, hearing Luke basically tell her the same thing.

"So you're ready to move on, is that it?" Her voice was choked with emotion and the strain of refusing to cry in front of him.

"Affirmative."

"Alone."

Luke nodded. "It's what I do best."

No, what he did best was break her heart into a million pieces.

"Come back later," Luke growled at the man who walked through Maguire's front entrance.

The crusty old attorney who'd worked for his father wasn't intimidated. Instead, he was all business. "I can't do that. Your father was very specific in his instructions that I was to give this letter to you the moment the six-month period was over. And that you were to read it before the terms of the will would be considered fulfilled."

Eager to get this mess over with, Luke ripped open the envelope.

Luke, if you're reading this it means that I've kicked the bucket and you've completed the six-month requirement of my will. I wanted you to come home again and knew this was the only chance of that happening. Some people say you can't go home again. I'm not one of them. I know you blamed me for your mother's death, and you know that I blamed you. We were both wrong. I'm not the kind of guy to get all mushy, so I'll just say that life is shorter than you think, and the years go by without you even realizing it.

What, you were expecting some brilliant words of wisdom from me? I don't have 'em. I could tell you to keep Maguire's, but that would probably just make you sell it. So all I'll say is good-bye.

Tommy Maguire

Luke crumpled the letter into a ball. Even at the end, the old man couldn't sign off as "Dad."

At least he'd gotten one thing right. Luke *had* blamed him for his mother's death. His father had never insisted she see a doctor. One of them might have found her heart condition and saved her. That's what the childhood Luke had always thought. Now the adult Luke wasn't so sure.

Either way, it was time to let go of the past and lay those old ghosts to rest. There was no changing things now.

Having fulfilled his responsibilities, the lawyer made a hasty exit but was soon replaced by an infuriated Adele. "I come into work and find a For Sale sign out front." Her hands were clenched into fists, as if she wanted to take a swing at him. "You couldn't tell me beforehand?"

"I couldn't tell anyone. My father's idea, not mine. Blame him."

"You've spent enough time blaming him."

Luke didn't even wince at the blow. It was a truthful statement. He realized that now. "You're right."

"If you knew all this time that you'd be leaving, why did you hook up with Julia? I thought things were serious with you two."

"Because I'm a no-good bastard."

"I'm not letting you off that easily. You want to know what I think?"

"Not at all."

"I'm going to tell you anyway."

"I had a feeling you would."

"I think you're afraid. I think you're scared spitless."

"Of what?"

"Of what you've got with Julia. Of the fact that you've fallen for her. Fallen hard."

"You're crazy."

"Am I?"

"And even if you were right, it wouldn't make any difference."

Adele fixed him with a stare. "And why's that?"

"She could do better."

"Than a former FBI agent?"

Now he was the one who fixed her with a stare, one of his narrow-eyed ones that got people to talk. "How did you know?"

"Your dad told me."

This came as a total shock to Luke. "He knew?"

"He paid a private investigator to check up on you. Make sure you were still alive."

"He didn't say anything about that in the letter he left for me."

Adele shrugged. "Your dad was a hard man to figure out. A hard man, period. But he was proud of you in the end."

"Proud that I had a gambling problem?" Luke scoffed. "Glad that I burnt out and left?"

"You're a good man, Luke. I don't know why you have such trouble believing that. Julia knows you're a good man."

Luke stared down at his nearly empty glass of Jack Daniel's with brooding intensity. "She doesn't know the real me."

"On the contrary. She saw through all the walls you put up around you. She might not know what life experiences *made* you the way you are, but she got to know the real you, all right. And don't you think otherwise."

"Well, *she* thinks otherwise now."

"Broke her heart, did you?"

Luke didn't answer.

"That's what you wanted, wasn't it? Make her hate you instead of love you. Because that's something you're more comfortable with. Being hated. Not being loved."

"What are you?" he growled, "A Dr. Phil clone?"

"Fine, you don't want to talk about it right now, we won't. Instead, let's talk business. Tyler and I want to be your business partners. We'd each buy one-third of Maguire's from you. What do you say?"

"I thought you wanted to marry the town sheriff."

"Who said anything about marrying him? Yes, I like him. A lot. But I also value my independence."

"And here I was, thinking you were an old-fashioned girl." Luke felt much more comfortable discussing this than his private life. Adele had been hitting far too close to the bone with her observations there.

"Sorry to disillusion you. But getting back to Maguire's, you can see that the new menu has been a success. Not only the sweet potato fries but also the beer-battered fish and chips and the traditional fare like the pot pies, the meat loaf, and of course the chicken and waffles."

"If you're not from around here, I don't know if you can get used to that last combo."

Adele ignored his mocking comment. "Adding the local Pennsylvania microbrewery beers was also successful, despite your initial misgivings. The bottom line is that Maguire's is doing better than it ever has. It seems a shame to stop things now. Just when they're going so good."

Luke was well aware that Adele's words could also apply to himself and Julia.

Two days later, Julia curled up on her living room couch, her soft velour READ pillow crushed against her chest as tears chased down her face. She'd held it together through the remainder of the work week, but now that it was Sunday, she was coming undone.

She should have seen this coming, this train wreck break-up with Luke. She'd been kidding herself, letting their relationship slide along without preparing herself for the fact that Luke didn't share her vision of a future in Serenity Falls.

He'd been kidding her, too. Instead of coming clean with her, he'd let her believe that they had a chance. Not that he'd said anything. But he should have. Should have warned her this was coming. Given her some hint instead of dropping the bomb on her out of the blue.

She ignored the first knock on her front door, but the second one was a demanding banging that indicated the person was not going away. Maybe it was Luke?

No, it was Adam Kemp.

"I didn't like the way we left things after our lunch," he began before actually looking at her. "What's wrong with you?"

"Men!" Julia hiccuped and angrily swiped the tears from her cheeks. "You all stink!"

Having made that brilliant observation, she pivoted from the door and headed back to the comfort of her couch and pillow.

"I took a shower this morning, so I'm not going to take that comment personally," Adam noted as he cautiously entered her living room.

"It's always all about the money. That's all you care about. That and sex."

"Ah. Boyfriend trouble. Here." He shoved an expensive handkerchief into her hand. "Take this and try to control yourself."

Julia derived great pleasure from completing a honking blow of her nose into his fine linen handkerchief before shoving it right back at him.

"No, no," he hurriedly said. "You keep that. Now what's this about money?"

"That's all he wanted. He only stayed in town for the money."

"What money?"

"From his father's will."

"Who are we talking about here?"

"Luke."

"Right. The man who refused a million dollars from me."

"What?!"

"I offered him money to walk away from you."

"He just did."

"Not for the money. There must be some other reason."

"Gee, thanks."

"You'd prefer to think he left you for money?"

"I don't know!" she wailed.

Adam started looking alarmed. "Hold on there, now don't go off the deep end on me. Let's look at this logically."

Half an hour later, Julia had calmed down some and was sipping the surprisingly good cup of coffee Adam had made for her.

"What's that noise?" he asked.

"I don't know. It sounds like it's coming from outside the house." Julia got up to pull the curtains aside and look. "Uh-oh."

Adam joined her. "Uh-oh indeed."

A dozen protestors had gathered on the sidewalk, holding quickly done handmade signs: YOU CAN'T BUY OUR FALLS! WE'RE NOT FOR SALE!

Julia opened her front door to find Walt standing there. "I told you it was him," he told the crowd as he pointed at Adam. "I recognized him from his appearance on the *Late Show* the other night hyping his new book. You're Adam Kemp. Don't try to deny it."

"I wasn't about to."

"Good. Because we want you to know that we'll move heaven and earth to protect our beautiful Serenity Falls waterfall."

"Not for sale," the crowd chanted.

"Stop that," Adam barked, clearly aggravated now. "I'm not here because of your stupid falls. I'm here because of her." He pointed to Julia. "She's my daughter."

Walt looked like he might pass out.

"Great," Julia muttered. "Now everyone will know. The media trucks are probably already on the way."

Edith stepped forward. "On the contrary. We do know how to keep a secret here in Serenity Falls."

"We're like Las Vegas that way," Mabel agreed. "What goes on here, stays here."

Angel softly closed the door to Toni's bedroom, relieved that the little girl had gone to sleep for an unexpected nap. Angel could use one of those, too. She'd been working long hours at the pancake house all week and then there had been that little jaunt into Philadelphia to see Adam the other day.

She hadn't had time to think lately, let alone to fully complete her usual meditation routine. Her chakras needed balance, and she needed sleep. But when Skye had phoned her and asked her to baby-sit this one rare afternoon she had off, Angel hadn't been able to refuse.

Skye seemed to be settling in well here in Rock Creek. That was a relief. At least one of the Wright women was happy.

Not that Julia didn't seem happy with Luke. But the tarot cards indicated trouble looming ahead for them.

Angel picked up the pink and lime green scarf she was knitting. Her hats and scarves were selling well at the store in Serenity Falls. In fact, she had a backlog of special orders, one of which she was trying to complete now.

The click of the knitting needles was reassuring to her. The pounding on the door wasn't. She opened it.

"Tyler." Angel was surprised to see him here at Skye's apartment. "How did you know I was here?"

"You weren't at Julia's so she suggested I come here. You still owe me a massage," he said abruptly.

"Oh." Angel blinked. "Well, you're right. I do. Do you want me to give you a massage now?"

"I want you to stop dating Phil. Are you in love with him?" Tyler demanded.

Angel shook her head, too stunned to reply verbally.

"Then ditch him. And ditch the khaki pants and severe clothes. I want the *real* Angel back with bells on your toes and laughter in your eyes. And I've wanted to do this from the very first moment I saw you . . ." Putting his hands on her shoulders, Tyler gently tugged her to him and kissed her.

Angel melted. This was her karma, her destiny, her cosmic soul mate. The radiant core of love that resided in the center of her personal consciousness responded. Her femininity bonded with his masculinity.

The feel of his mouth on hers was awesome. Well worth waiting for. She hadn't felt this way since she was a teenager, wild and free. But she wasn't a teenager any longer. She was a mother. A grandmother. Out to prove she was responsible.

"Wait." She took a step back. "We shouldn't."

"Why not? Are you interested in picking things up with Kemp again?"

"Are you out of your mind?"

"Some people might think so."

"Some people might think I'm not normal, either," Angel pointed out.

"You're not normal. You're *superlative*. Magical."

She blushed. "I don't know what to say."

"Say you'll stop seeing Phil."

"Why do you care?"

"Because I care about you. I've fought it. But it's no use."

"I've fought it, too," she whispered. "But I've just repaired the bridges with Julia, and I don't want to do anything that will rock the boat again."

"I understand."

"I know you do." She touched his cheek.

"But that doesn't mean I'm not going to fight for you, because I am."

"Oh Tyler . . ." She leaned forward to kiss him. The second time was even better than the first.

"Wait." This time he was the one who pulled away. "Before you make up your mind, it's only fair to tell you the truth. You deserve to know what you're getting into if you hook up with me."

Her heart sank. "You're married."

"No, of course not. Divorced, but that was a long time ago."

She resumed breathing. "Then what?"

"I haven't always been a handyman."

"Or an insomniac Rollerblader?"

"That either. In my prior life I was a prosecutor in Chicago."

"So that's why you told the town council that they had legal irregularities in their procedures. I heard the rumors even though I wasn't there myself."

"Did you also hear how everyone came to your defense, saying how much they loved your yoga lessons and what a difference they made?"

Angel nodded. "Julia told me about that, yes."

"Anyway, I was on the fast track to success, totally wrapped up in my work. Until that last case. The guy claimed he was innocent, but I'd heard that before. I was sure we had the right guy. Totally positive, without a doubt. But while he was in jail awaiting trial, a new piece of evidence turned up, exonerating him of the crime."

"So you made a mistake. You're only human."

"It was more than a mistake." Tyler's words were gritty with emotion. "The night before, the guy hung himself in his jail cell."

"Oh Tyler . . ." She put her arms around him, offering him comfort and sanctuary.

"I walked away. Left that life behind."

"I don't blame you."

"You should." His voice was muffled against the top of her head. "Someone should blame me for that innocent man's life."

"You're already blaming yourself, and have been for a long time. No, I'm not going to blame you. Instead, I'm going to love you."

"Thanks for coming so quickly, Algee." Julia welcomed the reinforcement she'd called in for assistance. After thinking things through, she knew what she had to do. She needed to figure this out because something didn't make sense to her. Why had Luke come to Philadelphia to get her if he planned on dumping her? He never had answered that question. "Adam, this is Algee. A friend of Luke's. Algee, this is my father. Adam Kemp."

"The rich guy?"

Julia nodded. "That's right."

"Is your father?"

"It's a long story."

"I'm sure. Heard there were protesters here earlier today."

"There were, but that's not why I called you over here. I wanted to talk to you about Luke. You've seen the For Sale sign in front of Maguire's, right?"

Algee nodded cautiously. "Right."

"Did he tell you he was going to put the place on the market?"

"No. But then he doesn't tell me his plans."

"But you're friends."

"Yeah, so?"

"So you know him better than most people."

"So do you."

"I thought I did," she muttered.

"I warned the dude that you were his weakness. His kryptonite."

"Do you think that's why he dumped me?" Julia asked.

Algee was vehement. "No way!"

"Way. He dumped me two days ago."

"No, I'm saying no way he'd dump you for that. Being his kryptonite, I mean."

"Maybe it had something to do with his

FBI background," Adam suggested.

"What?" Algee and Julia said in stunned unison.

"He didn't tell you about that either, right?"

Julia shook her head. "Let me guess. You had him investigated."

"Naturally. Any man who's interested in my daughter has to pass certain criteria."

"You had no right trying to bribe him," Julia belatedly reprimanded her father. "Try that again, and there will be consequences."

"My man Luke was with the FBI?" Algee said.

Adam nodded. "For almost a decade. Apparently, he did a lot of undercover work for much of that time. I couldn't get any details on that, naturally. I did discover he had a gambling problem resulting in a large debt just recently paid off. No indication of continued gambling. I could show you the file if you like."

Julia shook her head. She wasn't going to invade Luke's privacy. "I love him. And I'm not going to sit here crying without fighting to keep him. I've got to take action," Julia stated.

"Luke is a man who understands action more than words," Algee agreed.

"I was impressed with the guy when I first

met him," Adam said. "After turning down my offer of the money, he threatened to kick my butt if I hurt you."

Julia's heart melted. "He did?"

Adam nodded, his smile rueful. "It was a memorable moment. I haven't had anyone speak to me that way for some time now."

Julia remembered the grand gesture Luke had made on Valentine's Day, creating a magical prom experience for her. Maybe he didn't love her. Maybe he was no good at relationship stuff. Maybe he wanted to be alone. Or maybe not. His words didn't match his actions.

A good girl would meekly walk away.

Julia refused to do that.

"The bottom line is that I liked the guy," Adam was saying.

"Then pull up a chair and help us strategize," Algee said.

Julia nodded. "We need a plan."

"Remember, always bargain from a position of strength," Adam told her.

"And remember that Luke is a man who understands action more than words," Algee added.

"I'm not punching him again," Julia said, just in case he got any ideas.

"You don't have to. Not with boxing gloves. But with your feminine wiles . . ."

"What are you suggesting?"

"I'll leave that to you." Algee grinned. "I'm sure you'll come up with something . . ."

Luke couldn't believe it. Someone had stolen his Harley! And on a Sunday night, too. Right there from the alley behind Maguire's. Serenity Falls had a thief in its midst.

He was mad as hell. It wasn't enough that he'd lost Julia, now he'd lost his sweet set of wheels as well!

He ran up the stairs for the cell phone he'd left there. The door banged against the wall as he stormed in . . . and stopped in his tracks.

There was his Harley.

In the middle of the living room.

With Julia draped across it.

Wearing very little.

Luke's tongue stuck to the roof of his mouth, and all the blood rushed from his head to his crotch. The combination of both conditions left him temporarily unable to speak.

Finally he managed to get out a few gruff words. "What are you doing here?"

"Isn't that usually my line?" she replied in a husky, phone-sex kind of voice.

He couldn't tear his eyes from the racy red lace bikini panties she wore beneath a cropped top football jersey of his favorite team — the Steelers. Her bare midriff and bare legs showed plenty of creamy skin. And the red stilettoes were a total turn-on.

Noticing his attention to her attire, she tugged at the jersey, lifting it to show even more. "I know how much you like football."

He remained speechless.

"And I know how much you *love* your Harley." She stroked the machine the way a lover would.

Luke just about went ballistic as her fingers caressed the chrome. He wanted her so badly he could hardly see straight.

"But I don't know why you think you can get rid of me this easily." She placed her hands on her hips and glared at him.

"What?" he croaked.

"I think you're trying to be noble."

That got his attention. "I don't have a noble bone in my body."

"Of course you do. Don't even bother trying to tell me how bad you are. I've heard it all before from the people in this town."

"They're right."

"No, they're not. You gave me a prom. You warned my billionaire father not to hurt me or you'd kick his butt."

"So?"

"So Algee told me I was your kryptonite. Your weakness."

"And you're here to test that theory?"

"No, I'm here because I don't want to be your weakness. I want to be your strength. The way you're my strength."

With a groan, Luke yanked her into his arms. He was only human after all.

She completed him.

"I kept thinking I'd get over you once I got you in my bed," he muttered in between kisses. "When that didn't happen, I got worried."

She smiled. "So you tried seducing me on the pool table, the dining room chair, the shower —"

"And I still never got over you. I never will."

"I hope not. If you're leaving Serenity Falls, I'm going with you."

"I don't deserve you." His voice was rough with emotion.

"Maybe not, but you're stuck with me," she retorted with bad-girl sauciness.

He scooped her into his arms. "Have you ever made love on the back of a Harley?"

"No."

Luke flashed that bad-boy grin at her.

"Are you ready for the ride of your life?"

Julia grinned right back. "Are you?" she countered.

"Let's find out . . ." he murmured against her mouth.

A week later . . .

"Don't worry about a thing," Angel assured Julia as she gave her a big hug. "I'll take good care of your house while you're on the road."

"And I'll take care of Maguire's. With help from Tyler," Adele told Luke as he revved up the Harley, clearly eager to get going.

"And I'll take care of the rest of the town," the newly selected town council member Algee stated.

"And Julia, a job at the library is yours whenever you return," Frasier stated.

"I'm going to miss you." Pam gave her a final good-bye hug.

Julia swung her denim-covered leg over the Harley's seat with newfound confidence. Her roots were still here. But that didn't mean she couldn't take off and fly every once and a while.

Most of the town had turned out to see them off, including Walt, who was busy on his cell phone. "Listen up, folks!" he suddenly shouted excitedly. "We got it! Serenity Falls is on the top ten list of America's Best Small Towns. We're number nine, which leaves us room for improvement next year."

Julia didn't know what the next year would bring, but she knew she'd be spending it with the man she loved, the man who loved her, and that was enough for her. More than enough!